MAGNUS OPUM

JONATHAN GOULD

Booktrope Editions
Seattle WA 2014

Copyright 2012, 2014 Jonathan Gould

This work is licensed under a Creative Commons Attribution-Noncommercial-No Derivative Works 3.0 Unported License.

Attribution — You must attribute the work in the manner specified by the author or licensor (but not in any way that suggests that they endorse you or your use of the work).

Noncommercial — You may not use this work for commercial purposes.

No Derivative Works — You may not alter, transform, or build upon this work.

Inquiries about additional permissions should be directed to: info@booktrope.com

Cover Design by Lliam Amor

Previously published as *Magnus Opum*, Self-Published, 2012

This is a work of fiction. Names, characters, places, brands, media, and incidents are either the product of the author's imagination or are used fictitiously. Any resemblance to similarly named places or to persons living or deceased is unintentional.

Print ISBN 978-1-62015-214-0

EPUB ISBN 978-1-62015-310-9

DISCOUNTS OR CUSTOMIZED EDITIONS MAY BE AVAILABLE FOR EDUCATIONAL AND OTHER GROUPS BASED ON BULK PURCHASE.

For further information please contact info@booktrope.com

Library of Congress Control Number: 2014906273

To Fiona – for coming along with me on the journey

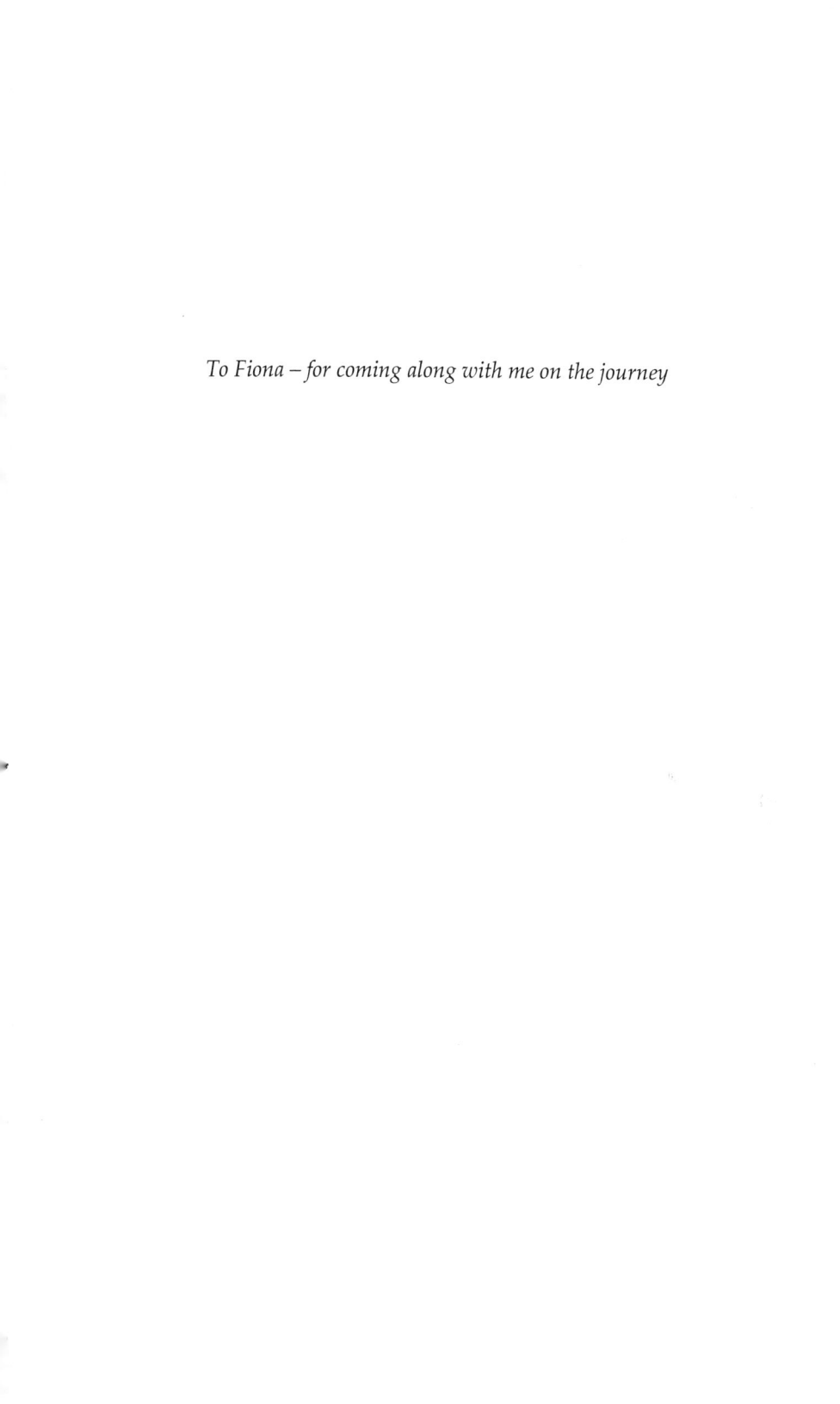

Table of Contents

The Grompets 7
Doosie News 16
Plergle-Brots 25
Sweet Harmody 35
Sharbalons and Krpolgs 46
The Blerchherchh 59
The Great Oponium 68
Ferelshine 78
The Pharsheeth 88
Parghwum Pass 99
Hargh Gryghrgr 109
Klugrok 118
The Shkroulch 128
Urqhuarest 141
Plombeth Jelly 154
Whounga Sunrise 165
Trupitompsit 177
Barglefest 188
Acknowledgments 198
Book Club Questions 199
More Great Reads from Booktrope 200

The Grompets

FAR, FAR OVER the Mounji Mountains, past the shores of Lake Kroulchip where the boulcher fish bellow, across the misty, musty Plains of Plartoosis, and beyond the depths of the dingy, dungy Drungledum Valley, lies the small homely village of Lower Kertoob.

If you happened to be passing on a bright Tuesday afternoon, as spring slowly drifted into summer, you might have seen Magnus Mandalora with his borse, out ploughing in his pflugberry field.

A borse, as you would well know, was the primary beast of burden used by the Kertoobis, the small and homely race who inhabited Lower Kertoob. It looked a little like a cow and a little like a pig and not an awful lot like a horse at all. However, the most striking thing you would notice, if you should happen to see a borse for the first time, was that the two legs on the left were substantially shorter than the two legs on the right.

This meant that a borse was not the most practical sort of animal to use to pull a plough, displaying an annoying tendency to reel off to the left at the slightest notice. Though there were a number of far more suitable creatures, such as the powerful jingloo, the extraordinarily endurable truffelong, and the seldom seen but much discussed diperagoff, the Kertoobis had never considered any of them as alternatives. They were determined to stick to their borses, even if it meant that ploughing a field was a constant battle to keep the wayward beasts going in anything resembling a straight line. That was just the way things were done in Lower Kertoob, and once you got used to it, it really wasn't such a difficult thing to manage.

Unless you happened to be Magnus Mandalora on that particular Tuesday afternoon.

Around the field Magnus staggered. Around and around in ever slower circles. Any attempts at keeping his borse on the straight and narrow had been well and truly abandoned. So what was going on here? Why was Magnus incapable of performing a task that most Kertoobis had mastered by the time they were teenagers? Could it be intentional? Was he perhaps the temperamental artistic type, unwilling to limit himself to straight furrows and seeking a more creative way to decorate his field? Or was there a simpler explanation? Could it be that, when it came down to it, Magnus was just no good at ploughing?

The answer to all of these questions was no. Magnus was in fact an expert plougher, highly regarded throughout Lower Kertoob for the straightness of his furrows. However, there was a very good reason why on this day Magnus's course was marked instead by a single spiral, making gradually for the centre of the field. There were things on Magnus's mind. Strange, shocking things that prevented him from concentrating on the job he was supposed to be doing, leaving him instead stumbling aimlessly forward like a sleepwalker as his borse dragged him around and around the field.

Suddenly, the plough collided with a large rock, stopping the progress of the borse with a jerk. The shock seemed to rouse Magnus from his trance, and he looked around, blinking in disbelief. He was standing in the middle of a wide brown field, surrounded by ever decreasing circular furrows. This would not do. Everybody knew that pflugberries would never thrive if planted in spirals. He would have to start the ploughing again from the beginning, but not today. Not while last night's news was still so fresh in his mind. There was only one logical course of action to take now. It was time to eat.

Magnus found a nice piece of sloping ground on which to tether his borse–there was no point tethering a borse on flat ground, as it was liable to tip over–and then wandered off to look for some food.

* * *

The village of Lower Kertoob was, as the name suggested, built at the bottom of a shady green hill. When the Kertoobis first arrived there many years ago, there had been talk of establishing another village at the top of the hill, to be called, of course, Upper Kertoob. There were even plans to found a series of In-the-middle Kertoobs on the slopes of the hill as well. As it turned out, life in Lower Kertoob was so idyllic that nobody ever got around to actually making a start on any of these other Kertoobs. Still, the intention was not forgotten, and to that day, the hill was always referred to by the inhabitants below as Upper Kertoob.

Passing under the flanks of Upper Kertoob, Magnus soon found himself in the centre of the village. On the main street of Lower Kertoob, there were no permanent shops. Instead, the road was lined with a series of small, temporary food stalls, each one selling the same item: pflugberry pies.

Magnus paused for a moment, scanning the colourful stalls and trying to decide which one to buy from. Klinkor Grepula had a stall, and his pies were always especially fruity, but Magnus had bought a pie from him three days ago. Gretla Pazuko also had a stall, and her pies had that crust that melted in your mouth, but Magnus had purchased two pies from her in the last four weeks. He noticed that Osllo Yakuli had just finished setting up a stall right in front of him. Osllo's pies were a bit dry, and the crust was usually somewhat flaky. Then again, Magnus hadn't bought a pie from Osllo in nearly a month. It was definitely his turn.

Magnus walked up to Osllo's stand.

"Afternoon, Magnus," said Osllo quietly. "What will you have?"

This was a blatantly unnecessary question as there was only one item on the menu, but the Kertoobis being a polite race, it was one that was always asked.

"Pflugberry pie, thank you," replied Magnus, also speaking softly. He knew why Osllo was peering at him intently as he carefully wrapped the pie. He also knew why all the other Kertoobis had stopped what they were doing to stare at him as soon as he appeared. He wasn't going to be the one to mention it first.

Finally, Osllo's curiosity got the better of him.

"Is it true?" he asked in a hushed tone.

"Is what true?" replied Magnus evasively.

"It's all around the village," said Grilda Ivandoo, who had snuck up behind Magnus without him noticing.

"Everyone's saying it," added Flybus Bassoni, who was every bit as good at sneaking as Grilda.

"Everybody's saying what?" said Magnus testily, knowing full well what everybody was saying.

"They're saying…" Osllo paused for a moment, reluctant to say the words. "They're saying Jangos has got the Grompets."

"The Grompets!"

The shocked murmur came from behind Magnus. He looked around to see just about everyone in the village standing behind him with looks of concern and amazement on their faces.

"I don't know what any of you are talking about," protested Magnus in annoyance. "How much for the pie?"

"Thirteen greplacks," said Osllo as he handed over the steaming hot pie. Magnus's question had also been unnecessary as pflugberry pies had been thirteen greplacks for as long as anybody could remember, and as far as the Kertoobis were concerned, they always would be. Still, it was a very effective way of indicating that there was nothing left to discuss. The conversation was over.

* * *

Rather than eat his pie in the village square as he usually liked to do, Magnus decided to take it back to his home where he could enjoy a bit of privacy.

Home for most Kertoobis was a little five-sided house, known as a kertottage. Each of the five walls was painted in a different colour, with the brighter sides facing towards the street and the duller sides facing towards the back. The two street-facing walls each had their own separate front door, so you weren't stuck with going in and out of the same old door every day. The other three walls were filled with an array of oddly sized and shaped windows, to provide numerous different views of the world around.

Inside the kertottage, a very particular floor plan was always followed. There was a master bedroom as well as a spare bedroom because Kertoobis loved sleepovers. Then there was a lounge room, a dining room, and a baking room for making pflugberry pies.

You may wonder why Magnus had to go into the village to buy a pie when he could just as easily have gone home and baked one himself. The answer is that Magnus, like all Kertoobis, liked to make sure he kept his fellow villagers in business. "How is anybody in the village supposed to make a living if I don't offer them my custom?" is the sort of thing he would have said should anyone have ever asked that question. And if Magnus ever found himself low on money, he knew exactly what to do. He would bake a few pies and set up a stall on the main street to sell them. In this way, the economy of Lower Kertoob was constantly ticking over.

Magnus sat in his lounge room, munching thoughtfully on his pie. Despite his protestations in the village, he couldn't deny to himself the truth of the rumours. Jangos really did have the Grompets, and there didn't seem to be anything he could do about it.

As he picked up another slice of pie, there was a knock on the left front door. At first, Magnus was reluctant to answer it, fearing it would be more Kertoobis come to bother him. As the knocking persisted, Magnus eventually got up and opened the door. There stood Jangos, a somewhat harried expression on his face.

"Well this is a fine situation," he said. "One brother has the Grompets, and the other is losing his hearing. What will they say in the village?"

"I'm sorry, Jangos," said Magnus. "There's nothing wrong with my hearing. I just wasn't in the mood for visitors."

"Then you'd better let me in quick. I'm quite the centre of attention at the moment. If the others discover that I'm here, you're going to have more visitors than a frazzletoad has beauty spots."

Magnus hurriedly showed his brother in and quickly shut the door behind him.

"Isn't there anything I can say?" he asked as he followed Jangos into the lounge room.

"You could say, 'Gosh Jangos, why don't you take a seat and make yourself comfortable.' Or you could say, 'Hey Jangos, perhaps you'd like to share some of that pie with me, even though it looks rather dry and flaky.'"

Magnus chuckled. This was just like Jangos, always able to lighten the situation with a joke. As he offered his brother a seat and handed him a piece of pie, he frowned again.

"You know what I meant. Isn't there anything I can say that might make you reconsider?"

Jangos shook his head.

"Don't even try. I've decided once and for all."

"But why, why, Jangos?" Magnus wanted to know.

"I'm bored," Jangos replied.

"Bored with what?"

Jangos waved his arms around. "Bored with everything."

"Have you been using both doors?"

"Both doors, ha." Jangos laughed. "I've even cut out a third door round the back. And about twenty extra windows. It still doesn't help."

"Well, what about trying some sleepovers?"

"I've hardly spent a night at home for the last month. I need something more than that. All I ever seem to be doing is ploughing pflugberry fields, picking pflugberries, baking pflugberry pies."

"Sounds pretty good to me," opined Magnus.

"To you maybe, but not to me. If I keep this up, I'm going to end up turning into a pflugberry. I want some excitement and adventure. I want to climb to the tops of the high peaks of Phrongia and delve down into the great Cavern of Kristobul. I want to see the sun rise over the iridescent cliffs of Whounga Canyon."

Magnus could not believe he was hearing such words from out of his brother's mouth. On the whole, Kertoobis were the most settled race you could possibly imagine. Their idea of excitement was sitting around on the main street discussing the pros and cons of using fresh or preserved fruit in pflugberry pies. Their idea of adventure was going out through the left door and in through the right door every day except Wednesdays, when they liked to reverse the pattern. But every so often, strange things happened to individual Kertoobis. They would get a kind of wanderlust, a desire to go out and see the big wide world around them. This desire was so inexplicable to the average Kertoobi that a name had come into use to describe it, a name that was uttered with amazement and fear. That name was the Grompets and Jangos had as bad a case of it as Magnus had ever heard.

"So there's nothing I can say that will make you change your mind?" said Magnus.

Jangos shook his head again. "Absolutely nothing. I've decided to leave tomorrow."

"But so soon," Magnus cried out in horror. "You won't stay just a little bit longer?"

"It's easier this way. I'm tired of being harassed and bothered. I'm sick of every second Kertoobi in the street coming up and asking me the most inane questions." He paused and then whined in a high- pitched voice. "What does it feel like to have the Grompets, Jangos? What does it feel like to want to leave the village, Jangos? Jangos, what does it feel like to have completely lost your mind?"

"You can't blame them," said Magnus. "It's hard for most of them to understand. It's hard for me to understand."

"I suppose you're right," said Jangos. "That's why I figure it's better if I leave as soon as I can."

"Where do you think you'll go?"

"I haven't completely decided yet. I'll probably head out west to avoid the Plergle Swamp and then make for Sweet Harmody."

"Sweet Harmody," sighed Magnus. For a second, a strange feeling had come over him, an overwhelming desire to see for himself the legendary city of the Cherines. It only lasted for a second. Then Magnus remembered the things he really loved: ploughing pflugberry fields, picking pflugberries, baking pflugberry pies. Voom. The feeling was gone.

Jangos must have noticed the faraway look that passed briefly across his brother's face.

"You see, Magnus," he said. "There are many great and wondrous things to see in the world."

"But there are also many fearsome and terrifying ones," cried Magnus, retreating even further away from the uncomfortable urge he had just felt. "Oh, Jangos, please be careful. Stay away from the gloomy pits of Trushlow."

"I've no intention of ever going near them," assured Jangos.

"Avoid the darksome den of the dingebats."

"It's definitely not on my itinerary."

"And watch out for the... the... the other things."

Other things. Jangos looked down for a moment. He knew that Magnus was right. There were other things out there. Things far worse than the gloomy pits of Trushlow and the darksome den of the dingebats. Things that were rarely, if ever, mentioned by name in the small homely village of Lower Kertoob.

"I'll be careful," said Jangos after a while. "I've also been thinking a bit about those other things. But they're not going to stop me. I still have to go."

"Well, if I really can't talk you out of it, will you at least do me one favour?" asked Magnus.

"Anything," replied Jangos.

"Make your last night in Lower Kertoob a sleepover."

"Over here?"

Magnus nodded.

Jangos smiled. "With pleasure. In fact, I was rather hoping you'd ask. My kertottage is currently being mobbed by a swarm of curious Kertoobis. I had no plans to go back there tonight."

"But what about your stuff?"

"All packed. I've hidden it just outside your front doors."

Magnus got up and helped Jangos bring his pack into the kertottage. The rest of the evening passed in silence. Magnus couldn't think of anything else he could do that might prevent Jangos's departure. There were a number of treatments recommended for the Grompets but these generally involved ropes, chains, shackles and large buckets of water, none of which Magnus was keen to impose on his brother. At this point, there was nothing left to say on the matter. Jangos was leaving.

* * *

The next morning, Jangos was ready to go before the sun had risen. Half in a daze, Magnus helped him load the pack onto the right side of Jangos's favourite borse, an excellent way to counteract the natural lean to the left. Then he gave his brother a big hug and watched gloomily as Jangos and his trusty steed began to stride down the main path out of the village.

"Don't forget to write," called Magnus as his brother disappeared into the mists of the morning.

Magnus could just make out Jangos turning and nodding.

"Of course I won't." The words floated out from the fog. Then he was gone.

Magnus knew that the road Jangos was on headed down towards the vast Plergle Swamp. A short way out of the village, it turned to the west, skirting the edges of the swamp, and then straightened out on its way towards the great city of Sweet Harmody.

Thoughts of that renowned place were almost enough to produce a tiny pang of jealousy. Almost, but not quite enough. Mostly, Magnus felt fear and concern for his brother. Of those Kertoobis afflicted with the Grompets, most were just gone for a short while. A brief taste of the outside world was all that was needed to convince them that nothing was better than life in Lower Kertoob. But some stayed away for months, or even years. And some were never ever seen again.

Doosie News

FOR THE NEXT couple of months, Jangos was as good as his word.

About a week after he had left, a bird with bright lilac wings and bulging green eyes, a messenger flythrop, flew in through one of the round windows of Magnus's kertottage. As it landed on the table, Magnus was excited to notice a small piece of paper tied to one of its legs.

Magnus hurriedly untied the paper and opened it out to reveal a not particularly well drawn picture of a kertottage. The drawing bore a vague resemblance to pretty much any of the kertottages in the village, but Magnus knew that if the flythrop had chosen his kertottage to fly into, then the message was definitely meant for him. Messenger flythrops were frequently used as a delivery service due to their rare gift of being able to read minds through pictures. No matter how unskilled the drawer was, the birds were always able to instantly recognise the correct destination for the various messages they carried.

Magnus turned the paper over. He knew who this letter had to be from, even before he began to read the words on the page.

Dear Magnus,

Well, who would believe it? I'm actually here in Sweet Harmody, and it's truly beyond anything I could ever have imagined. Everything about this place is so magnificent and astounding, I feel like I'm walking around in a dream. I'm so bruised from pinching myself, I think I'm starting to look like a pflugberry. And as for the Cherines, they are the most incredible hosts. It seems like every day is full of songs and poetry and beautiful art. I'm quite speechless just thinking about it.

Okay, you're right. There's nothing in the world that could actually leave me speechless. It's just that everything here is so gloriously splendid, it's hard to find the right words to describe it. I'm so glad I found the courage to leave Lower Kertoob. I know now that it was the right thing for me to do. My only regret is that I miss you and wish you could be here with me. Maybe one day you'll understand. Till then, take care. You'll be hearing from me again soon.

Your loving brother,
Jangos Mandalora

Magnus put down the letter. Part of him was crying, but another part was laughing with joy. He still found it difficult to comprehend what Jangos was doing, but as he read the letter he could almost hear his brother's voice leaping out of the page. The sense of delight and wonder in those words made him feel happier than he had been at any time since Jangos had left.

*   *   *

Over the next few months, the letters from Jangos became a weekly occurrence. As the other Kertoobis began to notice the regular arrival of the messenger flythrops, the reading of these letters developed into a major social event. Magnus's kertottage was crammed to the rafters, as almost every Kertoobi in the village squeezed in, keen to hear the latest installment in Jangos's travels.

And the stories were definitely worth hearing. The crowd gasped with amazement and awe at his descriptions of such scenic marvels as the glistening gardens of Glen-Arbee and the sweeping sands of the Drushida Dunes. They chuckled and chortled at anecdotes, such as his encounter with the sluggerinth, a beast with such a bizarre appearance that even it couldn't stop laughing at itself, and his visit to the bottomless crevice of Kertunia, down which he managed to accidentally drop his shoes, sunhat, and several pints of pflugberry juice. But nothing could compare to the excitement as Jangos's journey brought him closer to one particular destination, the sight that was universally accepted as the most magnificent and wondrous ever to be seen: the sunrise over the iridescent cliffs of the fabled Whounga Canyon.

Then the letters stopped. Just like that. Every day Magnus scanned the sky for the arrival of another messenger flythrop, but none ever came.

At first, he wasn't too concerned. Jangos was clearly having such a fantastic journey, it wasn't surprising if he couldn't always find the time to write. But as the weeks went by, he became more and more worried. This was not like Jangos. Not like Jangos at all.

Magnus's concerns were not helped by the behaviour of the other Kertoobis. In the weeks after the final correspondence, there was a steady stream of knocks at his doors as the other villagers politely asked if another letter had arrived. However, as more and more time passed, whispers started floating through the village. Magnus began to find that he was given strange looks as he walked down the main street to buy his lunch. Although nobody was actually rude to him and nobody would ever refuse to sell him a pflugberry pie, people regarded him with more than a small degree of alarm and suspicion. A brother who had disappeared into thin air was a highly dubious thing for a respectable Kertoobi to have.

*   *   *

One Friday afternoon, about three months after Magnus had last received news of his brother, some travellers passed through Lower Kertoob.

This was not an unusual occurrence. The road that passed through the village was long established, having once served as a trade route linking Sweet Harmody with the old grop mines to the east. However, as the mines had been exhausted many years ago, the road was not heavily used, and so it wasn't every day that passers-by entered the village. Still, with the infrequent travellers and the occasional tour parties, the Kertoobis were not totally isolated from the outside world.

These particular travellers were a couple of Doosies. As they strolled leisurely down the main street, it didn't take long for a sizable crowd to build up in their wake, eager for stories.

Being Doosies, the travellers were only too happy to give the Kertoobis exactly what they wanted. Of all the races, Doosies were the biggest storytellers and gossips you could ever meet. They had three ears– two in the normal places and another on the back of their heads–so they could hear absolutely everything that was said by anyone in the vicinity. In addition, they had long, prehensile noses, perfect for sticking into other people's business. Unfortunately, they only had one eye and not a very good one at that, so there were often substantial discrepancies between what they heard and what had actually happened. Not that this ever got in the way of a Doosie telling a good story. In fact, Doosies were so efficient at passing news from one to another that they were the primary source of information for pretty much all other races. As soon as one Doosie heard something, it was usually only a matter of hours before pretty much every other Doosie in the land also knew about it, which explained the popular Kertoobi rhyme:

*If you're after the newsy,
Then speak to a Doosie.*

Not a particularly good rhyme, but it did neatly sum up the way Doosies always seemed to know absolutely everything about everyone. It also summed up the great appeal of having a couple of Doosies in the village.

When the two short, but sturdily built, figures reached the village square, they sat down and began recounting a tale to their enraptured audience. The story involved the Geruntings, a fearsomely shy folk who had spent the last twenty years building the tiniest city ever, so they could live their lives without being noticed by passers-by. The city, truly one of the great marvels of its age, was filled with intricately designed palaces, shops and dwellings, none of which was higher than a few inches tall. Unfortunately, upon its completion, the Geruntings, who happened to be a race of fifteen-foot tall giants, quickly discovered that there was no way they could actually reside in the city they had so painstakingly created and were forced to remain out in the open, painfully exposed to all who passed.

The Kertoobis all giggled with delight at the completion of the story. "Please tell us another story," cried several members of the audience.

"I have another story," proclaimed one of the Doosies in his rich, deep storyteller's voice. "And this one will be extra special. I believe it involves somebody from this very village."

An excited gasp went through the village square. It was rare indeed for a Kertoobi to be featured in a Doosie's story.

"Is there anybody in this village named Magnus Mandalora?" boomed the other Doosie.

Magnus was not in the square at the time, but it didn't take long for a host of Kertoobis to summon him out of isolation. Suddenly, he found himself in the rather uncomfortable position of being something of a celebrity again.

"What is this?" he demanded of the Doosies. "I haven't done anything. How could I be in one of your stories?" As he spoke, Magnus began to get a feeling that he knew what this was going to be about. It was not a good feeling at all.

"Calm yourself, my good Kertoobi," said the first Doosie. "You are not the one I was referring to."

"But you do have a brother known as Jangos, if I'm not mistaken," said the second.

"Yes, I do," said Magnus. "Do you know where he is? Can you tell me if he's all right?"

The Doosies exchanged knowing glances. The first one puffed up his shoulders, a sure sign that he was returning to storyteller mode.

"Three bodies were recently discovered on the road leading to the rim of the fabled Whounga Canyon, famous for its iridescent cliffs," he declared solemnly, before signaling for his companion to take up the story.

"Two of those discovered were members of the mighty Cherine race, resident of the noble city of Sweet Harmody. The third was a member of that most charming and good-natured, although occasionally distressingly unworldly race, referred to by themselves, and coincidentally most others as well, as Kertoobis."

"Upon close examination," continued the first, "a letter was found on this body. A letter addressed to a certain Magnus and signed, 'Your loving brother, Jangos Mandalora'."

At these words, a second gasp filled the square, but this time it was a gasp of shock.

"Perhaps you would like to hear the contents of this letter?" enquired the second Doosie.

"Yes, tell us please," the Kertoobis called out in horrified fascination.

"No!" cried one voice over the top.

Everyone in the square turned to face the speaker. Magnus Mandalora was shaking. When he finally managed to speak again, his voice was as cold as the frozen wastelands of Vardoom.

"I do not wish for you to tell me the contents of my brother's final correspondence."

"Don't blame you in the least," rumbled the first Doosie. "If it was my brother who had been murdered, I wouldn't want the whole world to know."

"Did you say murdered?" said Magnus, struggling to keep his voice steady.

"Undoubtedly murdered," confirmed the second Doosie. "From all the signs, it was clear that the party had been ambushed and slaughtered by a roving band of Glurgs."

A final gasp reverberated through the square. This was not a gasp of excitement. It was not even a gasp of shock. It was a gasp of outright terror.

The Doosies grinned with satisfaction. They were always chuffed to get a reaction to a story, no matter what sort of reaction that might be.

"And that, my Kertoobi friends, is the end of our tale," said the first. "Thank you so much for your kind hospitality."

"We'd love to chat some more but we must be on our way," said the other. "For such intrepid newshounds as we, there can be little rest."

With that, the two Doosies stood up, hoisted their packs onto their broad backs, and strode importantly out of the village square and down to the road that led to Sweet Harmody, leaving Magnus to endure the stares of his fellow villagers.

For a long minute nobody said a word. Silence enveloped the town square. Then, at last, Magnus turned and began walking slowly away. Suddenly, his whole world was different. The village was blurry and unclear, as if it had been enshrouded by the mists from the dreaded Plergle Swamp. Eventually he managed to stagger back to his kertottage. He reached out, groping blindly for one of the front door handles, opened the door, and then collapsed onto the front mat.

Nobody followed.

After about half an hour, Magnus came to. He crawled into the lounge room and sat himself down. The whole time, his mind was racing around in circles like an untethered borse.

It had to be a story. It couldn't be true.

Magnus tried to persuade himself that the whole thing was just an invention of the Doosies. It was well known that most of the stories told by those incorrigible gossip-mongers were wholly, or at least seventy-five percent, fabricated. Like that first story. Everyone knew that the Geruntings were not really shy, fifteen-foot tall giants, but a race of tall but canny tourist operators who ran a large and extremely well-frequented miniature village-based theme park. That was the fun part of listening to Doosie stories: trying to figure out which bit was real and which bit was made up.

Try as he might, Magnus could not convince himself that this news was the fanciful imaginings of the Doosies. Everything about the story fitted: the fact that Magnus had not heard from Jangos in months; the location where the bodies were discovered, on the way to the Whounga Canyon; and the letter, especially the way it had been signed, exactly like all of the other letters Jangos had sent. There could be no doubt about it. This had to be one of those rare occasions when the Doosies had actually gotten their story correct. Jangos was almost certainly dead.

A tear slowly dripped down Magnus's face.

"Jangos, why did you let this happen to you?" he sobbed. "Why did you ever leave the village? Why did you have to get the cursed Grompets?"

Magnus still struggled to comprehend the urgings that had led Jangos to his doom. What was there in the outside world that you couldn't find here in Lower Kertoob? Sure there was excitement, and adventure, and amazingly marvellous sights to see. What was that against the safety and surety that village life offered? If Jangos had only been content to stay at home, there was no way he would ever have been ambushed by a murderous band of...

Magnus found it difficult to even think the word, let alone say it. It was one that was not often uttered in the village. The Glurgs. The most horrifyingly revolting, detestably repugnant creatures ever to have defiled the world. Vicious and savage and ruthless and cruel.

The Glurgs were the scourge of all other races, the enemy in a great struggle that had gone on for as long as history had been recorded.

A great wave of fury swept over Magnus. He hated the Glurgs for what they had done to his brother, hated them like he had never hated anything before. He wanted to hurt them like they had hurt Jangos. He wanted to kick them and beat them and bash them and mash them till nothing was left of the whole accursed race but the slimy, squalid mulch they had been born from.

Suddenly, Magnus's eyes jerked open, but they were no longer tear-stained. They were now cold and hard, filled with a new purpose. Outside the village, the battles against the Glurgs raged on. Other races continued to join in the fight while the Kertoobis lived their sheltered lives. Such a life was no longer good enough for Magnus. He was not prepared to sit around at home mourning while others waged war on his behalf. He was going to stand up and play his part. After what the Glurgs had done to him, this was personal. He was going to make them pay the price for their brutal crimes.

Slowly, he got back to his feet, wobbling slightly but then standing firm. So many emotions swirled within him. There was fear, stronger than any he had ever faced in his life. He was going to have to leave Lower Kertoob and go out into the world, and the merest thought of that provoked a terror so frighteningly intense, it threatened to drown him like a wave on the shores of the great Sea of Floushing. Yet, even that mortal dread was held at bay by the anger and hatred that burnt in his heart, giving him the strength to stand tall when he might otherwise have collapsed like a quivering lump upon the floor.

But that was not all. There was a different feeling that rose up from the bottom of his toes, gaining strength as his mind strayed towards thoughts about the world that lay beyond the edges of his village. It fluttered around inside his stomach, but it was not fear. It was something new and wholly unexpected. Even as he stood, battling to retain his composure, images of the marvels Jangos had witnessed entered unbidden into his mind: the glistening gardens of Glen-Arbee, the sweeping sands of the Drushida Dunes, and the glorious city of Sweet Harmody. Above all, he couldn't help seeing the one sight that his brother had wanted to view more than any other, but which had led instead to his downfall. The ultimate scenic marvel above all others: the sunrise over the iridescent cliffs of Whounga Canyon.

Was it possible that the outside world was not merely a dark and threatening place? Could it be that he, Magnus Mandalora from the small homely village of Lower Kertoob, might actually entertain a desire to see for himself these great and wonderful sights? Was this strange, overwhelming feeling that same uncontrollable urge that had driven his brother away from the village?

Suddenly, Magnus cried out.

"Jangos, what have you done to me? Is this my inheritance from you? Have you passed on the Grompets to me?"

Magnus wasn't sure this was the legacy he really could have wished for from his beloved brother.

Plergle-Brots

MAGNUS SPENT THE WHOLE of the next day preparing.

First things first. He would need supplies. This could only mean one thing. Pflugberry pies. Lots of them.

He took a quick glance outside. Five Kertoobis were standing in front of his doors, each holding a large orangey-brown fruit with spiky purple leaves growing out of the top. This was a prompanapple, a gift that was traditionally given to those in mourning. They tasted absolutely vile, and no Kertoobi in their right mind would ever countenance eating one. However they did stay fresh for an extraordinarily long time, so it was always handy to have a few around, just in case someone close to you lost a loved one.

Magnus quickly stepped away from the window before he was noticed. He did not want to have to deal with anybody today. Not yet anyway. Fortunately, he already had a good supply of pflugberries in his pantry, so he did not have to go out into the fields to do some picking. For the next three hours, Magnus rolled pastry and mashed up berries and placed each completed pie into the oven.

Cooking complete, Magnus stepped back to regard his work. Fifteen steaming hot pflugberry pies sat on the wooden table in the middle of the room. Magnus found himself a large pack and carefully placed the pies inside, then slung the pack over his shoulder and stole another look out the window.

There were now about twenty Kertoobis lined up outside the doors, prompanapples at the ready. Magnus took a deep breath and prepared to open the left door and face them. Before his hand even reached the door handle, he stopped.

His original plan had been to cook up a big batch of pies, sell them in the village and use the proceeds to buy as many pies as he could afford for the road. Once he started to think about the attention he would receive as soon as he left the kertottage, he began to have second thoughts. True, there would be lots of well-meant expressions of sympathy, which in any other situation he would probably have quite appreciated. But there would also be so many annoying questions. How do you feel? What are you going to do now? Why did you bake so many pflugberry pies? Too many questions Magnus did not even begin to want to answer. Besides, he had no space in his cupboards to store so many prompanapples.

He hurried back to the baking room. A radical plan was forming in his head. He wasn't going to sell the pies. He was going to take them along and eat them himself. If anyone else in the village should ever find out about this, they would be horrified. This was the most un-Kertoobi-ish behaviour imaginable. Magnus didn't care. He could no longer muster up any interest for a town whose residents were primarily concerned with such pressing issues as which was the most brightly painted kertottage, whose borse had the least lean, and whether pflugberry pies cooked better under moderate or high heat. Lower Kertoob was too small to hold Magnus Mandalora any longer. He now had his sights on a much bigger picture.

Magnus went to his bedroom. He opened the closet and scanned the contents, looking for the sort of clothes that would be most suitable for a heroic quest with no immediate end in sight. Unfortunately, this proved to be a much harder task than it sounded. Kertoobis were just not the sort of race to go running around on heroic quests, so generally, their wardrobes were not fitted out with the sort of gear required.

Eventually, Magnus settled on a pair of bright red trousers, a purple shirt with matching vest and a heavy green traveller's cloak. He also found a belt with a bright silver buckle to hold up his pants and a copper brooch delicately carved into the shape of a pflugberry to tie up his cloak. Finally, he took out his sturdiest pair of ploughing boots and gave them a thorough polish before placing all of these items at the foot of the bed. Fully prepared for a quick getaway, he allowed himself one final peek out the window.

There was now a crowd of 200 prompanapple-proffering Kertoobis milling impatiently outside, evenly split in front of each front door.

No doubt the crowd would soon lose patience and clear out. Magnus felt no inclination to share his plans with any of them. He was hoping to slip away early the next day and be well clear of the village before the sun had even begun to contemplate the thought of rising into the sky.

* * *

Magnus was roused from a heavy sleep by a knock at the door. He leapt out of bed, hurried to the front doors and hurled them open. There, standing in the moonlight, was the most wondrously joyous sight Magnus had ever witnessed. It was Jangos.

"I can't believe it. You're alive!" cried Magnus.

"Take more than a bunch of smelly old Glurgs to do me in." Jangos laughed as he stepped inside and held out his arms.

As the two brothers embraced, Magnus couldn't remember ever feeling so happy. Jangos was back. He would not have to leave the village after all. Everything was just as it should be. He clutched onto Jangos with all his might, even though Jangos felt cold and wet and slimy and stank like the cesspits of Swertania.

Magnus let go and reeled back. This was not his brother. It was a monster, a brute with bulging red eyes and a wide, twisted, slavering mouth crammed with foul yellow fangs. With a cruel laugh, the monster lunged at Magnus, a short dark blade in its mangled claw...

...Magnus woke with a scream. Morning was still a good way off, and an icy breeze was blowing in through the open window above the bed. For a long while, Magnus cowered beneath the sheets, all thoughts of heroic quests swept from his mind. It was clearly far too early for any right-minded Kertoobi to be thinking about rising. Better to lie in till the sun was bright before considering leaving the safety of the bed. As for journeys and adventures, well they would just have to wait until tomorrow.

As the terror of his dream slowly receded, Magnus grimly reminded himself that he was not any right-minded Kertoobi. He had a mission. If he did not take the first steps now, he would never take them. With a shiver, he forced himself out of bed.

He dressed himself hurriedly. Then he went to the kitchen, took up his pack, and slung it over his shoulders, adjusting the weight till it felt comfortable on his not particularly broad back. Ready at last, he strode to the front doors and cautiously opened the one on the right.

Darkness enveloped the village, illuminated only by the pinpricks of the night's last stars. As expected, yesterday's crowd had vanished, save for three particularly hardy souls who were lying on the ground, their prompanapples rolling around the bottom of the front steps in time to their snoring. Magnus took a deep breath, raised one foot into the air, and brought it down again in front, being careful to avoid the slumbering bodies below. He had taken his first step. The journey had begun.

Lower Kertoob slept as Magnus passed through. At first, he made for the stables, but halfway there he changed his mind. Taking a borse seemed more trouble than it was worth. Better to travel light.

When he reached the village square, Magnus took the road that led off to the south-west. As the kertottages began to thin towards the edge of the village, he couldn't help thinking of that other morning when he had watched his brother walking down the same road. That morning seemed like it was another lifetime away, yet everything was so eerily similar. The air held the same chill, and the same fog had risen up from the nearby Plergle Swamp.

Magnus shuddered and tried to brush the mists away from his face. The Plergle Swamp had an evil reputation amongst the Kertoobis. Every so often an unwary traveller would accidentally stumble in, but very few of these travellers would manage to stumble out again. Fearsome beasts were said to lurk within its depths. Beasts that had become the subject of numerous Kertoobi tales. Many an unruly Kertoobi child had been rapidly brought into line after being threatened by their parents with stories of the terrifying Plergle-Brots.

At last, the road cleared the last of the kertottages. It passed beneath the looming shadow of Upper Kertoob and then began to lead down to the source of the swirling mists.

Magnus did not care to be passing so close to the Plergle Swamp, but there really wasn't a choice. For a wanderer heading out into the big world for the first time, there was only one direction that could possibly make sense, and that was towards the noble city of Sweet Harmody. The Cherines had been at the forefront of all the great Glurg Wars, so it made sense to consult with them before making any further plans. Unfortunately, the only road that would take him there would also lead him right to the boundaries of that fearful swamp.

The fog seemed to grow thicker as Magnus left the safety of the village behind. Even as the sun slowly rose into the sky, a cold clammy soup filled the air. Magnus could barely discern the nose at the end of his face, and considering that Kertoobis actually have particularly short noses, this should give you some idea of how hard it was to see anything. He struggled on through the haze, occasionally brushing against trees or stepping through deep puddles. Blind to any sense of progress, he was forced to rely on the cold scrape of his boots on gravel to reassure himself that he was still heading in the right direction.

After an hour of stumbling, Magnus stopped, feeling somewhat perplexed. He should be well clear of the swamp by now and heading up towards the security of higher ground. How was it that he should still be enshrouded in these mists?

He crouched down and put his hands on what should have been hard, gravelly road, to find that his worst fears were realised. All he could feel underhand was soft, damp ground. As if to add a theatrical touch, a gust of wind suddenly blew a gap in the fog, revealing fully the horrifying reality. Magnus was standing on a small muddy bank, surrounded by pools of turgid brown water. From out of these pools the thick, wrinkled trunks of old swamp-grompar trees loomed like sinister beasts. Their slimy black leaves reached out like deadly fingers, while their vast twisted roots grasped for his feet.

Magnus fell to the ground in dismay. How could this have happened? He had been so careful to make sure he stayed on the road. How had his feet betrayed him? He raised his legs and saw straight away that his boots were studded with pebbles. Stones from the road had stuck fast to the sides, probably glued on by the polish he had so diligently applied the night before. This was the gravelly sound he had continued to hear, even as he left the road and continued to walk on and on into the centre of the Plergle Swamp.

Panic began to consume him. What was he to do? How was he to get out? Magnus had no idea which direction he had come from, nor how far he had actually strayed from the road. After barely an hour, his quest had already turned into a disaster.

Suddenly, he heard a sound. A rustling, coming from directly behind. He leapt around, eyes wide with fear. There was nothing to see.

Another sound, this time to his right. Again he jumped, his heart pounding beneath his purple vest. Again there was nothing.

The noises now seemed to be coming from everywhere. Now in abject terror, Magnus spun around and around, not even sure what he was looking for. Nobody in Lower Kertoob had ever seen a Plergle-Brot, at least nobody who had survived the experience. Would they come flying out of the trees or creeping out of the water? Did they have fierce jaws and fiery breath, or long, scaly arms with claws like scimitars?

The noises were really close now. They seemed to be coming from directly under his feet. Magnus willed himself to look down and then let out a massive sigh of relief.

There was something there, but it was not at all what he had expected. The creature was small, barely ten inches in height, and covered in soft pink fur. It had long, oval-shaped ears, big, inquisitive round eyes, and a tiny mouth. All in all, it was the least frightening thing he had ever seen.

Magnus sat down, his fears washed away. He had kept scarier toys in his bed as a child.

"Hey, little guy, what's your name? My name's Magnus," he cooed to the cute little creature.

The creature opened its mouth, and a small squeaking sound emerged. It walked up to Magnus and pointed up towards his collar.

"My brooch. Would you like to look at it?"

The creature nodded excitedly.

Magnus unclasped the brooch and handed it to the creature. For a moment it admired its new prize, humming softly. Then it tossed the brooch over its shoulder and came back to Magnus. It squeaked again and pointed to Magnus's shiny belt buckle.

Magnus chuckled. "Sorry, you can't have my belt as well."

He reached over to pick up the brooch. Immediately, the creature raced back to stand over the brooch. Magnus jerked his hand back in surprise.

"Hey, little guy, you can't keep my brooch," he said. He reached over again to try to pick it up. Again the creature stood its ground, not letting his hand get near.

Magnus stepped back. The creature stepped away from the brooch and approached again, its eyes still fixated on Magnus's belt.

Magnus thought for a moment. He could probably take back the brooch by force but he didn't want to hurt such an endearing little animal. Then an idea came to him. He took off the belt and handed it to the creature with one hand, while using the other hand to keep his pants from falling. Again, the creature hummed in contentment as it examined another trophy. Magnus quickly made a lunge for the brooch. Too late, the creature had dropped the belt and was now standing on top of the brooch. Thinking quickly, Magnus lunged back for the belt. Thinking even more quickly, the creature was back at the belt. Not thinking of anything much, Magnus fell to the ground, his pants around his ankles.

As if this was a signal, another three of the little creatures leapt out of the mist. Two made a grab for Magnus's trousers while the third began rummaging in his pack.

"Hey, get out of there!" cried Magnus, but it was too late. His pies were already laid out on the ground. He dived to try to catch the creature but only succeeded in flopping face first into the mud. With a cry of joy, the two creatures wrestled his trousers off and began dancing around, each holding onto one of the legs. However, these too were quickly tossed down onto the ground as all four leapt onto Magnus's back and began trying to remove his vest and shirt as well.

Magnus staggered back to his feet, swatting at the furry little beasts whose surprisingly sharp claws were slowly but surely prising open all remaining buttons. But for every one that he managed to shove away, it seemed that another three were ready to take its place. Magnus was rapidly being smothered in a soft pink blanket of groping claws and searching teeth.

With a cry of rage, he finally managed to brush the last of the creatures away, but to no avail. He now stood on the wet, swampy earth completely naked. In front of him, all his possessions lay in a series of heaps on the ground, closely attended by about twenty of the little creatures.

Magnus sat down again, contemplating his next move. Fortunately, it didn't take long for the situation to appear resolved. The creatures quickly lost interest in their ill-gotten gains and began to disappear back into the swamp.

Relieved by the end of this struggle, Magnus crawled towards the nearest pile. Instantly, it was surrounded by a quivering pink wall of fur.

He changed direction and headed for another pile. Same result. Every time Magnus tried to approach his things, the creatures would bare their teeth and wave their claws and growl an unearthly fierce growl.

Magnus was at his wits' end. He was freezing cold and exhausted from wrestling with these pint-sized brutes. Nothing he tried seemed to make a difference. Here he was, embarking on a quest to take on the might of the Glurgs, and already he was struggling to defeat a tribe of plush bedtime toys.

Suddenly there was a great cry. Magnus looked up. A bright light seemed to fill the clearing, casting away the gloom of the swamp. In the centre of the light stood a tall and extremely well-built figure. He had massive shoulders and a bulging chest that seemed to burst through a gleaming battle vest. His eyes were piercing blue, his chin rigid and firm, and his cheekbones magnificent, while his flowing blond hair shimmered and shone with every shake of his head. In short, he was the most perfect specimen of a being of any kind that you could ever possibly see.

"Begone, vile Plergle-Brots," the figure roared, in a voice that echoed through the swamp like a great trumpet. Then he swung his sword at the little pink monsters. Heads, arms, and legs flew everywhere, while the few survivors squealed in terror and hurried away to the safety of the swamp-grompar trees.

The figure turned to Magnus and smiled. He motioned towards the scattered belongings. "You come ill-prepared to take on the perils of the Plergle Swamp, friend Kertoobi."

"Th-those were Plergle-Brots?" stammered Magnus, when he was eventually able to locate his tongue.

"Evil, vicious, ruthless beasts," nodded the figure, who Magnus knew could only be one of the mighty Cherines.

"But they're so…little…and furry."

The Cherine laughed. "Little and furry and deadly. Begone, get," he cried again as a couple of the Plergle-Brots crept out from the trees and began motioning towards his lustrous sword. "Believe me, friend Kertoobi, if I had not arrived, you would never have retrieved any of your things. And how long do you think you could have survived, freezing and naked within the depths of this dark place?"

Magnus could see exactly what his new companion meant. He shuddered to think about the fate that would have befallen him if this saviour had not appeared. Hastily he retrieved his clothes and began to dress himself.

"Feeling better?" asked the Cherine.

Magnus nodded. As he buckled his belt and fixed the brooch back onto his cloak, he began at last to feel warmth again. "But what did they want to do with all my things?" he wondered.

"Nothing," the Cherine replied.

"Nothing? But why—"

"The Plergle-Brots have need for nothing," the Cherine interrupted, "yet they want everything. Not because it may be of use to them, but merely for its own sake. They have an insatiable hunger, a greed for anything that is not theirs. You see even now how it overcomes their fears," he added, flicking his sword and neatly decapitating a Plergle-Brot that had snuck out and was grasping at the buckles of his boot. "But see also how once they have gained what they seek, they pay it no further regard, their lust having moved on to the next object of their desire."

"They certainly seemed interested when I tried to take my things back," muttered Magnus.

The Cherine laughed again. "Indeed, the only way their interest in anything can be rekindled is by attempting to take it away, for suddenly it is as if the thing is no longer theirs again. My friend, you will not easily prise anything from a Plergle-Brot. They have been trapping the unwary since time unknown, stripping them of all they have and leaving them to perish in this dismal waste. If you should spend any time exploring this detestable swamp, you will find it littered with their refuse, easily taken and just as easily discarded. However, time within the Plergle Swamp is not something I would recommend. I suggest we depart now, before they return in numbers even I may not be able to repel."

Magnus couldn't think of a better idea. He took hold of the firm hand offered and then followed as the Cherine found a sure path out of the swamp. It was only when they reached the safety of the road that the Cherine stopped and spoke again.

"I'm glad I was able to find you, friend Kertoobi. Forgive my rudeness for the situation was dire, but it is on my conscience that I make a proper introduction. My name is Shaindor and I make for Sweet Harmody. Are you to return to Lower Kertoob or will you accompany me?"

"My name is Magnus Mandalora, and I will accompany you," Magnus replied. "I wish to see for myself your wondrous city."

Sudden compassion softened Shaindor's shining blue eyes. "Magnus Mandalora, your loss is known to us in Sweet Harmody," he said solemnly. "You will indeed find welcome there."

Sweet Harmody

AFTER ABOUT AN HOUR of steady walking, the fog began to lift as the road rose away from the Plergle Swamp. It took a lot longer for Magnus to summon the courage to take a look behind at the fading misty blur, now far back in the distance. As each step carried them further away from the perils of that gloomy mire, he could not help thinking how extraordinarily lucky he had been to be rescued in such circumstances.

"How was it that you came to be in the Plergle Swamp at my hour of need?" he asked the Cherine beside him.

"It is a most remarkable thing," Shaindor replied. "It certainly was not my design to ever venture into that evil swamp. But as I was passing, I heard a strange noise, a sort of scratching, gravelly sound, which I felt compelled to investigate. I thought perhaps it might be the seldom seen but much discussed diperagoff, but in fact, it turned out to be you."

A scratching, gravelly sound? That could only have been the stones stuck to Magnus's boots. The very thing that had brought him into peril had also been the cause for his salvation. Magnus excitedly relayed this information to Shaindor who frowned.

"An extraordinary series of events, I agree," he said. "But we Cherines believe that everything happens for a reason. It seems, Magnus Mandalora, that we were destined to meet. I suspect at some point we shall discover why. Till then, let us away to Sweet Harmody. It is a long journey, but I think we will meet no further peril on this road."

Shaindor was right. Although it was a trek of ten days and nights to reach the city of the Cherines, the journey passed uneventfully. They shared the road with many fellow travellers: Klunkarians with their five stumpy legs and long braided hair, which they were constantly tripping over; Shabandors, towing wagons full of trinkets for sale, their shifty eyes on the lookout for the next sucker; as well as the obligatory Doosies, ears wide open and noses sniffing around for fresh gossip. But nothing or nobody they encountered was a threat in any way. Gradually, the blackness over Magnus's heart began to lift, and he began to feel a lightness of being that had seemed lost forever after the terrible news of several days previous.

Undoubtedly, his new travelling companion was a significant factor in this improvement in his spirits. This was not the first time Magnus had encountered a Cherine. Touring parties from Sweet Harmody made occasional trips to Lower Kertoob, and these visits always produced a great joyousness throughout the village. Much pflugberry wine would be consumed, and the night would always end with an enormous pflugberry pie fight. It was widely known, even amongst the Kertoobis, that spending time with a Cherine was exceptionally good for the soul.

At the end of each day, Magnus and Shaindor would make camp by the side of the road, light a fire, and warm up another pflugberry pie. When dinner was complete, Shaindor would entertain Magnus with songs about his wondrous city:

> *I walked the fair streets of Sweet Harmody town,*
> *From its gate to its glittering heart.*
> *For each house on those golden-paved lanes of renown,*
> *Is a wonder of glorious art.*
>
> *I climbed the great towers of Sweet Harmody town,*
> *And gazed out from those spires so high.*
> *Far away to me now seemed the land so far down,*
> *As my heart soared so near to the sky.*
>
> *I supped with the folk of Sweet Harmody town,*
> *The Cherines of such glory and fame.*
> *For their beauty sublime and their wisdom profound,*
> *Are the source of their widespread acclaim.*

Magnus would lie back and enjoy the sound of Shaindor's voice, now soft as a gentle summer rain. He would slowly drift off to sleep, his dreams filling with mighty towers topped with spires and the wise words of his new friend.

For the first nine days of the journey, the course was relatively flat. However, just past lunchtime on the tenth day, the road began to rise as it passed over a range of high, grassy hills topped with rocky ridges.

"The green hills of Gronadine," murmured Shaindor. "They provide a protective ring around the noble city. It will not be long before you shall at last see it for yourself."

As the road grew steeper and steeper, Magnus found himself beginning to tire, but the words of his companion spurred him on.

"Not much further now. Be strong and follow, for you shall soon be witness to a sight you will not ever forget."

After three trying hours, with the sun now sinking before them, they finally approached the peak of the range. Just before they reached the highest point, Shaindor stopped and turned to Magnus.

"The moment is almost upon us. Only a few steps are left till we reach the top of the pass. It is best that this be done properly. Close your eyes now that I might guide you. Then, when I say the word, you shall view the noble city in all its glory."

Magnus did as directed, shutting his eyes tightly and relying on his friend to guide his steps. As the road beneath him levelled out, he could feel the evening breeze cooling his forehead. Then Shaindor cried out:

"The time has come. Open your eyes, and behold Sweet Harmody!"

Magnus unclenched his eyes and then gasped. Unfurled before him was a vision of truly unsurpassed splendour.

The hills atop which he was now standing swung away to left and right and then met again in the near distance ahead, defining a deep, oval-shaped valley. The last wisps of sunlight were creeping over the far range and resplendent in their fading light, in the very centre of the valley, stood the city of the Cherines. Beneath the gathering dusk, it seemed to swim before Magnus's disbelieving eyes. The lights of its towers sparkled in a gleaming display of many-coloured jewels, while its great walls shone milky-white like the finest mother-of-pearl.

Magnus could only stand motionless, his eyes wide and his mouth gaping.

After a moment, Shaindor nudged him.

"If you are at a loss for words, may I make a few suggestions: breathtaking, ethereal, magical, inspiring, and earth-shattering."

"It's beautifagnificextraordimazing," Magnus murmured at last, trying to find the right word and managing only to mash a whole bunch of them together into something that barely made any sense at all.

Shaindor nodded, seeming to understand what Magnus was trying to say. "And it's even better from inside. Come with me, Magnus, and let me show you."

He took Magnus by the hand and led him down into the valley towards the radiant city ahead. Darkness had well and truly fallen when they arrived at the walls, now glowing translucent in the moonlight. Passing through the gates, Magnus entered, for the first time, the noble city of Sweet Harmody.

It was exactly as Jangos had described. Magnus felt as if he was floating in a dream of pure bliss. His feet barely touched the stones of the streets which, as Shaindor's song had stated, truly were paved with gold. They shimmered in the light of many fires, filling the air with a lustrous haze. Through this brilliance, faces of unmatched loveliness peered over, greeting him with warmth and kindness.

In a daze, Magnus allowed himself to be led down a maze of winding paths. Eventually, Shaindor stopped and opened a door. He guided Magnus inside, down a short corridor and into a room with a large and extremely welcoming bed.

"Here are your lodgings, Magnus. I'd say sweet dreams, but here in Sweet Harmody, that is assured."

Magnus was fast asleep before his head even hit the pillow.

* * *

Magnus woke slowly. He stretched his arms and legs, embracing the softness of the sheets and the plushness of the mattress below. He had never slept in such a comfortable bed.

"Awake at last, sleepyhead." Shaindor laughed as he came into the room.

Magnus yawned and stretched again. "I could lie here all day. This bed is magnificent."

"Nothing but the best for our guests. The sheets are finest spun shafkron and the mattress is filled with lienkor down."

Magnus gasped. Shafkron and lienkor down! Both items were rare and extremely valuable. Shafkron was a thread spun from the hair of a little-found rodent known as a shafrat. Each shafrat had but one hair which grew at the rate of half an inch every ten years. Lienkor down, on the other hand, was not so hard to find, given that the lienkor was an extremely common, fifteen-foot-high bird covered in brightly coloured feathers from beak to tail. However, removing the feathers from a lienkor was a tedious and often highly dangerous task. The birds were obsessive about politeness, requiring you to say "pretty please with sugar on top" for every feather that you plucked. And if they did not feel that your manner conveyed the correct tone of deference, they were liable to eat you.

Magnus got up and dressed himself, amazed to notice that all of the mud from the Plergle Swamp and the dust from the road had been removed from his clothes. He followed Shaindor back through the corridor, admiring the walls covered with delicate artwork and interspersed with shiny mirrors.

"Are all Cherine dwellings as magnificent as this?" wondered Magnus.

"Magnificent," Shaindor chuckled. "This is a mere cottage, plain and simple by the standards of Sweet Harmody."

At the end of the hallway, there was a small dining room. Here, Magnus and Shaindor shared the last of the pflugberry pies. When they had finished, Shaindor stood up.

"You have seen Sweet Harmody by night. Now it is time for you to experience it in the full light of day."

Upon leaving the house, Magnus found the brightness overwhelming. The sunlight upon the cobblestones blazed so fiercely that he was forced to shield his face. But gradually, as his eyes adjusted, he was able to begin taking it all in, overpowering as it was to his simple Kertoobi senses.

A pool of light rose up from the ground, flowing over the walls of the buildings that lined the narrow street. The sides of these buildings were detailed with the most intricate and exquisite of carvings and studded with a myriad of gems and precious stones. It seemed that not a single surface on any structure had been left unadorned, save for the mirrors of various sizes and shapes that hung at intervals, reflecting the light from all around until the whole street was immersed in a golden glow. Through this glow the great spired towers rose, their full majesty revealed against the deep blue sky.

For the next few hours, Shaindor guided Magnus on a tour of Sweet Harmody, revealing wonder after wonder until Magnus's brain struggled to take any more of it in. As morning passed into afternoon, the streets gradually grew wider until Magnus found himself on a broad boulevard that ran directly into the centre of the city. He felt himself seeming to shrink into insignificance as the towers rose, taller and grander on either side. At the end of the boulevard was a vast plaza, lined with green lawns and full of imposing statues. On the far side of this square stood the mightiest tower of all. The glittering heart of the noble city.

"Yonder is the palace of the Prodiva," said Shaindor, pointing across the plaza towards the far tower.

"What is a Prodiva?" asked Magnus.

"Not what, but who. The Prodiva is the ruler of Sweet Harmody, the leader of all the Cherines," Shaindor replied. "Come with me now, Magnus. He has heard of your arrival and wishes to meet with you."

The plaza was so wide, it seemed to take a lifetime to get from one end to the other. Eventually the companions reached the massive marble doors of the towering palace where two Cherine sentries stood, clad in shining armour. They nodded as Magnus and Shaindor approached and then stood aside as the doors slowly swung open.

"Welcome to the Great Hall of Sweet Harmody," said Shaindor in a voice soft with reverence.

Magnus could see why even Shaindor was awed. The scale of the Great Hall was beyond anything he had ever witnessed. The walls, lined with enormous coloured tapestries and shimmering mirrors, seemed to stretch on forever. But it was the ceiling that most caught Magnus's attention. Over its entire surface, an immense mural had been painted, an awe-inspiring battle scene filled with noble Cherine warriors brandishing mighty swords.

"The battle of Phrill," explained Shaindor, his voice echoing as they began the long journey down the length of the hall. "The greatest victory of my people. There, see Gronfel the Brave, leader of the Cherine armies on that glorious day." He pointed up towards a particularly noble-looking Cherine brandishing a particularly mighty looking sword.

Incredible as the painting was, there was one thing about it that Magnus did find quite odd. The Cherines were all poised as if in battle, thrusting and slashing with their swords, but there didn't seem to be anybody or anything they were thrusting and slashing against. It was as if they were just making poses rather than participating in an actual battle.

"But who are they fighting against?" Magnus asked. "There don't seem to be any enemies."

Shaindor stopped and turned to Magnus, his face grave. "We Cherines create only works of beauty. It would not be right to stain the perfection of this majestic hall with a depiction of that which they fought against." He then turned, adjusted his hair in one of the mirrors, and continued walking.

Magnus didn't say anything. He had a pretty good idea whom that enemy must have been. Since meeting Shaindor, he had managed to clear his mind of the evil that lay outside this city, and of the horror that had led to his brother's death and spurred him on to his own journey. Quickly, before such dark thoughts could return, he hurried to catch up with Shaindor.

At the far end of the hall, Magnus saw a huge stone throne, decorated with a massive bejewelled flower. On the throne sat without a doubt the most splendid and dignified Cherine that Magnus had yet seen. His eyes twinkled with wisdom and his whole bearing bespoke great power and majesty. He was clad in a white robe with red trimmings, but across his chest he wore a red sash, inscribed with the same flower as was emblazoned on the throne above. Behind the throne, slightly to the right, stood another Cherine. He wore a robe of reverse colour, red with white trimmings, and he held himself in a fashion that suggested quiet, understated dignity.

"Great Prodiva, I present to you Magnus Mandalora from the small homely village of Lower Kertoob," said Shaindor, bowing low as he addressed the Cherine on the throne.

"Greetings, Magnus," said the Prodiva in a soft voice. "Deep is the sorrow that we in Sweet Harmody feel for your loss. My name is Lipherel, and though I may be ruler of this mighty city, I should be your servant if that could go some way towards mending the sadness you must feel."

Magnus felt himself awed by these words and could barely manage an awkward bow as he mumbled in reply.

"There's nothing you need to do. It wasn't your fault."

"But in many ways I fear it was," said the other Cherine, speaking even more softly as he came out from behind the throne and stood alongside.

Magnus could only gasp in shock. "Surely not."

"Consider this," the other Cherine continued. "Your brother was travelling with an escort of Cherines, but they were not able to protect him. That in itself is a failing. More telling is the location where the attack took place. From the earliest days, we Cherines have been charged with the creation and preservation of beauty in all its forms. This duty includes the stewardship of all places of great natural wonder. If the safety of visitors to the Whounga Canyon, the finest spectacle in all of the world, can no longer be assured, then surely we have failed in this duty."

Lipherel motioned towards the other Cherine. "Magnus, this is Phraedon, Chief Judge of Sweet Harmody."

Phraedon bowed before Magnus. "A humble servant of the great Prodiva, now forever in your debt as well."

"I fear he has taken this most personally," said Lipherel.

Phraedon shook his head. "It is not merely about me. This is a threat that hangs over all our people. The Glurgs grow strong and bold. They strike now in places they have never dreamed to strike before. Their menace spreads over all lands like a black cloud—"

"But fear not," interrupted Lipherel, sensing Magnus's growing unease. "The Cherines will not allow it to spread further. We are even now massing our forces. An army is being summoned, the like of which has not been seen for many a year."

"Indeed," added Phraedon. "The loss of your brother to you is a tragedy beyond repair. But to us it is a warning sign, a call to action. We shall not rest until this threat is removed forever."

"But enough of that," said Lipherel quickly. "Such words and actions are of no interest to our visitor." He turned back to Magnus. "Anything we might do to lighten your mood, so we shall do. Though mere objects cannot compensate your loss, still I would offer you anything you may desire. Speak and you shall have it."

"There really is no need," muttered Magnus. "Just a chance to enjoy your wonderful city would be enough."

"He speaks fine words for a Kertoobi," said Lipherel. "So I decree that you shall have the freedom of our city. But eventide now awaits. Will you do us the honour of joining in our supper? We have nothing on the menu as fine as pflugberry pie, but perhaps you will find something to your satisfaction."

Magnus most definitely found dinner to his satisfaction. Fifteen different courses were placed in turn before him, each one more delectable than the last. Magnus tried his best not to gorge down these gastronomical delights and to instead copy the fine manners of his hosts, but figuring out all of the rules of Cherine etiquette, such as exactly which piece of cutlery to use, how large each individual bite should be, and how many times to chew before swallowing, was not easy. As he agonised again over which of a multitude of knives and forks to pick up, he suddenly found himself transfixed by a voice that rang through the dining chamber.

He looked up to see a Cherine maiden standing at the head of the table, her golden hair cascading down over a long dress of ivory white. Her voice was soft as lienkor down and as clear as the crystal peaks of the ice fields of Flairn as she sang her song of heroism and grace:

> *Red dawn rose o'er the field of Phrill,*
> *The wind blew clear and still.*
> *Brave Gronfel gave his last command,*
> *And strove to make a final stand,*
> *Upon that fateful hill.*
>
> *Encased in armour, fitted tight,*
> *And polished gleaming bright.*
> *Beneath his helm his hair stood firm,*
> *With layers, blow-wave and a perm,*
> *As forth he strode to fight.*
>
> *And even as his foes did swarm,*
> *Beneath that sun so warm.*
> *Great Gronfel raised his sword up high,*
> *And with a mighty battle cry,*
> *He showed his finest form.*

His blade did flash with style and flair,
He smote with studied care.
And with each strike he raised his shield,
For his reflection so revealed,
To check his face and hair.

And as night fell upon that plain,
All Gronfel's foes were slain.
Yet not one hair was out of place,
No scar besmirched his noble face,
His armour bore no stain.

By the song's end, Magnus had been lulled into such a state of total relaxation, he was barely able to keep his eyes open. It took a series of taps on his shoulder to stir him out of his reverie.

"Magnus, this is Tharella."

The voice was Shaindor's. Magnus opened his eyes. Standing beside Shaindor was the Cherine who had been singing. Up close, her beauty filled Magnus's eyes with a light that was blazingly brilliant and somehow also soothingly gentle.

"Greetings, Magnus," said Tharella. "I knew Jangos and I miss him. He made us laugh, and laughter is a blessing, especially in such dark times. But perhaps you also bring a gift to Sweet Harmody?"

"Surely my lady, I don't have any gifts," said Magnus. "I'm not Jangos, and I do not think I could make anyone laugh. Certainly not now."

"I share your pain," said Tharella. "And yet you are not wholly right. Everyone has their own gift. They just need to know where to look in order to find it. But you are tired. I think it is past the time for you to be in bed. I should upbraid Shaindor for keeping you up so late."

"It was worth it to hear your song," replied Magnus.

Tharella smiled, sending warmth flowing through every corner of Magnus's being. Then she turned back to Shaindor.

"And what about you?" he said. "Your day rapidly approaches. Do you feel you are ready?"

She nodded. "I believe so. As ready as anyone could be."

A black, starless night lay over Sweet Harmody as Magnus and Shaindor left the palace and began their journey back across the plaza.

Even in the darkness, Magnus could see all was not still. Movement caught his eyes. The glint of fleeting moonlight on armour and sword. The sound of thudding feet. A great army marched in that square.

"You see the truth in the Prodiva's words," said Shaindor. "Sweet Harmody is not idle. Battle will soon be rejoined."

Magnus shuddered. He had not yet told anyone, not even Shaindor, of his real reason for leaving Lower Kertoob. If he was true to himself, it was not a secret he would be able to keep for much longer.

Sharbalons and Krpolgs

OVER THE NEXT FOUR DAYS, Magnus took in the sights and sounds of Sweet Harmody. He spent hours exploring the streets and lanes, delighting in particular in visiting the artisans' quarters where the great craftsmen resided: artists, sculptors, metal workers, and jewellers, all expert in the creation of objects of extraordinary beauty. Within the shops and workshops that lined the twisting alleyways, Magnus could see Cherines hard at work, shaping fine metal into complex but delicate designs, cutting jewels into pieces of immaculate shape and worth, and carving ivory and alabaster into intricately detailed figures.

"You see that the magnificence of Sweet Harmody does not exist by chance," said Shaindor. "It takes the labour of many to maintain our city in the state that you find it."

Much of Magnus's time was spent with his new friend, who proved himself a most helpful and informative guide. But even when left to his own devices, Magnus never found himself alone for long. The Cherines being so friendly and welcoming, he was regularly invited into other homes, particularly when mealtimes came around. And after eating, there would always be much music and singing.

Despite the joys of the noble city, Magnus still could not shake off the dark feelings that hung over his heart. The sight of armoured troops marching through the city was becoming a frequent occurrence, and news regularly came in of ever more brazen and deadly Glurg attacks. The blackness that was spreading in the world outside the walls of the city could no longer be avoided.

On the fifth day, Shaindor roused Magnus especially early.

"Awake, Magnus. Today is an important day."

"What could be more important than a good sleep?" groaned Magnus as his eyes gradually adjusted to the morning light.

"Today is the day of the Sharbalon. Come quickly. This is an event you will not want to miss."

After a hurried breakfast, Magnus followed Shaindor outside and onto the wide avenue that led towards the centre of the city. A vast throng already filled the street, making for the Prodiva's palace.

"What is a Sharbalon?" asked Magnus as he struggled to avoid being swept off his feet by the rushing flood of Cherines.

"The Sharbalon is the ceremony by which we choose a new Prodiva," replied Shaindor.

"What's wrong with the old one?" wondered Magnus, thinking back to his encounter with Lipherel some days ago.

"There is nothing wrong with the old one. Lipherel has performed his duties with grace and dignity. But it is our way that the office of Prodiva can be held for one year only before it must be passed onto a new candidate. Here, be careful..."

Shaindor reached out to pull Magnus up, preventing him from drowning in a sea of perfectly manicured feet.

As they reached the central plaza, the crowd was able to spread out a bit, giving them some much needed space and allowing Magnus to continue with his questions.

"Why can a Prodiva serve only one year?"

"Three reasons," replied Shaindor. "Reason one is that we believe every Cherine to be wholly unique, possessed of their own individual and wonderful talents. By choosing a new Prodiva each year, we ensure that a new set of such talents is brought to the role. Thus the city and its people are constantly replenished and renewed."

Magnus nodded. This seemed like an excellent reason.

"Reason two. Even for those as wise as the Cherines, power is a temptation that may be hard to resist. By limiting the length of time any one may hold office, we ensure nobody can gain more power than would be good for them, or for the city."

Magnus nodded again. This seemed like an even better reason.

"And what is the third?"

Shaindor grinned broadly. "The third reason is that it allows us to have a Sharbalon every year. And as you will soon discover, a Sharbalon is a truly wondrous event. Come now, let us enter the Great Hall."

Magnus and Shaindor walked through the palace doors and passed into the Great Hall. As they followed the crowd down the length of the hall, Magnus was amazed to see that rows and rows of chairs had been laid out. At the far end of the hall, just before the throne, a platform had been raised, bounded on both sides by curtains of scarlet.

"Here, we have an excellent position," said Shaindor as he guided Magnus to a seat and then sat beside him.

Magnus looked around. It seemed that the whole city was now seated within the Great Hall. Lipherel still sat on his throne, gazing beatifically over the room, but this time nobody was standing behind him.

"Where is Phraedon?" asked Magnus.

Shaindor pointed to three seats set slightly forward, just below the front of the platform. "See, he sits with the other judges."

Magnus looked more closely. Although only their backs were visible, he could see that in the central seat there was a Cherine in the familiar red robe trimmed with white, while on either side sat two other Cherines, clad in red robes without trimming.

"They will make the final decision on which candidate shall be the new Prodiva," explained Shaindor.

"How do they choose?"

"There are three trials which all candidates must fulfill. The candidate who wins will be the one who most clearly demonstrates the values we hold of highest order: skill at arms, wisdom and beauty. But quiet now. The ceremony begins."

At that moment a surge of music filled the hall. A single Cherine stood up on stage and announced the beginning of the first trial: the test of arms. He then shouted out the name of the first candidate:

"Fermwell!"

The Cherine called Fermwell leapt out through the curtains on the left side of the stage, clad from head to toe in shining battle gear and brandishing a fearsomely sleek sword. He bowed low to the audience and then proceeded to demonstrate a series of expertly executed thrusts, parries, and stabs, all the while moving nimbly over the stage.

At the completion of this display, the crowd clapped politely. Fermwell bowed again and then walked off through the curtains on the right side of the stage.

The announcer returned to the stage and called the name of the second candidate:

"Yeaborn!"

Yeaborn strode onto the stage and followed a similar routine to Fermwell's, revealing a comparably adept level of military prowess before bowing and departing to further applause.

Seven more candidates followed, each swinging and jabbing and cutting with dexterity and proficiency. When the name of the tenth and final candidate was announced, Magnus gasped.

"Tharella!"

Tharella appeared through the curtain and stepped onto the stage. Now dressed in shimmering armour, she seemed to Magnus even more lustrous. As with the other candidates, she bowed, then lifted her sword and began to slice it through the air. Her movements as she danced across the stage in battle against an invisible foe were precise and skilful, yet also fluid and graceful. At the end of her demonstration, the roar of applause was more than for all the other candidates combined.

The announcer returned to the stage to declare that the first trial had ended and there would be a short break while the candidates prepared for the next.

Magnus looked around again, noticing the judges now involved in feverish discussion. Before long, the announcer came on again to declare that the second trial, the test of wisdom, was to begin.

Once again Fermwell was the first candidate to appear. However, this time the battle gear was gone. As he reached the front of the stage, the judge sitting to the right of Phraedon stood and asked a question:

"Why should you be selected as the next Prodiva?"

Fermwell stood in thought for a few moments before replying. "Because I have the strength, the courage and the wisdom to lead my people to victory," he cried out at last to the great approval of the audience.

The judge thanked Fermwell for his response and sat down. The judge sitting on Phraedon's other side then stood up and asked a question:

"If there was one aspect of the world you could change, what would it be?"

Fermwell did not have to think about this, firing off an answer without even taking a breath. "If I had the power, I would henceforth remove all ugliness from the world."

As before, the judge thanked the candidate, speaking loudly to make himself heard over the cheering of the crowd. Finally Phraedon stood up. He waited, allowing the crowd to quieten, before asking his question:

"What is the one word that you believe best sums you up?"

This question seemed to be the most challenging of all. Fermwell considered for a long time, searching for the right word, before eventually replying. "I believe that word would be 'inspiring'."

The crowd seemed to think he had made a good choice and gave Fermwell a great whoop of support. Fermwell accepted Phraedon's thank-you with a bow and then walked proudly off the stage.

So the ceremony continued for the next eight candidates. Each appeared on stage to be asked the same three questions, and each replied in fairly like manner. For the first question, all answers revolved around either leading the people to victory or sharing their great wisdom and talent. For the second question, elimination of unsightliness was the constant theme of all responses. For the final question, the words bandied around included noble, fearless, and magnificent.

Finally, only Tharella remained. She glided through the curtains, seeming to float above the surface of the stage. Then she stood silent, radiating serenity as she waited for the first question:

"Why should you be selected as the next Prodiva?"

She did not even need to think. Her voice was clear and confident as she replied, "Because however grim the days become, I will never allow the light that shines inside our people to burn out."

The crowd responded with the loudest cheer that had yet been heard within the hall. Tharella did not move as she waited for them to hush so the second question could be asked:

"If there was one aspect of the world you could change, what would it be?"

Once again, she did not need to spend any time in consideration. "I would set myself always to the creation of beauty, for it is by creating, not destroying, that we can make the world truly beautiful."

The crowd again erupted with delight at this response. It took a full five minutes before there was sufficient quiet for Phraedon to ask his final question:

"What is the one word that you believe best sums you up?"

This time she did not reply immediately. Her eyes searched carefully around the hall as she contemplated, eventually coming to rest upon the mirrors that lined the wall. Then she looked back at the judges and answered. "Reflective."

This was clearly the best answer yet. The crowd stood up as one to give Tharella a deserved ovation. She bowed low before them and then was gone.

At the end of the second trial, the judges once again conferred while the candidates prepared for their final challenge. The trial that Shaindor assured Magnus was the hardest of the three to fulfill. The test of beauty.

"What do they have to do?" asked Magnus.

"Nothing," replied Shaindor. "That is what makes it so difficult."

For a third time, Fermwell returned to the stage, this time clad in a robe of glittering gold. He stood for several moments at the front of the stage, twisting and turning only slightly to ensure that the sparkle of his garments would reach all corners of the hall. He then walked off to the side, but instead of passing out through the curtains, he remained on stage, waiting stationary while the next candidate emerged.

So the candidates reappeared in turn, each done up in the finest of vestments. One at a time, they sashayed up to the front of the stage and stood, allowing the judges and audience to bask in their splendour. Then they walked to the sides of the stage, alternating left and right, to form a backdrop for the remaining candidates.

Magnus held his breath in anticipation for Tharella to emerge. At last she was called, the final candidate to appear. Unlike the others, her robe was simple, bearing no ornaments or decoration. Yet her radiance was such that she lit up the Great Hall like a torch glowing in the darkness of the deep caves of Corbellum. Much cheering had greeted the other candidates, but for Tharella there was only awe-struck silence.

The hush remained as for the third time the three judges consulted. Their discussion was more animated now, as if they had irreconcilable differences of opinion.

"You see now how they debate the merits of each candidate?" said Shaindor.

Magnus didn't see how it could be a difficult choice to make. One candidate was so clearly superior to the others. "What happens if they cannot agree?"

"Then it is up to the Chief Judge, wise Phraedon, to cast the deciding vote."

At last the judges ceased their conferring. As one, they stood up and ascended to the stage. Here they turned to the audience and Phraedon declared, "People of Sweet Harmody, the verdict of your judges is now at hand."

Before announcing the victor, the judges in turn congratulated several of the candidates for particularly impressive performances in individual trials:

"Fermwell, you showed great skill and valour in the test of arms."

"Gaiholm, your answers to the questions displayed true insight."

"Yeaborn, your rare beauty is beyond dispute."

However, there could be no doubt as to whom the winning candidate must be. "It is now my proud duty to declare that the victor in our Sharbalon today is…" Phraedon paused for dramatic effect, gazing out over the hall and its expectant masses, before turning back to the stage to utter the final, inevitable word. "Tharella!"

Again, the music surged, and the crowd rose to their feet, cheering wildly. Tharella stepped forward to the front of the stage, standing before Phraedon.

"Are you ready now to take the oath of office?" Phraedon asked.

Tharella nodded.

Phraedon held up an ancient scroll from which he proceeded to read. "Do you swear to uphold the laws of the Cherines, to protect and defend our noble city and its people against all enemies, and to tirelessly strive for the victory of beauty and the destruction of all who oppose it?"

"I swear," said Tharella in a voice that rang out through the Great Hall.

As Tharella took her oath, Lipherel at last rose from his throne and walked up to stand beside her. He removed his red sash and placed it over her shoulders.

"People of Sweet Harmody, behold your new Prodiva," he called.

Tharella bowed low and then turned and walked back to the throne. As she sat down, Phraedon again turned to face the crowd.

"People of Sweet Harmody, it is a long time since we, your judges, faced such a grave choice. The task for Tharella shall be great for even now our enemies gather, seeking to cast a shadow of horror over all the lands. Let us always remember the significance of this day, for even as we were victorious then, so shall we be victorious again."

"Such things will be dealt with in time," said Tharella. "But for now, let us take advantage of this glorious day. Good people of Sweet Harmody, my first order to you as your new Prodiva is to enjoy to the fullest the remainder of this Sharbalon."

With a great cheer, the crowd rose and began filing out of the hall. Out in the plaza the party had already begun, with music playing and Cherines dancing and singing. But Magnus could not help thinking of Phraedon's final words.

"What is the significance of this day that Phraedon wants us to remember?" he asked Shaindor.

"The Sharbalon always falls on the anniversary of the battle of Phrill," Shaindor replied. "It is thus that we celebrate to mark the greatest day in our long, proud history."

And celebrate the city did. It was close to dawn when an exhausted Magnus was finally led back to Shaindor's house and a welcome bed.

"My people have chosen well," commented Shaindor after wishing Magnus goodnight.

Magnus nodded. "The Cherines are indeed lucky to be led by such a wise and gracious ruler."

* * *

In the days that followed the Sharbalon, an air of heavy expectancy settled over the city. At all hours, the clatter of feet and the ringing of arms could not be avoided as the great army went through its paces. But this was all it seemed to be doing. There was not a hint of when it would march through the gates to take on the enemy whose strength seemed to grow with every passing day.

"They have reached even to the vale of Yallaron," cried folk on the street. "Never in our lifetime have the Glurg armies drawn so near to Sweet Harmody. Surely it is time that our forces marched."

Magnus began to find the atmosphere stifling. It became harder and harder for him to savour the pleasures of the noble city. Every day that passed brought him closer to the time when he would have to declare his true intentions.

On the fourth day after the Sharbalon, Magnus could bear it no longer.

"I wish to speak to the Prodiva," he said to Shaindor as they breakfasted together.

"What about?" asked Shaindor.

"I cannot say. But I would like to see her today. Is there something I need to do to make an appointment?"

Shaindor shook his head. "Tharella will always welcome you. But will you meet her alone or shall I accompany you?"

"Yes, I'd like you to come with me," said Magnus.

The Great Hall had by now been cleared of the trappings of the Sharbalon. Tharella sat still on the throne, the sash of office across her breast, while Phraedon had returned to his position behind.

"Greetings, Magnus," said Tharella. "Is there something you wish from me today?"

"Yes, there is, great Prodiva." Magnus swallowed before finally managing to force the words out. "When the Cherine army marches from Sweet Harmody, I want to go with them."

A gasp came from beside him. He looked around to see Shaindor, eyes wide in horror. Magnus forced himself to continue.

"I too wish to wage war on the Glurgs."

Tharella frowned. "This is a most serious request. I fear that you do not truly understand what you are asking for."

"On the contrary, my lady, I understand full well."

"But this is madness," cried Shaindor. "Surely you are not serious."

"I've never been more serious in my life."

"You have no conception of what you are saying," Shaindor continued, clearly upset. "You cannot imagine the true terror of the Glurgs. Merely the sight of one would still your heart with fright. They are ghastly of face, vile and twisted in body. They glory only in violence and pain, destruction and death."

"Shaindor is right," said Tharella. "This battle is not for you, Magnus."

"But it is for me," insisted Magnus. "They killed my brother. I have to do something."

"It is noble for you to offer us your aid, but we cannot accept it," said Tharella. "The enemy is too strong for you. Leave this fight to the Cherines. If it is vengeance you seek, we shall deliver it for you."

"Listen to Tharella," begged Shaindor. "She speaks the truth."

"Stay if you wish in Sweet Harmody," added Tharella. "You will always be welcome here. But when you go from this city, return to Lower Kertoob. You and your people have no need to fear. Your village is precious to us, and we will ensure it comes to no harm."

Magnus looked down at his feet in shame. He knew the words of the Prodiva made sense. What use would he be in a great battle against the power of the Glurg armies? But he couldn't just slink back to Lower Kertoob like a drog with its leg between its tails.

"There must be something I can do," he pleaded.

Tharella shook her head. "There is nothing."

"There may be something."

It was Phraedon, now stepping out to stand beside the throne. Magnus looked up with sudden new hope.

"Magnus," continued the Chief Judge. "Do you know anything of the Krpolg?"

"You cannot ask this of him," said Tharella quickly. "It is far too dangerous."

"This Kertoobi offers his aid," said Phraedon. "The Krpolg has troubled us now for many months. Do we find now a solution to this problem?"

"But he's just a Kertoobi."

"A Kertoobi with perhaps the very skills we require to complete this mission."

"What is a Krpolg?" asked Magnus. He looked quizzically at Shaindor, but his friend seemed utterly confused by this exchange.

"For a long time now," said Phraedon, "we have been concerned about the growing strength and confidence of our enemy. Many times in the past they have risen in might to attack, but always we have been able to hold them off and drive them back to their stronghold at Hargh Gryghrgr. But now there is something different. They attack with a fierceness we have not experienced before. Whole stretches of country that we long held have now been taken from us. And we think that the answer has something to do with the Krpolg."

"So what exactly is this Krpolg?" asked Magnus again.

"We do not know," replied Phraedon. "We have heard stories and rumours that it is some sort of new weapon the Glurgs have devised. Something so powerful that nothing can stand in its way. Something so awesome that the very thought of it gives them the confidence to fight with a power ten times what they were previously capable of."

"That is why we have held back our army," added Tharella. "Not knowing what we face, prudence seemed the wisest option. We do not wish to send our forces out on a suicide mission."

"But we cannot hold back forever," said Phraedon. "Soon we must march, Krpolg or not. And the more we know of what this deadly new weapon may be, the better prepared we will be for that fateful day. This is how I believe you may be able to aid us."

"You need me to help you find out more about this Krpolg," said Magnus.

"Indeed," replied the Chief Judge. "Unfortunately, our sources of information are less reliable than we might wish."

Magnus nodded in understanding. He had a pretty good idea of the sources Phraedon referred to. The problem they faced could be best expressed by the popular Kertoobi rhyme:

> *If you seek for the truth, of course,*
> *Never make a Doosie your source.*

Not a particularly good rhyme, but it did illustrate the difficulties before them. The Cherines needed reliable information and they needed it soon. This left one major unanswered question in Magnus's mind.

"So, how do you think I might be able to help you discover what the Krpolg is?"

Phraedon frowned. "This is the bit where it starts to get dangerous. What we really need is for somebody to enter into Hargh Gryghrgr in secret and find out first hand."

Magnus reeled back in dismay. To actually enter into Hargh Gryghrgr, the terrible fortress of the Glurgs!

"But s-s-surely this is a task a Cherine could accomplish," he eventually managed to stammer.

"Unfortunately not," said Tharella. "We require someone to pass, quietly and unannounced, into the Glurg city. We Cherines have many outstanding talents but passing quietly and unannounced is not one of them."

"Imagine a mighty Cherine warrior such as Shaindor," added Phraedon. "He could make an audacious and bold assault on the very gates of the stronghold, but to what effect? Even he could not storm the might of Hargh Gryghrgr alone. However a Kertoobi such as yourself might just be able to sneak in under their guard."

"But I do not even know where Hargh Gryghrgr is or how to get there."

"You would not be on your own for the whole of this quest," said Phraedon. "We will send a guide to show you the way as far as possible, and to protect and defend you from whatever dangers you should happen to meet on the road."

"This is insane," said Shaindor, still violently shaking his head. "Magnus, you do not need to do this."

"Indeed, he does not," agreed Phraedon. "There is no obligation to take on this task. And we will not regard you in any lower esteem should you refuse."

Magnus looked from Phraedon and Shaindor to Tharella, searching in her face for some clue as to whether he should assent to this mission.

"I cannot give you the answer you seek," said Tharella. "Only you can make this choice. But think wisely. This journey is fraught with peril."

Magnus wished he could curl up into a little ball and hide away. He wished he had never left that delightful bed of shafkron sheets and lienkor down. He wished he was back, safe and sound, in his little kertottage in Lower Kertoob.

At the same time, he didn't. The fire in his heart still raged as strongly as on the day he had set out. He had already survived the Plergle Swamp and made it to Sweet Harmody. There was no way he was going to turn back now. Before he even had the chance to think about what he was saying, the words had already spilled out of his mouth.

"I'll do it."

For a moment, nobody in the Great Hall spoke. Finally it was Tharella who broke the silence.

"If I could, I would continue to dissuade you for all it was worth, but I see you are determined. Whether you succeed or fail, your courage shall always be remembered in Sweet Harmody."

"Let us not speak of failure," said Phraedon. "We shall succeed. Too long have we allowed the ugliness of the Glurgs to defile our fair lands. It is time their vile stain was erased forever."

"But for now," said Tharella, "I would suggest you return to Shaindor's house to rest. You will require all your strength for the road."

The Blerchherchh

MAGNUS WAS GIVEN THREE DAYS to prepare for his mission. The very first thing he was required to do was change his garb.

"Your Kertoobi clothing is most appealing and charming," opined Phraedon, "but woefully unsuitable for the journey you must undertake. It is far too bright and colourful and will surely attract attention. For this mission, you will require an outfit that will allow you to pass unseen by even the sharpest eye."

Phraedon sent Magnus to the best tailors in Sweet Harmody who, after careful measuring, produced some new clothes for him: a travelling suit, complete with shirt, pants and cloak, all cut from the drabbest schnottzerskin. The schnottzer was a large animal of such uninteresting appearance that it had resided in near plague proportions and in close proximity to Sweet Harmody for millennia without ever being noticed. It probably would have remained undiscovered had not a particularly short-sighted specimen mistaken a rather tall Cherine, by the name of Glishorn, for a blumphera bush, the usual food source for these otherwise docile creatures. The bumbling beast had nibbled off both arms and most of a right leg before the unfortunate Cherine became aware of the creature that was ingesting him.

Magnus was also provided with a new pack which was somehow miraculously crafted to feel almost weightless when placed on his back, regardless of how fully laden it was. And to ensure sustenance on the road, he was supplied by the greatest chefs in the city. However, there was one dish even they were not prepared to attempt to cook. Instead, Magnus was handed a whole carton of pflugberries, less fresh than he would normally have liked but still quite useable, and given the freedom of the best equipped kitchens in the city in order to ensure an adequate supply of pflugberry pies for the journey.

On the evening of the final day before his departure, Magnus received one final summons from the Prodiva. Finding his way unaided to the Great Hall, where as expected Tharella and Phraedon awaited, Magnus was happy to see that Shaindor also stood alongside.

"Before we continue with what must be done," said Tharella, "I feel it is my duty to offer you one more opportunity to change your mind. Do you still wish to proceed with this mission?"

Common sense told Magnus exactly how to respond to this question. Here was a final opportunity to do the reasonable thing. There would be no honour lost. It had been an act of courage to even say 'yes' in the first place. Now it was time for the fantasy to end and for Magnus to return to the real world. He did not even hesitate as he spoke:

"Yes, I still wish to proceed with this mission."

"I thought as much," said Tharella. "And though this is grievous to me, I have something to tell you which brightens my heart a little. As we have said previously, you shall not embark alone from Sweet Harmody. Therefore, I henceforth inform you that to assist you as well as he might, Shaindor will accompany you."

Magnus's heart leapt at this news. He rushed forwards to embrace Shaindor, crying, "I couldn't ask for a better guide."

"I was in great pain when I heard you make your choice," said Shaindor. "But then I remembered the circumstances of our first meeting, and how our fates have become intertwined. I began to understand that perhaps there was a good reason for you to embark on this quest, ill-advised as it would seem. And I knew at that moment that you would not be leaving Sweet Harmody without me beside you."

"And a wiser, truer guide than Shaindor you will not find," said Tharella.

"Indeed," added Phraedon. "If anyone could lead you underneath the watch of the Glurgs and to the very walls of Hargh Gryghrgr, he is the one. But there is one more gift we have for you before you depart." He reached underneath his robe and offered to Magnus a small sword.

Magnus took the sword and held it before his eyes, marvelling at the glint of its steel and the sharpness of its blade.

"Understand that this is no ordinary weapon," said Tharella. "It was owned once by Gronfel the Brave."

"Gronfel the Brave!" exclaimed Magnus. "Surely this was not the mighty sword he wielded at the battle of Phrill?"

Tharella and Phraedon chuckled.

"Surely, it was not," said Phraedon. "The sword that Gronfel wielded on that day you would not even be able to lift. But this was, it is said, the blade he used to open the many letters of commendation he received after that famous victory."

"And for that we hold it in no lesser regard," added Tharella. "Use it well when you need to, though I pray those times be few. But come now. It is near to dinner time. As you will not soon be dining again in the noble city, I wish to make this a meal to remember."

Once again, the dinner was extraordinary. Preoccupied with his mission, Magnus was unable to stop himself wolfing it down without any regard to the complicated etiquette he would normally have been obliged to follow. Fortunately, the other Cherines, even with their finely tuned table manners and delicately measured out morsels, were not upset in the slightest by this exuberance, cheerfully encouraging him to eat his fill. After the food was removed at last, the music and singing began. Magnus might have sat and listened all night had Shaindor not gently lifted him and whispered in his ear:

"Come Magnus. Though the night is but young, the hour has come for us to retire. Our journey begins tomorrow. Let your last sleep in Sweet Harmody be a good one."

* * *

Magnus was still dreaming of the magnificent feast when Shaindor shook him awake next morning.

"Why do you wake me so early?" he protested. "Surely the sun has not yet risen."

"I fear we shall not see the sun today," said Shaindor. "But come, I have let you rest enough. It is past the time when we should be on our way."

The darkness of the morning matched Magnus's mood as he reluctantly got out of bed and dressed in his new travel clothes. After a perfunctory breakfast, he said farewell to Shaindor's cosy dwelling, and together they made their way along the narrow, twisting lanes.

When they reached the gates, Magnus paused, reluctant to leave the noble city, until Shaindor took him by the hand and led him through the mighty archway and into the world outside.

Slowly, they crossed the valley and began climbing up into the green hills of Gronadine. Magnus could not stop himself looking back over his shoulder to catch just one more glimpse of the city, still shining like a lone beacon in the cloudy gloom. But after half an hour, they reached the heights of that encircling range and began to go down the other side. And then Sweet Harmody was gone.

Magnus drew his cloak around him and shivered. Whilst basking in the brightness and warmth of Sweet Harmody, he had lost all sense of time passing. Now, back in the outside world, reality was quickly returning. Summer was long gone and winter was setting in. The sky was grey, and a light rain fell as they descended from the hills and began following the road that led south-west from the city.

Once they had left the green hills behind, the land grew wilder around them. Carefully tended fields soon gave way to unkempt bushland, which in turn was gradually replaced by light forests of scraggly trees. Shaindor and Magnus spoke little, pushing on as best they could, though the weather showed little sign of improving. By early afternoon, the forests were getting thicker, and the road began to descend into a narrow crevice. Soon, the pair found themselves at the bottom of a deep, dark ravine. High, mossy cliffs rose up on either side, and heavy gnarled trees, bent and twisted with age, prowled all around.

"The dingy, dungy Drungledum Valley," said Shaindor. "A place of ill repute into which my people seldom venture. But haste has forced us here. This is the quickest way to the path we must follow. Come, let us hurry. I do not think we wish to tarry."

So saying, Shaindor and Magnus increased their pace, hurrying through the shadows of the valley as quickly as their legs could carry them. Or at least as quickly as Magnus's legs could carry him, for Shaindor was regularly forced to stop and wait for his less able companion to catch up with him. Even so, after several hours Magnus found he had reached the limits of his endurance.

"As dingy and dungy as this place is, I cannot go any further," he moaned as he sat himself down on a large, wet boulder.

Shaindor was reluctant at first to stop, but after several entreaties he agreed to allow Magnus a ten minute breather.

"How many days before we get near to Hargh Gryghrgr?" asked Magnus when he had begun to get his breath back.

"It is difficult to say," replied Shaindor. "It has been many years since any of my race journeyed near to its loathsome gates. But we do not make directly for there."

"Really? Why not?"

"I have been charged with more than one errand as part of this journey. Of course, my first priority is to guide and protect you, and nothing shall ever divert me from this task. But between here and your ultimate destination, there is another task I am required to perform. It lies on the way to Hargh Gryghrgr but not in a straight line. For this reason, we have been forced to make a slight diversion from our original course and enter into this dismal valley."

"What exactly is that other task?" wondered Magnus.

Shaindor did not reply. His head was cocked to one side and he was concentrating hard. After a few seconds, he turned to Magnus. "Did you hear something?"

Magnus raised his head and listened as hard as he could, but heard nothing. He shook his head.

"I definitely heard something, coming from somewhere yonder," said Shaindor, pointing to the cliff behind.

Magnus strained his ears but still could hear nothing. "But your ears are so much more sensitive than mine."

Shaindor nodded. "You are right. And there's something about this place that my ears do not like. Neither do my eyes. Turn around and tell me what you see?"

Magnus stood and looked around. Behind the large rock upon which he had been sitting lay another boulder, slightly higher as the ground began to rise. Behind this was a series of further stones embedded into the cliff wall, each set directly above the one below like a rough sort of staircase. As Magnus scanned his eyes up the wall, his insides contracted. Just above the topmost step, there was a big round opening, a dark cave high on the cliff face. There could be no doubting now the sounds coming out of that cave – a kind of scraping, rasping, dragging noise, getting louder and louder.

"The seldom seen but much discussed diperagoff?" said Magnus, more in hope than anything else.

"I think not," said Shaindor. "I do think, however, that we should get out of here, fast."

They both turned to run, but it was already too late. The noise above had reached fever pitch. Whatever was in that cave had just about reached the entrance.

"Quick, hide," said Shaindor. He dragged Magnus over to the far side of the valley where they attempted to duck down behind the trunk of one of the rotten old trees.

The thing in the cave emerged slowly, gradually taking form in the darkness of the valley. It was huge, green and utterly hideous. Its broad, twisted body writhed with bulging, quivering muscles, while its gangling arms and legs each culminated in a bristling tangle of razor-sharp claws. Atop a giant, misshapen head, vicious eyes glowed as fiercely as the flames of the fiery holes of Theringdol, and beneath these were not one, nor even two, but three gaping mouths, each filled with a fearsome array of teeth and fangs of all conceivable sizes and shapes, as well as a few that were actually quite inconceivable.

"Is that a…a…a Glurg?" whispered Magnus in horrified fascination.

Shaindor shook his head, then made a strange noise in his throat. "Blerchherchh."

"What?" said Magnus.

Shaindor made the noise again, "Blerchherchh." Then he held his finger up over his mouth. "Shhhh."

The creature began to climb down the stone steps, its blazing eyes peering over towards their hiding spot. It opened all three mouths simultaneously, and from out of them, three monstrous voices echoed across the narrow space.

"Mmmmm! Do I hear dinner?"

Magnus was now shaking so hard that the tree they were hiding behind began to quiver. Shaindor quickly put an arm out to steady him as the creature reached the floor of the valley and began to lurch towards them.

"What have we here?" it roared. "Something sweet or something savoury? Shall I boil you or shall I fry you? Or shall I wrap you up in pastry, baste you with oil, and put you in the oven until you're nice and crisp and brown?"

The creature had virtually reached their hiding spot by now. Suddenly, Shaindor took his hand away from Magnus's back. He let out a mighty yell and leapt to his feet.

"Begone, cruel Blerchherchh, lest you wish to get a taste of my steel in each of your foul mouths."

The Blerchherchh let out a blood-curdling laugh. "Seems to me there's more than just a taste here. You look like you'll make a hearty feast. For starters, I'll bake your brains and roast your heart in a thick and spicy stock." With that, it made a lunge towards Shaindor. Just in time, Shaindor swung his sword, striking the grasping claws with a loud, reverberating clang.

"Then I'll mash your kidneys and pickle your pancreas," roared the monster, as it again rushed towards Shaindor. Again, Shaindor was able to drive the brute away, but it did not seem too perturbed by this show of resistance.

"I'll steam your stomach and broil your bladder. I'll flambé your intestines and serve them up with a light but cheeky dipping sauce," it cried as it circled Shaindor, reaching out every so often with an expectant claw which was always quickly rebuffed by Shaindor's steely blade.

"I'll make dumplings from your duodenum and sausages from your spleen. I'll dice and slice your gizzards, I'll..."

Without warning, the Blerchherchh suddenly charged at Shaindor, this time catching him just a little off his guard. Shaindor was just able to repel the attack, but in doing so, he lost his footing and fell heavily on his back.

The Blerchherchh laughed a cruel laugh. With one swing of its claw, it sent Shaindor's sword spinning away across the valley floor. With another swing, it sent Shaindor spinning across the valley floor as well. Headfirst, the Cherine crashed back to earth. There he lay, senseless and motionless, now utterly at the creature's mercy.

Before Magnus could even stop himself, he had let out a loud gasp of horror. The Blerchherchh paused and then turned towards him.

"What is this? Are there more treats in store?"

Realising that his hiding place no longer offered any security, Magnus jumped up and began running over to the far side of the valley, trying to put as much distance as he could between himself and the ruthless monster. The Blerchherchh watched him, a lascivious grin etched over each of its mouths.

"How delightful," it drooled. "Is this dessert? Or is it perhaps an appetiser before the main meal?"

Then it began striding, slowly but purposefully, towards Magnus, all the while licking its slavering lips.

"I'll smoke your tonsils and julienne your tongue."

Magnus had now reached the far wall of the crevice. In desperation, he searched for hand and footholds.

"I'll sauté your sinuses and poach your pituitaries."

Magnus scurried up the cliff face as quickly as he could.

"I'll sugar-coat your eyeballs and wrap them up as little petit fours."

Magnus heaved himself up onto a little rock ledge, but this seemed to offer very little respite. By now, the Blerchherchh had crossed the valley. It thrust its claws deep into the cliff face and began to effortlessly climb up the rock wall. In a moment, the probing, questing claws had reached the level of the ledge. In another moment, the hideous head emerged, barely inches away from him, its three great jaws wide in anticipation.

With absolutely no idea as to how to actually use it, Magnus drew his sword and made to strike with all his force against the ghastly face that leered before him. But before he had even raised it, he felt it lifted easily from out of his grasp.

"What is this? A toothpick? How thoughtful. Just what I'll need to get the last morsels of you from between my teeth."

With that, the Blerchherchh swung a claw towards Magnus, who leapt out of the way, only just in time, as the flash of steel swept past his face. The Blerchherchh laughed and lunged again at the defenceless Kertoobi, who jumped to the side, leaving the fearsome claw to scrape instead against the hard rock of the cliff face behind.

"How you dance, little one," chuckled the Blerchherchh. "Please keep still now. I'm getting hungry."

For a third time, the monster thrust its claws at Magnus. Again, Magnus attempted to evade those razor-sharp talons, but this time, he was not quite quick enough. The end of one of the claws caught the edge of his cloak, leaving him pinned against the wall and unable to move. Frantically, he tried to unclasp the cloak and set himself free, but to no avail.

"The game is up, little one," gloated the Blerchherchh. "It's time for you to become my dinner." It lifted its other claw, preparing for one final blow.

The blow never came. Instead, the Blerchherchh let out a roar of pain and raised both claws into the air, leaving Magnus to fall back onto the floor of the ledge. When Magnus raised his eyes again, he was delighted to see the Blerchherchh writhing in agony as, from below, Shaindor struck again and again at its legs. The monster tried to evade the blows, but in such an awkward position, perched halfway up the cliff face, there was little it could do against the Cherine's slashing sword. As it twisted around and down, in order to strike back, it succeeded only in completely losing its balance.

Down came the Blerchherchh. Down the cliff face it fell, tumbling past Shaindor, who deftly leapt to the side as it passed. Then, on across the floor of the valley, it rolled. With a thud, it crashed against the bottom of the stone staircase that led up towards the cave. And then it did not move.

Shaindor looked up towards Magnus, still balanced high on his rock ledge. "Jump," he commanded.

Magnus obliged. He threw himself off the ledge and into the safety of Shaindor's arms.

"Is it…? Do you think it is…? Have you killed it?" Magnus stammered.

Before Shaindor could reply, the Blerchherchh let out a low, blood-curdling moan.

That was all the information either of them needed. Within a second, Magnus was off at a sprint. Shaindor paused just long enough to retrieve Magnus's sword, then he quickly followed. Together they ran, with no respite at all, till the ground began to rise and the gloom began to clear and they were far away at last from the horrors of the dingy, dungy Drungledum Valley.

The Great Oponium

NIGHT WAS FALLING when Magnus and Shaindor finally stopped running. The forests had cleared, and they were now standing on a wide grassy plain. Shaindor found a small copse which seemed to offer some cover and suggested they make camp.

As he warmed his hands over the fire, Magnus had many questions for Shaindor.

"What was that monster, the Blerchherchh?"

"The Blerchherchh is a creature of folklore and legend," said Shaindor. "A ravenous beast with a hunger for the flesh of all other creatures. But before today I had not heard any substantive stories that pointed to the existence of such a monster. Nor had I any inkling that it should happen to dwell so near to Sweet Harmody."

"You mean to say your people didn't even know that such a creature lived in the dingy, dungy Drungledum Valley?"

"As I mentioned to you before, my race seldom descend into that dark chasm, and only haste drove us there today. Had I known that such a monstrosity haunted that place, I would not have led you into its depths. But I agree that it is exceedingly strange that this brute should have dwelt long under our noses without us becoming aware of it. I suspect that the Blerchherchh is only a recent arrival to these parts. My fear is that it has been driven out of its old abode by the spread of forces even more terrible."

Magnus did not need to ask what forces Shaindor might be referring to. He knew that, horrific as the Blerchherchh was, there were beings even more cruel and evil. The path he had chosen was going to lead him directly into their realm.

After a short while, Shaindor spoke again. "Such things are the stuff of nightmares. Better that we do not mention them again." Instead, he began to sing one of his songs of Sweet Harmody. As Magnus fell under the spell of his voice, thoughts of that noble city with its magnificent walls and towers erased the dread of the day's encounter, sending him into a deep and untroubled sleep.

The next morning, Shaindor again roused Magnus early. They ate a quick breakfast and then hurried on their way. The plain they were passing through seemed never-ending. Its low brown grasses stretched as far as the eye could see, with only the occasional tree to break the monotony.

"You make good progress, Magnus," commented Shaindor. "If we keep up this pace, we should reach the Shrine of Oponite by the day after next."

"The Shrine of Oponite?" murmured Magnus in amazement. "Are we going to see the Great Oponium?"

"You have heard of the Great Oponium?" said Shaindor.

"Even in Lower Kertoob the unsurpassed wisdom of the Great Oponium is well known."

Shaindor stopped for a moment and looked earnestly at Magnus. "Among all the races, there is none that can compare to the wisdom of the Cherines. And yet it is said that even we are as fools beside the extraordinary mind of the Great Oponium. Thus I have been charged to seek him out for counsel, for with his superior intelligence he can surely advise us of strategies that will enhance our chances for success. Such is the mission I was telling you of yesterday. But before we move on, I feel now that there is another task I must fulfill."

"What is that?"

"Your stand against the Blerchherchh yesterday was truly brave, but it would have counted for naught had I not been there to save you. And we will meet more fearsome enemies before this quest is done. It's time we did something about sharpening up your fighting skills. Come."

Shaindor led Magnus towards one of the lonely-looking trees that stood in the middle of the grasslands. It rose only slightly higher than Shaindor, with two branches that hung limply on either side like floppy brown arms.

"The brigalong tree," said Shaindor. "It provides no fruit, very little in the way of shelter, and its branches have no worth as timber." He paused to demonstrate by raising one of the branches and then allowing it to flop lifelessly down again. "And yet this tree is amongst the most useful of all plant life, as you shall shortly see."

Magnus regarded the brigalong tree, wondering what about the despondent bush could possibly be valuable.

"Draw your sword," instructed Shaindor.

Magnus did so.

"Now strike the brigalong tree."

Magnus raised his sword and struck the tree with all his might. To his surprise, a small noise came out of the tree. A strange sort of giggle.

"Harder, harder," urged Shaindor. "You can do better than that."

Magnus tried again. He swung his sword, putting everything he could into it. Again the tree giggled, slightly more loudly this time, and its branches waved around in seeming amusement.

"Come on, Magnus. Put a bit of force into it. You're just tickling it. Here, watch this."

Magnus held his sword above his head and smote the tree with a furious force.

"Owwwww!" The tree let out a loud wail of pain, and its branches writhed in anguish.

"You see," said Shaindor. "That is what you need to do."

For the next hour Magnus practiced his swordcraft on the brigalong tree. At first he could do little more than make the tree chuckle and wriggle. But under Shaindor's expert tutelage, he soon began to improve.

'That's the way," said Shaindor approvingly as Magnus began to make the tree wince just a little bit amidst its giggles. "Swing from the hips. And put more shoulder into it. You'll soon get it. Time we got moving now. There will be plenty of time for further practice." He pointed across the plain where numerous brigalong trees dotted the landscape before them.

So Magnus and Shaindor proceeded for the rest of the day. Every few hours they would pause from their journey at another forlorn-looking brigalong tree so Magnus could continue improving his skills. By the end of the second day, while still not able to produce the great howls of pain that Shaindor could elicit, he was starting to generate a variety of yelps and whines.

"You make excellent progress," said Shaindor. "Even the brightest of Cherine children could not make a brigalong tree moan as you do."

"Is this how all Cherine children learn their skills?" asked Magnus.

"It is a first step," said Shaindor. "Fighting a tree is not the same as fighting a fierce enemy on the battlefield. But all warriors must start somewhere, and this makes the brigalong tree of great value to our people. You will find one in every house where a child is being raised, for the skills of swordplay are of high import to our race."

"There is none who can match the mighty Cherines on the battlefield," agreed Magnus.

"And yet we do not love to fight," said Shaindor soberly. "We are drawn into battle but reluctantly. We fight only when we are forced to. Unlike our enemies, for they delight in the brutality of violence and warfare, desiring nothing but to inflict pain and suffering on all others. That is the difference between our races. We fight from necessity, but they fight from choice."

* * *

Over the following day, the landscape began to change. The brigalong trees were becoming sparser, and by the middle of the day there were no more to be seen. The grass began to thin out as well, as the land grew dry and rocky. In the distance, Magnus could just make out a high hill that stood out on its own. At the crown of the hill, there seemed to be a large circular object, like a great marble perched atop the peak.

"You see before you the Shrine of Oponite," said Shaindor.

As they drew nearer to the hill, the structure at its top began to take form. Sitting atop a short base, the shrine rose over the hill like a huge head guarding the plains around. Its massive sphere was constructed of smooth, grey bricks, decorated with mystical signs and symbols in ink of black, decipherable to no-one but the extraordinary mind that dwelt within.

Early next morning, the travellers arrived at the foot of the hill and began to climb the steep path to its peak. The dry and dusty trail twisted around the slopes and up into the shadow of the mighty ball at its summit. Eventually, they arrived at the walls of the base on which the shrine balanced. Here they found a wooden door, locked tight but with no visible doorknob. Beside the door, some words were written:

"Knock here all ye who seek enlightenment."

Shaindor knocked three times on the door which, after several minutes, slowly swung open to reveal two towering figures, clad in tight silver robes. So gigantic were these two in virtually all aspects, from elephantine arms and legs to hulking necks and torsos, they looked as if they had both been pumped full of the expanding gases that emanated out of the murky mires of Mithroparg. Oddly enough, the only features of these figures that were not of a totally stupendous size were their heads, which, by way of contrast, were so tiny as to be almost unnoticeable. However, the effect of these miniscule craniums was somewhat lessened by the colossal spherical headpieces that each wore, giving the impression that their heads were indeed as disproportionately large as the rest of them.

The two figures looked down upon the travellers.

"Greetings, seekers of knowledge. Welcome to the Shrine of Oponite," said one of them in a voice whose softness belied his size. "We are the Oponiots, keepers of the shrine and servants to the Great Oponium."

"Greetings, wise Oponiots," replied Shaindor. "We request an audience with your master, for we require the wisdom of his counsel on a matter of grave importance. My name is Shaindor and this is Magnus Mandalora from the small homely village of Lower Kertoob."

"Doubtless your names and the purpose of your visit are already known to the Wisest One," said the second Oponiot, also speaking in the same quiet manner. "High above, he now awaits your arrival."

"Follow us now, but be warned," added the first. "You are soon to meet with the Lord of Learnedness, the Sultan of Sagacity. Best you cast out all foolish thoughts from your mind before you enter his chamber, for he sees all," and it seemed to Magnus that both Oponiots cast a long look in his direction before directing them through the doors and into the shrine.

The Oponiots led Magnus and Shaindor down long, winding corridors and up steep, narrow stairways, the walls of which were marked by more of those seemingly unintelligible symbols. Finally, just as Magnus was beginning to think he could not lift his feet up another step, the stairs ended, and they found themselves standing within a vast chamber. The grey walls arched away and up, forming an enormous dome high above their heads. And in the centre of this chamber, upon a great seat, sat a most imposing figure.

It was not the body of this figure that was so impressive, for though it was cloaked in long, flowing robes, embroidered with more of those inscrutable symbols in all of the colours of the rainbow, it was otherwise of a wholly unexceptional nature. The feature that truly made this figure so remarkable was the head. It was of a most incredible size, filling nearly all the space within the chamber. The face was lined and wrinkled, as of great age, and a white beard flowed down over the robes and onto the floor. But the eyes were bright, twinkling and dancing in the dim light.

The two Oponiots strode forward, chanting in turn:

"The depths of his knowledge are unfathomable."

"The heights of his wisdom are unscalable."

"The breadth of his understanding is immeasurable."

"Behold the wisest of the wisest of the wise. The Great Oponium!"

"Welcome, pilgrims," said the Great Oponium. "Come stand before me. The Wisest One I am called, and the Wisest One I truly am."

Shaindor immediately stepped forward. "Greetings, oh Great Oponium. I am Shaindor of the Cherines, and this is my friend Magnus Mandalora—"

"From the small homely village of Lower Kertoob," said the Great Oponium. His voice was old and cracked, yet leavened with a lightness of humour.

"Indeed," said Shaindor. "At the edge of doom we come to you to seek your guidance on a matter of great urgency."

"Speak your matter," said the Great Oponium. "Tell me what you seek, such that I might share with you the fruits of my infinite mind."

Shaindor at once began to explain the purpose of the mission, beginning with the rising fears of the Cherines as the power of the Glurgs began to grow.

As he listened, the Great Oponium sighed. "Nobody knows better than I the long history of warfare between your races. But do go on, for I sense in your words a new threat. Something not before anticipated in your struggles against their foul blackness."

"So is your great wisdom revealed," said Shaindor admiringly. "It is true that we believe we are faced with a new threat. The Glurgs seem to have gained a fierceness and a strength we have never before encountered. We have good reason to believe they have devised some sort of deadly weapon, which they think will give them mastery over us. We even have a name to give to this weapon – the Krpolg."

"Interesting," said the Great Oponium. "That the Glurgs should have devised a weapon of evil is not a surprise to me. But still, can you be sure this is the case? Is it perhaps not possible that they have gotten better at fighting and you have gotten worse?"

"With respect to your overwhelming wisdom, this is a possibility I cannot countenance," replied Shaindor. "The power of the Cherines is as it always was. We are certain that there is another factor at play. Something we have not encountered before."

The Great Oponium considered Shaindor's words. "But why should you believe it is as a result of this thing, this Krpolg? Do you mind telling me upon what evidence you base your presumptions?"

Shaindor quite clearly did mind answering this question, but under the probing gaze of the Great Oponium, it was not something he could keep secret. "We do not know anything for sure. We have merely heard rumours of such a thing from the Doosies."

"And it is well known that the veracity of stories spun by the Doosies can never be doubted," said the Great Oponium, smiling slightly. "But tell me, Shaindor of the Cherines, why do you bother coming to see me when you already possess information from such a reliable source?"

Shaindor bristled at the suggested slight but continued nonetheless. "Of course we do not believe all the words of the Doosies. That is the reason for this mission." He went on to describe the plan to send Magnus as a spy into Hargh Gryghrgr in order to learn more about the true nature of the Krpolg.

The Great Oponium listened carefully to Shaindor's description of their mission, eyes closed in deep concentration. When it was finished he opened his eyes again and fixed them upon the Cherine. "So, now you have explained your mission. Tell me what you seek, for doubtless I have the answers you require."

"We wish to gain the benefit of your counsel," replied Shaindor. "What say you about our plan? Can you, in your wisdom, tell us what chance we have of succeeding?"

"What chance you have of succeeding? An interesting question. Yes, a most interesting question."

"But do you have an answer?"

"I do indeed." The Great Oponium chuckled before replying. "None."

"Did I hear you rightly?" asked Shaindor, somewhat taken aback. "Did you say none?"

"Absolutely none," confirmed the Great Oponium, now breaking into a chortle.

"You don't think it's a good plan?"

"It's the most ridiculous plan I've ever heard. It's beyond madness. It's beyond stupidity. You'd have to be an idiot, a moron, a simpleton of the highest degree if you actually believe it might have even the vaguest chance of success," laughed the massive head.

"Well then, perhaps you can tell me what is so terrible about it?" said Shaindor, utterly nonplussed by this reaction.

"What, you cannot even see it for yourself?" said the Great Oponium.

"No, I cannot."

"Then you are clearly a bigger nincompoop than even I originally took you for."

Magnus until now had stood back, saying nothing and feeling hopelessly small and unimportant. Now, stung by this slander on Shaindor, he felt he could no longer keep his silence.

"Shaindor is not a nincompoop. He's a great warrior of the Cherines," he cried.

Slowly, those glittering eyes turned towards the Kertoobi.

"Are you suggesting that I am wrong?" There was mocking humour in the voice that echoed around the chamber.

"No," gulped Magnus. "I didn't mean—"

"Are you saying you know more about these things than I do?"

"No," said Magnus, trying to avert his eyes from the intensity of the gaze that bored down upon him. "I would never dream of—"

"Tell me, my little friend, is it to you that people come from far and wide, to seek the wisdom of your counsel?"

"No it isn't." By now Magnus was wishing he could find a very large hole in which to duck down into.

"Of course it isn't. It's me. I'm the one people travel to from faraway lands, such that I may deliver to them my incomparable insights." The Great Oponium then turned back to Shaindor. "But I am afraid there's little more I can say to you. The strain of lowering myself to such a feeble level of discussion is giving me a headache. My inestimable brain requires some stimulation of a more nourishing nature."

"But you have not yet given us the counsel we require," cried Shaindor in dismay. "There is more that we would ask of you. You say our mission is foolhardy. Can you tell us what plan of action we should take?"

"I am sorely tested by such foolish questions," replied the Great Oponium. "Of course I can tell you. I'm the Great Oponium."

"Then what say you, oh Wisest One?"

The Great Oponium regarded the two companions carefully. "Listen well, Shaindor of the Cherines and Magnus Mandalora from the small homely village of Lower Kertoob, for I shall say this only once. Clear now is the path I see that lies before you. Simple are the choices I determine that you must make. So they should also be to you, had you even half the intelligence I bear. However, that is clearly not the case. Your meagre brains are no match for mine. Your miniscule minds have but a shadow of the mastery I possess. Thus it is that even though I have given my counsel, I doubt very much that you have the wit or capacity to act on it as would be required."

Having said his piece, the Great Oponium leant his head back and closed his eyes. And though Shaindor begged and pleaded, the massive head remained silent.

"Come, come, the audience is over," chanted the Oponiots as they began hustling Magnus and Shaindor out of the great chamber. "The Wisest One has shared the fruits of his wisdom. We must now leave him in peace."

"I do not understand," Shaindor protested. "I fail to see the meaning in his counsel."

"But he answered your questions plainly and precisely," said one of the Oponiots.

"And that you fail to realise this," said the other, "is merely an indication of the gap in understanding between yourself and the great one above."

"Then perhaps you can help us make sense of this counsel," said Shaindor. "Wise Oponiots, please explain to us the meanings hidden behind the words of your master."

The Oponiots stopped and looked at each other. After an awkward silence, they turned back to Shaindor.

"It is not for us to stand in his stead," said one.

"We are but humble servants," agreed the other. "But if you wish to consider further his words of wisdom, you may like to spend the night in this shrine, for perhaps proximity to his penetrating mind will help to bring the enlightenment you seek."

Shaindor was clearly torn. Indecision crossed his face as he debated internally the worth of remaining at the shrine of Oponite to ponder the words of the Great Oponium. After a while, he looked up again.

"A fool I already feel after my audience with the Wisest One. I think a fool I will remain. Thank you for your hospitality, good Oponiots, but we must depart. The path of haste now seems the wisest path to follow."

With those words, Magnus and Shaindor departed from the Shrine of Oponite, with the counsel of the Great Oponium still troubling their souls.

Ferelshine

THE HILL OF the Shrine of Oponite, with its stupendous balancing ball, had long since receded into the distance when Magnus and Shaindor stopped for the night.

All that day they had talked little, for the audience with the Great Oponium weighed heavily over them. It was only after they had eaten and were sitting around the campfire that Magnus was able to say what he had been thinking for most of the day.

"I'm sorry, Shaindor. I made a fool of myself this morning. I should have kept my mouth shut."

"Do not blame yourself," replied Shaindor. "It could not be helped. Even I feel myself to be partly at fault for what happened."

"Even you?" said Magnus in disbelief.

"Even I," said Shaindor. "While I was in the room with the Wisest One, listening to his words, I found myself unable to think clearly. It was as if my own mind had seized up in awe of the superior intelligence before me, and I found myself feeling foolish and simple."

"Can you not find any meaning in his counsel?" asked Magnus.

Shaindor shook his head. "I am afraid that I find myself at something of a loss. From the day we left Sweet Harmody, I had been relying very much on his providing us with the guidance we needed. But all I can glean from his words is that he believes this to be little more than a fool's errand. And knowing this, I cannot say whether it is worth continuing even another day on our quest."

"But what then are we to do?"

Shaindor took a long time to answer. "Although the counsel of the Great Oponium fills me with grave reservations about the wisdom of our course, they do not provide me with any ideas for what alternative we might follow. Therefore, I can suggest nothing better than to continue on our path for now. And if in time we should at last derive meaning from those words, let us pray it is not too late for us to turn back and heed them."

Shaindor's doubts gave no comfort to Magnus. He eventually managed to fall asleep, but even then he dreamed of a massive head that hung above him.

"You have no idea what you have gotten yourself into. You shall not succeed. You cannot succeed," it taunted.

"Yes, I will succeed," cried Magnus. "You just watch me."

"Oh, I'll be watching you all right," said the head, and it began to laugh an evil, demonic laugh.

For the first time, Magnus recognised the face at the front of that massive sphere, its mouth twisted in cruel mirth and its eyes wide with scorn. He could not stop himself screaming:

"Jangossssssssssssssssssssssss!"

"Wake up, Magnus," said Shaindor. He was sitting above Magnus, shaking him gently.

Magnus sat up, rubbing his eyes. "What happened?"

"You must have been dreaming. You called out."

"I did?" Then the recollection of the dream came back to him and he shuddered. "It was horrible. I saw Jangos and he…he…"

"You do not have to tell me," said Shaindor. "It is nothing more than a phantom of the night. But see, the night is gone and now it is day. Put aside your fears. Rise, stretch and fill your stomach and you will feel all the better."

Shaindor was right. It felt good to be able to partake of a hearty breakfast, and by the time they were ready to move on, Magnus's night fears had disappeared.

As they set off, Shaindor spoke quickly. "I am afraid our visit to the Shrine of Oponite has taken us out of our way for very little advantage. We now have need for haste."

So they hurried along the rough stony road. At first, it was hard and uneven, scored with cracks and potholes. Before long, it began to become smoother and firmer underneath their feet, even as the country around grew greener and friendlier.

Late in the day, they arrived at a small village. The inhabitants were Gleeprogs, a race of highly evolved fish capable of living on land, although they were yet to evolve lungs and so were required to go around with large bowls of water over their heads. While they were greeted warmly, Magnus could not help feeling an undercurrent of unease and fear.

Over the next few weeks, they passed through rich lands of lush pastures and deep, flowing rivers. Many more villages lay on their road, but the further they travelled, the more unsettled was the behaviour of the residents of these hamlets. The Frungoles, a tribe who were renowned for their ability to go about their normal working day while fast asleep, were now fully aroused and aimlessly wandering the streets, unsure about how to behave in such an awakened state, while the Querks, a jocular race who were famous for the length and breadth of their conversations, would only take the time to say "hello" and then "goodbye" in one breath before scurrying back into their houses.

After this, there were no longer any signs of life in any of the villages that they passed. No lights in the houses and no movement in the town squares. All habitations had been well and truly abandoned. But the emptiness of the villages was more than made up for by the constantly growing traffic on the road itself. It seemed that the entire population of this region was on the move, surging past in the opposite direction. Their possessions were packaged up on wagons, and their eyes were lowered, save only for fearful, furtive glances. Shaindor and Magnus tried to make contact, but few were prepared to stop and talk. The main exceptions were the inevitable Doosies, and it was from these that the companions were able to derive information regarding the source of this uproar.

The residents of the surrounding villages were fleeing the advancing Glurg armies who, it was said, were progressing rapidly, destroying everything in their path. Shaindor pressed these informers for more information, particularly regarding the nature of the Krpolg, and discovered over the course of several encounters with different Doosies that it was in turn a device capable of projecting warriors five hundred feet into the air, a special type of sword that could fight on its own without needing to be carried, and a large tree with magical leaves that could turn metal into ice-cream.

After several days of pushing through the throng, the crowds on the road began to thin out, and soon they were gone completely. Magnus and Shaindor were once again left on their own.

"We have come to the edge of the no-man's-land between us and the Glurg armies," said Shaindor. "Best we tread carefully. Peril is now before us, very near."

Magnus felt a chill come over him as they trod along the silent road and through the skeletons of abandoned villages. Even the slightest noise was enough to send them scurrying behind the undergrowth on the side of the road, but in each case it turned out to be merely a small animal or bird. In the days that followed, there was no indication that the enemy was drawing near.

* * *

On the morning of the sixth day after they had left the crowds behind, Shaindor clutched Magnus's arm and pulled him off the road and into the fields alongside.

"Come with me Magnus. Though this is not part of our quest, there is a place close by I feel we must attend. And though this country may be dangerous, I do not wish to pass so near and not pay homage."

So saying, he led Magnus across the field. As they walked further away from the road, Magnus was surprised to see two lines of stones that seemed to mark out a path. The further they progressed along this path, the higher those stones reached, and soon Magnus felt as if he was walking along the bottom of a deep canyon. Just as they reached a point where the stones grew so high they began to block out the sun, they passed under an archway and back into sunlight.

As his eyes adjusted, Magnus found himself standing on a wide lawn. In the centre of this lawn, a tall stone obelisk stood, and at the far end there rose a high hill.

"Behold," said Shaindor. "We have come to the field of Ferelshine."

Magnus looked around. Given the level of solemn grandeur in Shaindor's voice, he had been expecting something a bit more impressive than this.

"What is the field of Ferelshine?" he asked politely.

"A place of great, if terrible, significance for my people."

Magnus waited for Shaindor to go on, but it was clear the Cherine was waiting for Magnus to speak again. Obviously this was a moment Shaindor wanted to extend for as long as possible. Magnus figured that he had better oblige.

"Why is this field so significant to you?"

"Because it is the site of one of the most critical events ever to have occurred. One of the key markers in our history."

Sensing that Shaindor was still not ready to reveal all, Magnus tried again. "And what exactly was this event?"

"On the field of Ferelshine, for the first time ever, we did battle with that vile and brutal race that has evermore been known as the Glurgs."

Magnus felt as if his eyes had just been opened. Far from standing in the middle of a nondescript lawn, he now saw himself at the centre of a great battle. "What happened here?" he asked excitedly.

Shaindor sat down and motioned for Magnus to do likewise. He began speaking, as if he were a teacher in a class and Magnus the student, and given the importance of this story to the Cherines, this was most likely how he had himself first heard it.

"Many years ago my race did not dwell in Sweet Harmody. Their home was a faraway realm, the name of which is no longer spoken, for what is remembered of this realm is not remembered well. It is said that it was a harsh land, bearing little of value. Few crops would grow in its soil, and there was naught in the way of beauty in its landscapes. So it was that my ancestors left that land in order to find somewhere more worthy of our noble race. For many years they travelled, over high mountain peaks and across desolate deserts. The journey was hard and some did not survive. But at last they arrived in a country that they deemed to be green, fertile and suitably picturesque. Then, at last, my people knew that their travails were over. They had found a good place to live. A great celebration was planned, to be held upon this very lawn."

"On this very lawn," mouthed Magnus in amazement.

"Indeed. The feast of Ferelshine it was called, for that was the name given to this fair place." Shaindor stood up and led Magnus to the stone obelisk. "See here, the story is told."

Magnus looked at the obelisk. Across its surface strange characters were carved, flowing delicately from one side to the other. He tried to follow the symbols, but it was not a language he had ever seen before.

"I cannot read this writing."

"It is the ancient script of the Cherines, which we use now only on special festive occasions. But I can tell you that what is written here is the Ballad of Ferelshine, which recounts what happened on that fateful day." Shaindor began to sing softly:

> At Ferelshine, decree was made to hold a joyous feast,
> Ten tables there were built with care, to hold two hundred each.
> Upon their sides, with skill and craft were carved the faces fair,
> Of Nespel, Wesprith, Qweferdine, and mighty Limbadair.
>
> Then for each top, a cloth was draped of ivory white so pure,
> All woven from the finest thread by hands both slick and sure.
> Fine cutlery was freshly forged from silver, gold, and copper,
> And set upon each table in a style correct and proper.

Shaindor broke off his song to look at Magnus again.

"You see the care that went into the preparations?" he said. "Even to carving onto the tables the faces of the four great leaders who had guided my people here: Nespel the Handsome, Wesprith the Wise, Qweferdine the Well-Mannered and Limbadair the Bold. Truly this was to be the finest feast in all of history."

"So what happened at this feast?" asked Magnus, eager to hear the rest of the story.

"Let me find the verses that describe the events of that day." Shaindor carefully followed the script as it wound around the obelisk. "There are another twenty or so verses that describe the preparations in more detail. Designing menus, sourcing of produce, seating arrangements. Here, this is the part." Shaindor raised his head and began to sing again:

> At last the guests took to their seats, before the feast so grand,
> But even as they raised their cups to toast their newfound land,
> From hilltop high, a clamorous cry destroyed the mood so bright.
> Then as their eyes were lifted, they beheld a ghastly sight.

"What did they see?" cried Magnus.

"The song does not explicitly say," replied Shaindor.

"Why not?"

"Remember what I told you before. We Cherines only create works of beauty. It would not be right to sully the words of a fine song with the depravity of the sight they witnessed. But our histories allow us to fill in the gaps left by the words. For it is known that what they saw was a party of Glurgs standing on that hill just above us. Can you imagine what that must have been like for my ancestors as they prepared to partake of this splendid feast? To see, for the first time, the hideousness, the utter repulsiveness of that misbegotten race?"

Magnus looked up at the hill and imagined what the sight of a group of Glurgs standing atop its peak might resemble. Try as he might, he had neither the experience nor the imagination to recreate such a scene. He could only shudder at the thought of what it must have been like.

"So what did they do?"

"Naturally there was not a lot of time to consider their actions. But even then, the four great leaders quickly consulted, as the song states."

> Said Nespel, "What are these we spy arranged upon this hill,
> With countenance so foul and crude, I fear I may be ill."
> Quoth Qweferdine, "Such action could not possibly be right,
> Though they appear quite hideous still we should remain polite."
>
> Cried Limbadair, "I cannot bear to view such filthy beasts,
> Let's draw our swords and slay them all ere we commence our feast."
> But in the last, wise Wesprith said, "We must proceed with care,
> For should these things be friend or foe, we cannot yet declare."

"So you see, even in such a gruesome situation, the instinct of my people was for peace. We did not wish to create a conflict with these Glurgs, disgusting as we found them. However, it very quickly became obvious that we had no choice in the matter."

"The Glurgs attacked you?" said Magnus.

"Indeed," replied Shaindor. "Again the song does not describe in detail the full horror of their unprovoked assault. However our histories relate how without any warning the Glurgs suddenly charged down the hill towards the tables, waving their arms wildly and screaming their vile battle cries. We were left with no other choice but to defend ourselves. Battle reigned on the field of Ferelshine."

"So what happened? Were you victorious?"

"In the end our might prevailed," said Shaindor. "The final verses of the ballad of Ferelshine describe the many great deeds performed that day, but we do not need to go into such detail. Suffice to say that one alone of my forefathers claimed particular honour that day. So let us pass now to the final verse." Shaindor followed the script around to the very bottom of the obelisk before completing the song.

> *The slashing blade of Limbadair has never since been matched,*
> *And so it rained upon those brutes till each one was dispatched.*
> *Now of the host arranged to eat, no dead nor hurt were seen,*
> *Yet still they knelt in mourning for the feast that should have been.*

"So they never got to have their feast in the end," mouthed Magnus.

"Regrettably not," said Shaindor. "The unexpected attack had left a rather unpleasant taste in their mouths. Not to mention a horrific stench, which caused all the food to wrinkle up and rot on the spot. And for this alone, we hold the Glurgs to account. But of more import to us is the fact that this was but the opening skirmish in the interminable war that continues to this day. An accursed war we did not choose, but for which our race has paid dearly. Unfortunately, it can have only one end. The total defeat and destruction of their race. For if there is even one of them still in existence, there is enough hatred and malice to keep this conflict alive."

Having finished his story, Shaindor sat down beside the obelisk. Magnus went to sit next to him, and together they contemplated the enormity of the events that had occurred here in silence. After a while Shaindor awoke from his reverie.

"We should not tarry here longer than we need. Time is short and I fear the enemy draws near."

They had not travelled far beyond the arched gateway and back down the path towards the road when Shaindor's words were proven correct. Without any warning, five figures leapt out from behind the great standing stones and onto the path before them–figures the likes of which Magnus could never have summoned up, even in his worst nightmare.

They were not large, standing barely higher than Magnus himself, but their features were so grossly distorted as to render them truly terrifying. The components of their faces seemed to have been stuck on at random and then twisted beyond all reason by some psychotic sculptor. Foul-smelling liquid oozed out of eyes, noses, cruelly leering mouths, and various other indescribable orifices. And each of their spindly, gnarled claws clutched a fearsome black dagger, poised and ready to strike.

Magnus barely had a chance to duck behind the nearest stone before the Glurgs, for there could be no doubt that this is what they were, attacked. At first, all he could do was cover his face and whimper as the battle raged. But after a minute or so, he summoned up the courage to open his eyes and poke his head back around the stone.

A whirl of movement met his eyes. Five hideous shapes leapt and lunged around the beleaguered figure of Shaindor, who spun and danced, swinging his sword like lightning to meet the advancing blades of his foes. Outnumbered or not, the Cherine was a fearsome opponent, and within a minute, he had succeeded in cutting down one of his attackers. A headless body fell to the path, the misshapen head rolling to a stop only inches from Magnus's face.

Holding his mouth to stop himself from retching, Magnus quickly crawled away from the grotesquely reeking object. This sudden movement caught the eye of one of the remaining Glurgs who immediately broke away from the fight with Shaindor and stalked towards him, dagger at ready. Magnus desperately rolled from side to side, narrowly avoiding the rushing blade as it came hurtling down again and again. All the while he was screaming:

"Shaindor, help!"

Shaindor somehow managed to extricate himself from the other three Glurgs. With three great leaps and two swooping slashes of his sword, he separated the Glurg from both its arms and its legs.

Magnus's relief was only short-lived. In taking his eyes off the three remaining Glurgs, Shaindor had left himself open to attack. In an instant, they pounced, sending Shaindor reeling back against one of the standing stones. Courageously, he fought them off, but it was clear that he was beginning to struggle. Any moment now, one of the Glurgs was likely to strike a killing blow.

As Shaindor battled to keep his foes at bay, Magnus felt a great surge of anger rush over him. These were the monsters that had killed his brother. He couldn't just watch while they struck down his friend and guide as well. Slowly, he raised himself to his feet and approached the whirling melee. With all of their attention focused on Shaindor, none of the Glurgs noticed him creeping up behind them. As he reached for his sword, he remembered Shaindor's advice:

"...Swing from the hips. And put more shoulder into it..."

Magnus swung from the hips, put as much shoulder into it as he could, and buried his blade into the back of the nearest Glurg. It went in easily, sending a stream of putrid black liquid splashing over him. The Glurg twisted around savagely, pulling the handle out of Magnus's hand. It let out a roar of fury and raised its dagger high above Magnus's head. Then it collapsed, lifeless, to the ground beside him.

A daze of exhilaration overwhelmed Magnus. He barely registered as Shaindor, the odds now well and truly back in his favour, was quickly able to finish off the two remaining Glurgs. It was only when the Cherine came over and patted him on the shoulders that he was brought back to reality.

"Congratulations," said Shaindor. "You just killed your first Glurg."

The Pharsheeth

THE INCREDIBLE THRILL Magnus felt after killing his first Glurg took a long time to dissipate. While Shaindor hastily buried the bodies, so they did not defile the sacred ground nearby, Magnus found he could not contain himself.

"It was all soft and mushy," he gibbered. "I thought it would be all hard and knobbly, but my sword went in so much more easily than I expected. And it fell so quickly. I thought it was going to get me. I thought I was a goner. And then it just fell. I must have really got it good."

'Indeed, you must have," agreed Shaindor.

"I did exactly what you said, Shaindor. I swung from the shoulder and put all my hips into it." Magnus repeated the movement for Shaindor's benefit.

"We'll make a warrior out of you yet," chuckled Shaindor.

"Do you think there are any more around?" Magnus muttered, fingering the handle of his sword and peering around eagerly.

"Mercy," said Shaindor. "Let us not be in too much of a hurry. At our next encounter, we may find more than five."

"We can take them, you and me," said Magnus. Noticing that Shaindor had succeeded in covering the pit with dirt, hiding the Glurg carcasses from sight, he began to stride towards the road. But Shaindor grabbed him and pulled him back. He held Magnus close and whispered into his ear.

"It is a big step you have taken, Magnus, but still only the first of many. Do not forget where we are or what we are facing. I do not think we should remain any longer on the road. It can no longer be considered safe."

Walking quickly, he led Magnus away from the path and the standing stones and into the shelter of the line of trees that ran alongside the road.

Signaling for Magnus to follow, he began to climb, eventually stopping at a large branch about halfway up. He took a quick look around and then turned to peer down at Magnus who was still struggling to make his way up.

"It is as I feared," he said softly. "The Glurgs we encountered were but an advance party. Their major force is coming up close behind."

By now, Magnus had managed to haul himself up beside Shaindor. He lifted his eyes to gaze out over the country ahead.

Before them, the road could be clearly seen, winding and stretching through a land of undulating hills. But something about the countryside seemed odd. It was as if the land itself had come alive, rolling and heaving like a shaken sheet, while the road writhed and twisted like a great snake. After squinting to look more closely, Magnus became aware that it was merely an illusion. The land itself was not moving. Along the road and across the hills, black figures were marching. A massive army whose end, far beyond the horizon, could not be observed, was rapidly advancing towards them.

Shaindor frowned. "This is not good," he muttered. "This is very, very bad. I begin now to discern the wisdom of the Great Oponium when he claimed this was an errand without hope. It is still many days march ere we begin to arrive near to Hargh Gryghrgr. And even should we somehow evade the Glurg armies over these meagre hills, beyond lies the misty, musty Plains of Plartoosis, a featureless, barren wilderness which will provide us with little shelter. It is not feasible that we should pass this way to the walls of Hargh Gryghrgr undetected."

"So what are we to do?" asked Magnus. "After we've come so far, are we to turn back now?"

"It pains me to consider it. See now what they do, the barbarous vandals," Shaindor growled with disgust, pointing out towards the advancing Glurg armies.

Magnus looked again. Before the head of the Glurg forces, the land remained rich and green. Behind, there was nothing to see but brown. The Glurgs were destroying everything in their path, ripping out trees and bushes and lighting fires to scorch the earth as they passed.

"Why do they do it?" he wondered. "It's just mindless destruction."

"Because that's what they are." Shaindor replied. "Mindless destruction is the only thing they know."

Magnus covered his eyes to blot out the horrible sight before him. It didn't seem right that these monsters could just march across the country, driving out the peaceful residents. Now he and Shaindor were also set to flee, powerless before the advance of the Glurgs.

"But isn't there something else we can do? Maybe another way we can find?" he pleaded.

Shaindor shook his head. "There is no other way, except…" He paused for a moment.

"What?" asked Magnus.

"I've just realised there is another way. To the east of Hargh Gryghrgr lie the mighty Mounji Mountains. They are difficult to cross, it is said, but not impassable. And although it is possible that they too will be patrolled by the Glurgs, I deem it unlikely, as the major body of their force seems intent on this destructive push forward. Yet, even if it were the case, the high mountains offer a better chance for protection than the desolate plains. If we can pass that way, we may be able to avoid the Glurg armies and approach Hargh Gryghrgr from behind. Then we just might have a chance of sneaking in through a back door."

"Do you know how to cross these mountains?"

"I do not. But I know where we can get the guidance we require. In the foothills of the mountains on their northern edge lies the forest of Krondeep. And in the depths of this forest dwell the Pharsheeth. Once, long ago, they were allies in our struggles against the Glurgs. It is said that none know the high passes of the mountains as they do. Come, Magnus. The enemy draws near. It will be a race to see if we can reach the shelter of the forest before they reach us."

Before he had even finished speaking, Shaindor was already clambering out of the tree and motioning for Magnus to do likewise. As soon as they hit the ground, they were off and running.

* * *

The next few days were a blur to Magnus. From the moment the sun came up till it sank glowing behind them, they did not stop running. Magnus had no idea where they were passing, nor what sort of countryside it might be. All he was aware of was the aching of his limbs and the shuddering of his breath as they ran on and on, each jarring step bringing them nearer and nearer to the great peaks that slowly rose up before them.

Always it seemed the enemy was on their heels. The signs of their presence were a constant throughout the journey; the rough clanging of their marching feet; the savage harshness of their cries; the foul stench of their nearness. On more than one occasion the armies of the Glurgs picked up their trail and engaged in a fierce pursuit from which escape seemed impossible. In the nick of time, they somehow managed to find some hollow or shelter to duck into, just as their foes shot into view.

Magnus could not tell how long this frantic chase lasted. It may have been sometime on the fifth or sixth or even the seventh day when he suddenly noticed that their surroundings had changed quite dramatically. The land was now gradually rising, while the trees were not only multiplying around them but also soaring to greater and greater heights above their heads.

Shaindor allowed himself to slow down as they moved into the welcome darkness of the trees.

"Well done, Magnus," he said. "We have won the race. Here now are the eaves of the forest of Krondeep."

"Do you think we are safe here?" gasped Magnus.

"Nowhere is truly safe anymore," cautioned Shaindor. "But the Glurgs will not take this forest easily. The Pharsheeth are a proud race and bold fighters. I doubt our enemies will try to enter here yet. Not when there are easier conquests to be made. Still, I would not like to count on it. Let us hurry on, for Pharnarest, the great city of the Pharsheeth, is deep in the forest and most likely several days walk away."

So the travellers wandered into the heart of Krondeep forest. As they passed further into that dark wood, Magnus found it difficult to keep focused on the path ahead. His eyes continually roamed up towards the tops of the trees, so miraculously high in the air. Shaindor, absorbed with making his way forward, did not even notice his companion's distraction until Magnus walked headlong into one of those massive trunks for the fourth time.

"The towering swigeresh trees of Krondeep forest. The tallest living things in existence. They're quite something," Shaindor commented.

Magnus could only nod in awestruck silence.

"It is said that these swigeresh trees have a love of the sun unmatched by any other form of life. This is the reason they have grown so tall, for should one tree grow to such a height that it blocks out the sunlight, then the others will quickly try to catch up and to overtake the first so that they in turn may take the greater share of the light they so desire. At the higher reaches, you will even see how they grasp and pull with their branches to hold the others back and claim for themselves an advantage."

"Is that right?" murmured Magnus, at last able to find his voice.

"I cannot say for certain, for it is said primarily by Doosies, and therefore, I would not be prepared to verify the truth of it. Still, it is a sight to behold. Let us stop for a while, so we can enjoy this wonder without putting your nose at any further risk."

Shaindor's instincts again proved to be correct. As they progressed further into the forest, there were no more signs of the presence of their pursuers. The only noises they heard were the continual rustlings of the swigeresh trees and the occasional scratching of verpigs, large rodents peculiar to Krondeep forest that gained sustenance by chewing on each other's fingernails.

"Tell me more about the Pharsheeth," said Magnus, when they at last stopped to rest. "What are they like?"

"I do not rightly know," replied Shaindor.

"But you said that you and they were once allies in your battles against the Glurgs."

"That is correct. But it was a long, long time ago. In the many years that have passed since, our races have become sundered. It is many years since any contact has been made with them."

"How could this have happened? Surely it would be better if all enemies of the Glurgs stuck together."

"There is wisdom in your words, Magnus," said Shaindor gravely. "Our histories do not clearly state the reasons for the split between our peoples. But what little that is recorded suggests that there was a time when we Cherines came to the conclusion that despite the common goals we shared, we could no longer benefit from our association. Since then, they have remained secure in their fortress within the forest. Yet, I fear that this security may be short-lived, for as the power of the Glurgs rises it will not be long before their armies will be advancing upon Pharnarest. It could be that this change in our plans is a blessing for both our peoples. Let us bring a warning to the Pharsheeth. In these days of peril, it is time that ancient disagreements were set aside and the alliance between us rekindled."

* * *

Over the next couple of days, Shaindor led Magnus through the maze of mighty trees, seeking for the hidden city of the Pharsheeth.

"It will not be an easy place to find," he said. "The Pharsheeth have lived in isolation for many generations. I suspect their citadel has been well designed to blend in with the forest around, so travellers may pass right under its walls and still be completely unaware of its presence."

For the first time ever, at least in Magnus's recollections, Shaindor turned out to be completely wrong.

They heard the city before they saw it. A noise, somewhat like the babbling of a hundred flowing streams, came drifting through the forest. Sometimes rising, sometimes falling, it never let up in its frenzied intensity. After following the sound for about half an hour, the companions arrived in a wide clearing and found themselves standing before the walls of Pharnarest. Even Shaindor could not stop himself gaping in amazement, for what they saw was completely unexpected.

Rather than trying to camouflage their city within the forest, the Pharsheeth seemed to have gone to every effort to make it stand out as much as possible. The walls were painted in all the colours of the rainbow, as well as a few others that the original designers of rainbows had never even considered. The arrangement of these colours was such that from one to the next, the maximum contrast was always obtained. Blue sat next to red, while yellow intertwined with purple. This effect ensured that the whole wall seemed to throb and pulse with colour.

It was not just the garish colour scheme that caught the eye. In form as well, the walls seemed to defy any sense of reasonable or cogent design. No two lines were parallel and no curves were smooth. Towers of all shapes and sizes jutted out at all kinds of ridiculous angles. Pharnarest appeared less like the great and ancient fortress Magnus was expecting and more like some sort of psychedelic fun park.

"Should we go in?" asked Magnus.

"Just give me a minute," said Shaindor, who was looking somewhat pale. Eventually, he managed to compose himself, and the two approached the manic walls where, amidst the swirling colours, it took them quite a while to locate the gates of the city.

Shaindor rapped on the gates. The tinny sound echoed over the loud hubbub from within the city but did not elicit a response. Shaindor knocked a second time. Again, no response. After the third knock, voices could at last be heard from within that crazy tumult.

"What was that noise?"

"I think someone's knocking on the gates."

"Visitors! Quick, open the doors immediately!"

Without any further delay, the gates of Pharnarest were thrown open. Then Magnus and Shaindor entered the city of the Pharsheeth.

Again, the first thing that hit them was the noise, now a great roar like the mighty Cataracts of Whetherwhog. Their eyes struggled to take in the sights before them, for the outer walls were merely a taster for the visual madness within. Every single building had its own peculiar structure and its own outrageous colour scheme. Multi-hued pyramids stood adjacent to polka-dotted trapezoidal prisms. Chequerboard towers that somehow leant in all directions at once abutted speckled, spherical lollipops. It was as if each building within the city had been designed by an individual architect, cut off from all others and then denied sleep until a suitable degree of derangement had been induced.

Amidst all of this rushed the Pharsheeth. Seemingly incapable of standing still, they dashed this way and that along the streets, conducting loud conversations with all others within their general vicinity. Several came right up to Magnus and Shaindor, circling them in a demented whirlpool.

"Who are you?"

"What are you?"

"Why have you come to Pharnarest?"

This constant movement made it difficult to get a definite sense of their appearance, although it could just be discerned that they had long, thin limbs with multiple joints, none of which ever stopped flexing, and round heads with big, wide eyes, topped by wiry, frizzy hair that stood high up above their scalps.

"We come with an urgent warning. We must speak to your leaders at once," gasped Shaindor. "Will you take us to them?"

"With pleasure," replied at least twenty voices as ever more Pharsheeth rushed over to them.

"They seem really friendly," said Magnus as the two were jostled and pushed along the veering, zigzagged boulevards of the city. "I don't think we'll have any trouble enlisting them to our cause."

Shaindor did not respond.

"I guess I'll leave it to you to do the talking so I don't embarrass myself, like I did before the Great Oponium."

"Actually," said Shaindor, "I was wondering if you minded doing most of the talking. I'm afraid I'm feeling a bit queasy."

Magnus glanced over at Shaindor. His normally peerless complexion had taken on a somewhat greenish hue, and he was breathing heavily. This seemed to Magnus to be an extremely poor time for Shaindor to be taken ill. He swallowed nervously at the expectations that had been placed on his narrow shoulders. Any future alliance between the Cherines and the Pharsheeth now rested on his ability to convince the rulers of Pharnarest of the threat that faced them.

Before long they found themselves in front of the most outrageous building of all, a bulging cornucopia of colour and movement so excessive that it looked like it had exploded out of the ground in one great multi-hued blast. The travellers were led into this building to find themselves in a hall of assembly, similar in size to the Great Hall of Sweet Harmody, but as gaudy and overdone as that other hall was tasteful and restrained.

At the far end of the hall stood a high, wide stage. Magnus and Shaindor were led up a small flight of steps to the top of this platform, where a tall Pharsheeth stood before them. His head and limbs still twitched and jerked slightly and his eyes rolled around unceasingly in their sockets, but he was definitely the least frenetic of all the residents Magnus had yet observed.

"Greetings, strangers. Welcome to Pharnarest," said the Pharsheeth. "My name is Gillibub, and I am the ruler of this city."

"Greetings, Gillibub," said Magnus, trying to sound as formal and authoritative as he could. "I am Magnus Mandalora from the small homely village of Lower Kertoob, and my companion is Shaindor, a mighty warrior of the Cherines, although I am afraid he is feeling slightly unwell at present."

Gillibub waved his many-jointed arms impatiently. "Is this the way we treat visitors when they are unwell? A chair, please, for our mighty warrior."

In a flash, a chair was brought and a relieved Shaindor collapsed into it.

"That's more like it," said Gillibub. "But it has been a long time since we last had a visit from the noble Cherines or those who travel with them. To what do we owe this honour today?"

Magnus cleared his throat, preparing to speak. As he did so, he happened to glance around. To his shock, he suddenly noticed that the hall was full of Pharsheeth. It seemed as if the whole city had followed them into the hall. He turned back to Gillibub, keeping his voice low.

"Is it really necessary for everyone to be in here?" he asked.

"But of course," said Gillibub, matching Magnus's quiet tone by yelling at the top of his voice. "We so rarely get visitors. This is a special occasion we all should share."

"It's just that I'm a little bit nervous," said Magnus, still trying to keep his voice down. "And the information I have for you is highly sensitive. I think this may be better done in private."

"Oh, nonsense," Gillibub laughed. "We're all friends here. Please speak now for the benefit of everyone."

Sensing that Gillibub would not be swayed, Magnus gave up. He summoned up his most confident sounding voice and began. "People of Pharnarest, we bring a warning of great peril—"

"Oh, let us guess what it is," interrupted Gillibub. "Come on, any ideas?" he called out to the crowd.

"The Qworbagger plague," shouted a voice from the audience.

"An invasion of stinging twipperflies," called another.

"The seldom seen but much discussed diperagoff," cried a third.

"No, it is none of those things," said Magnus. "I bring a warning that the power of the Glurgs is rising. Their armies are spreading out of Hargh Gryghrgr and will soon—"

"I'm sorry, can I just stop you there?" interrupted Gillibub again.

"What now?" said Magnus.

"I'm afraid the people at the back are struggling to hear you. Speak up a bit would you."

Magnus started again. "I bring a warning that—"

"No, no good. You need to project your voice, like this," Gillibub demonstrated by booming his voice out over the crowd.

"The armies of the Glurgs are spreading out from Hargh Gryghrgr," said Magnus, trying to boom the way Gillibub had done. "They have taken great swathes of the countryside and—"

"Sorry, you're losing us. Put a bit of expression into your voice. Don't just drone on and on in the same old monotone."

"The Glurgs have taken great swathes of countryside," repeated Magnus, doing his best to force his voice to rise and fall. "They are drawing nearer to—"

"No, it's not working," said Gillibub. "You're sending the crowd to sleep. Can't you do something to make it more interesting?"

"Like what?" said Magnus who was becoming extremely frustrated. He had urgent information to pass onto these people, and yet they seemed to have switched off completely. Many in the crowd were now chatting idly amongst themselves, and several were yawning.

"I don't know. Maybe try singing it instead of just saying it."

This seemed like the most nonsensical suggestion Magnus had ever heard, but by now he was prepared to do anything to get his message across. "The Glurgs are drawing nearer to the forest of Krondeep," he sang in a scratchy voice. "We fear it will not be long before even Pharnarest will come under direct attack—"

"Boring!" said Gillibub. "I don't mean to be rude, but I'm afraid you seem to have had a complete charisma bypass. Isn't there anything else you can do to get our attention?"

"But why should I need to?" cried Magnus in exasperation. "What I have to say is really important. Why should it matter how I say it?"

"If you have something to say to the Pharsheeth, then it matters a lot," said Gillibub impatiently. "If you cannot engage our interest, if you cannot entertain us, then we will not be prepared to listen to you. But come, there must be something else you could try. Can you juggle?"

"This is ridiculous," cried Shaindor, leaping from his seat and swaying unsteadily towards Gillibub. "Can't you hear what this Kertoobi is telling you?"

The sight of the majestic Cherine reeling across the stage was enough to transfix all in the crowd.

"Now that's more like it," said Gillibub. "Give the floor to the Cherine."

Shaindor was still struggling to stay upright, and the strain could be heard in his voice, but it didn't matter. There was not one inattentive ear in the hall as he spoke.

"The armies of the Glurgs draw near. Will the Pharsheeth join with us, restoring our ancient alliance to make battle against our common foe?"

A great hubbub rose up in the hall. Even Gillibub was not unmoved.

"How exciting and splendid," he cried in delight. "We're going off to war!"

Parghwum Pass

IT WAS EARLY the following morning when Magnus and Shaindor departed from Pharnarest. Neither had slept particularly soundly, for night seemed to make little difference to the Pharsheeth, and the cacophony on the streets did not cease even for a second. Amazingly, Shaindor's health began to take a turn for the better as soon as they left the gates of that frenetic city. Barely an hour after departure, his breathing had become more relaxed and he was soon back to his usual powerful and commanding self.

As his strength returned, he took to interrogating Biddira, the young Pharsheeth guide Gillibub had assigned to them, regarding her knowledge of the mountains. She responded with supreme confidence.

"I have been roaming the Mounji Mountains since I was a tiny Pharsheethling," she stated as her eyes darted wildly around her freckled face, seeming to rest upon everything except the Cherine beside her. "I have spent many days wandering the valleys, traversing the high peaks and creeping into clefts and crevices that no other of my race has ever entered. There is none in this world who knows these mountains as well as I do."

"It is vital that you understand our needs," insisted Shaindor. "We require the best path over these mountains. Can you find it for us?"

She just laughed at his urgency. "If you want the best path over the mountains, you have definitely come to the right Pharsheeth. The best path over the mountains is exactly where I will lead you."

As evening approached, the ground, which had been continually rising since they first entered the forest, now took a substantially steeper turn. By mid-afternoon the next day, the trees began to thin, and on the morning of the third day since their departure from Pharnarest, Magnus awoke to an awe-inspiring sight.

They had at last completely emerged from the darkness of Krondeep. Now, directly in front of them, loomed the massive peaks they had but glimpsed during their frenzied flight from Ferelshine. High into the sky they soared, putting to shame all that Magnus had once considered immense. The swigeresh trees seemed now to be but puny bushes, while even the great towers of Sweet Harmody arose in his recollections as nothing but children's toys.

"The mighty Mounji Mountains," breathed Shaindor, coming to stand beside Magnus. "Many a fine song has been written about their wondrous heights." Shaindor began to sing:

> *Oh Mountains of Mounji, so high in the air,*
> *When I climb your great heights I forget all my cares.*
> *I shall breathe your fresh breeze, dip my feet in your streams,*
> *And be carried away to a land of sweet…*

"Come on, come on," called Biddira. "Let us move. My feet itch to be amongst the mountains again."

Shaindor cut his song off. "You are right, good guide," he said. "Come, Magnus. I do not think you will find this road to be easy. But let us stay close to Biddira, for with her knowledge, we shall find the path we seek."

Biddira grinned as she led them on. "We shall make for the Parghwum Pass. In all my years, I have never found a better way than that."

* * *

As Shaindor's health had improved, so his ability to make accurate predictions had also returned. Magnus definitely did not find the journey into the mountains to be easy. Every step felt like a massive labour as he hauled himself up the steep winding paths along which Biddira led them. If not for the assistance of Shaindor, he probably would have given up early on the first day of their ascent. Fortunately for him, the admirable Cherine was forever by his side, offering words of encouragement and providing him with a strong and certain helping hand.

This support was particularly welcome because Biddira seemed to pay no heed at all to Magnus's difficulties. She continued to leap ahead, her nimble feet clinging surely to the narrowest paths and the slipperiest rocks. Shaindor frequently had to call out to her to halt her progress and wait for them to catch up as she threatened to dance out of sight entirely.

After many days of such toil, Biddira led them along a trail that wound up the side of a high ridge. Magnus, as usual several paces behind, struggled to drag himself up the final yards to reach the top. The cold wind battered his cheeks, its chill setting his teeth to chatter like the prattling goosefish of Mersfong Marsh.

From their high vantage point, a path led down into a wide, green valley, from the depths of which the roar of a rushing stream could be heard. On the far side of the valley, another great wall of rock rose, even higher than the ridge they were currently balancing on. About halfway along the top of this sheet of rock, a narrow defile could be seen, a small crack through which the sun gleamed warm and bright in the frigid air.

Biddira pointed to this break in the rock. "You see our destination," she said. "The Parghwum Pass. From there, we will begin the journey back down the other side of the mountains."

"Your knowledge is indeed proven to be profound, Biddira," said Shaindor. "Come Magnus, let us make for the Parghwum Pass." So saying, Shaindor took Magnus's hand and the two began to walk along the path that led down into the valley.

"Wait. Where do you think you're going?" called Biddira.

"Why, to the Parghwum Pass, as you directed," said Shaindor.

"But that's not the best way."

"It's not?" Shaindor seemed a bit taken aback.

"Of course not. This is the best way." Turning her back on the broad green valley, she began to stride further up the ridge.

Shaindor looked doubtful for a moment, but as she was about to disappear from view again, he had little option but to drag Magnus by the arm and quickly follow.

However, after another day of seemingly random traversing along this high path, Shaindor called out for Biddira to stop.

"Are you sure this is the best way?" he asked.

"Who is it that's been exploring these mountains from a tender age?" she replied.

"You," said Shaindor.

"Then why do you need to ask? Just a few more steps and we've made it." She pointed up to a point not far above them where the path disappeared over the peak of another ridge.

This information heartened the others, and with a few final steps, they made it to the high point Biddira had directed them to.

"Here we are at last at the Parghwum Pass," said Shaindor as he and Magnus sat themselves down to catch their breath.

Biddira laughed. "Does this look like the Parghwum Pass?"

Magnus looked around. This clearly wasn't the narrow cleft in the great wall of rock Biddira had pointed out the previous day. Instead they found themselves sitting on a snow-capped summit, the apex of a tremendous peak.

"Where are we?" Magnus asked.

"The famous high peaks of Phrongia," said Biddira, throwing out her arms expansively.

Magnus followed her arms and began to take in the scene around them. The peak atop which they were sitting rose out of the clouds, like a towering island. On every side, similar peaks were rising up, some higher and some lower, but all gleaming white beneath a sky that had never looked so blue. It was as if they were sitting in the middle of an ivory archipelago floating in an ocean of cloud.

Magnus tugged on Shaindor's arm. "I'm sure I've heard that name somewhere before."

"No doubt you have," said Shaindor, gazing out raptly at the spectacle about them. "The high peaks of Phrongia are often spoken of as one of the truly great wonders of the world. We are indeed privileged to be witnessing it for ourselves." And he began to sing:

> *Perched on the high peaks of Phrongia,*
> *Carried up to such marvellous height.*
> *My heart skips a beat as I lift both my feet,*
> *And I rise to the heavens in…*

"Alright, already, got to move," called Biddira. "We've still got to get to the Parghwum Pass, remember."

"Of course I remember," said Shaindor, sounding somewhat annoyed. "But this is a once in a lifetime opportunity. Can you not let us enjoy it for just a few more minutes?"

"Suit yourself, your mission," said Biddira airily.

It was with difficulty that Shaindor and Magnus were eventually able to drag themselves away from the wonders of the high peaks of Phrongia. With time pressing, they were forced to stand up and continue their journey. Once again, they found themselves being led back and forth amongst the winding mountain trails, with no apparent end in sight.

After two days of such fruitless trekking, Shaindor again called out for Biddira to stop.

"Are you really sure this is the best way?"

"Who is it who has spent virtually all their lives up amongst the high peaks?" she replied.

"You," said Shaindor, but he didn't sound all that sure.

"Then have no fear. We're practically there. Just around this corner." She pointed ahead to where the path disappeared behind a massive cliff.

Shaindor and Magnus quickened their steps and raced around the corner. When they got to the other side, they did not find themselves at the top of a high pass. Instead, the path disappeared into a gaping black hole at the foot of the cliff.

"This is a tunnel that leads direct to the Parghwum Pass?" said Shaindor.

"Oh no," laughed Biddira. "Something much, much better."

And then, before either Shaindor or Magnus could raise an objection, she had disappeared into the darkness.

Shaindor and Magnus looked at each other doubtfully, but there didn't seem to be a lot of choice. To be left, lost and alone amongst the peaks of the Mounji Mountains, was not an option. Reluctantly, they followed her into the blackness.

Within the hole, it was darker than night below the starless skies of the desolate sea of Scarpposia. Then a light appeared, spinning around in the darkness. Magnus could just make out Biddira standing before them, swinging a torch in wide circles. Suddenly, they were overwhelmed by a kaleidoscopic display of brightness, reflecting from all around in sparkling colour. It was as if they had entered a cave whose walls were lined with gems and jewels of the highest order.

"Welcome my friends," said Biddira, "to the wondrous Cavern of Kristobul."

"The Cavern of Kristobul," said Magnus. "I'm sure I've heard that name before as well."

"Assuredly you have," said Shaindor, whose eyes were glittering in the torchlight. "For as the high peaks of Phrongia, so the Cavern of Kristobul is also held to be another of the great marvels of our world."

Magnus looked around with delight as Biddira led them through the cavern, shining her torchlight on the mystical and magical shapes it contained. Intricate pillars rose up from the ground, and delicate chandeliers hung from high above. Every surface seemed to glow with unearthly light. It was like an underground city of astonishing beauty, a subterranean Sweet Harmody.

By Magnus's side, Shaindor began to sing softly:

> *Hidden away from the light of the day,*
> *Lies a realm both majestic and noble.*
> *For astonishing sights fill the enchanted nights,*
> *Deep, deep down in the cave of Kris…*

"Echo, echo, echo." Biddira's voice boomed through the cavern, cutting off Shaindor's song.

"What are you doing?" he demanded through clenched teeth.

"Making echoes. You should try it. It's really fun."

"Don't you think there are more appropriate ways to appreciate the magnificence of this place?" he said.

"Enjoy it any way you want. Probably best we were heading off anyway. The Parghwum Pass awaits."

Before she had even finished speaking, the torchlight was bobbing back towards the exit of the cave, leaving Magnus and Shaindor with little choice but to again hurry after her.

Back on the outside, the path continued to twist and turn in its seemingly aimless way. Magnus began to feel that each step no longer mattered. It was as if he was rooted to the spot while above him the same mountains circled around and around.

After a further three days of such futile rambling, Shaindor yelled out for Biddira to stop.

"Are you absolutely, positively sure this is the best way?" he demanded.

"Who is it who knows every valley, cleft and crevice in this mighty range?" she replied.

"You," said Shaindor, but he sounded far from convinced.

"Then don't worry. Just down this path and we'll be there." She indicated a point ahead where the trail began to descend.

By now, Magnus and Shaindor knew better than to take Biddira's word for it, so it came as no surprise to discover that, rather than a high mountain pass, the path actually led them down into a wide circular valley. But when they reached the valley floor, they found before them a sight the likes of which they could never have anticipated.

There was a lake unlike any they had ever seen. Its surface was perfectly still, as if a layer of glass had been laid out across the valley. Beneath that surface, the water sparkled and glistened like the purest crystal. So clear was the water in this lake that even the tiniest pebbles at the deepest depths could be plainly discerned, gleaming like diamonds beneath the shimmering sun.

For a third time, Biddira threw out her arms. "My friends, I present to you the jewel of the mountains. Behold translucent Lake Christolia!"

Magnus and Shaindor stared, spellbound, at the miraculous vision before them.

"It's the most beautiful thing I've ever seen," said Magnus.

"To think that I should witness with my own eyes translucent Lake Christolia," Shaindor murmured. He raised his arms, puffed out his chest, and opened his mouth. But before a note could come out, Biddira quickly interrupted.

"Here we go. He's going to sing again."

Shaindor's chest unpuffed and his mouth snapped shut. "I was not."

"Oh yes you were. You always sing whenever we get to one of these places."

"Well, maybe I do. Is there anything wrong with that?"

"It just gets kind of boring after a while."

"My songs are not boring. How dare you suggest—"

"Can we just go?" said Magnus. The bickering between Shaindor and Biddira had ruined the splendour of this place for him. Now he just wanted to get on with the journey.

So the following days passed in tense silence, with neither Shaindor nor Biddira even prepared to acknowledge the other. Magnus battled to keep up, dragging himself up cliffs and over ledges. High above, the mountain tops spun, while death-defying drops gaped below. It was almost impossible to believe it when, after climbing to a small cleft that seemed vaguely familiar, Biddira uttered the words they had begun to think they would never hear:

"Congratulations. We have reached the Parghwum Pass."

Magnus looked down. There was the wide green valley with the sound of water gurgling far below. There, on the other side, was the ridge they had scaled so many days before. As he regarded this sight, he couldn't help noticing another path that led up from the valley.

"What path is that?" he asked.

"Only the path you would have come up if you'd foolishly followed your own direction instead of listening to me," Biddira explained. "It goes down into the valley and then comes up again on the other side."

Shaindor's ears had pricked up at this information. "And how long would that have taken?" he demanded.

"About five or six hours," she replied breezily.

At that moment Shaindor looked as if he might explode.

"Are you telling me," he roared, "that we have spent days trekking and toiling over this tortuous trail when we could have crossed this valley in a mere six hours?"

"Yes," said Biddira. She looked extremely pleased with herself.

"Why would you do this?" Shaindor raged. "Why would you deliberately lead us on such a foolish journey? Why would you drag us so far from our path? Why would you—"

"With respect," she interjected, "I was only following your directions."

"But my directions were clear. You were to find us the most rapid path over these mountains."

"That is not what you asked me to do. You said only that you required the best path over the mountains."

"Well, perhaps you can explain how it could possibly be the best path when it has taken us over a week to travel a distance we could have crossed in a few hours?"

"Let me see," said Biddira, ticking off the details on her fingers. "First you climbed to the high peaks of Phrongia. Then you witnessed for yourself the Cavern of Kristobul. And finally, you got to take in the wonders of translucent Lake Christolia."

"But we did not have time for such sightseeing. When I requested the best path, it should have been obvious that I meant the quickest path."

"Not to a Pharsheeth," answered Biddira. "If you say you want the best path, we will lead you by the most exciting and spectacular path we can find. And let me add that I did not hear you complaining at the time. I could barely drag you away from those sights, such was your need for haste."

"Why, you disrespectful brat."

"Stupid, vain, pompous snob."

"Ignorant, obnoxious vulgar—"

"Stop!" cried Magnus. His voice echoed out over the valley, forcing the two combatants to look down and acknowledge his presence.

"Listen to the two of you," Magnus continued. "What would the Glurgs think if they saw you? They'd be laughing. They'd think the war was already won. We're on the same side, or have you both forgotten that? How are we supposed to get anywhere if we spend all our time fighting amongst ourselves?"

"How can you say that, Magnus?" protested Shaindor. "After what she has forced us to go through."

"Biddira did not deliberately seek to mislead us," said Magnus. "She thought she was doing exactly what you'd asked her to do."

"What I asked of her was simple to comprehend," muttered Shaindor.

"So it might seem to you. But look closely at your words, Shaindor. You said you required the best path across the mountains. To you, driven by the urgency of our quest, this could only mean the quickest path. But to Biddira, they suggested instead that we desired the most scenic and enthralling route. And so she has guided us truly and with great skill."

"But she has added days to our journey."

"I am aware of this, and yet I do not regret it. When I left my village, I had a desire to see for myself the sights and wonders of the world. Now I have witnessed three of the finest. So thank you, Biddira, for helping me to achieve my wishes." Magnus paused and, to Shaindor's amazement, he bowed before her.

"But now," he said, straightening up again, "it is time for the two of you to make up. Let apologies be made and this misunderstanding cleared up once and for all."

For a moment, silence reigned over that high wall of rock. Shaindor spoke first.

"Magnus's words are wise. I begin to see how my directions could have been misconstrued. I apologise, Biddira, for my harsh words. You have been a worthy guide who has led us well in the way you thought best."

"And I apologise to you, Shaindor," said Biddira. "Perhaps I was too hasty in my decisions, wishing to follow the path I desired rather than the path you needed. In future, I will strive to consider your requirements before my own."

Magnus grinned. "That's better. We must not forget who our real enemies are. We fight the Glurgs."

"We fight the Glurgs," agreed Shaindor and Biddira.

"And now that is agreed," said Magnus, "I wish to reiterate Shaindor's directions so there can be no room for confusion. We now request that you lead us by the quickest and easiest way down the other side of this range. If even the fuming fire mountain of Flumighon or the sparkling ice-caves of Imigoren lie before us, we should have no desire to see them."

"Such a task would be a challenge to any Pharsheeth," replied Biddira. "But I will do my best."

Hargh Gryghrgr

IF THE DESCENT of the Mounji Mountains passed without the viewing of any particularly spectacular attractions, it also passed without any further incidents. The trail was still a difficult one for Magnus to follow, but it was far less exhausting than the initial climb. The one who seemed to be having the most trouble was Biddira, for she clearly found that denying herself the allure of the numerous scenic detours available, in order to keep to the path she had promised, was much harder than she had anticipated.

Over the five days it took them to come down from the heights of the Parghwum Pass, another dramatic change in the scenery became apparent. When they had ascended the foothills of the mountains, they had been under the lushly forested eaves of Krondeep. However, the slopes on the far side of the range could not have offered a greater contrast. The further they descended, the sparser the vegetation around them grew, and by the time they took the final steps back onto level ground, there was no plant life of any kind to be seen.

They were standing on the edge of a wasteland that stretched away to the horizon. It was not smooth, as was the plain they had passed over to get to the Shrine of Oponite, but instead pitted and scored with deep holes and trenches. It was as if the very earth had been infested with a wasting sickness that had caused the ground to rot away, leaving nothing except a dried-out landscape of blisters and scars.

"You see before you the desolation of the Glurgs," said Shaindor, surveying their surroundings with distaste. "This is how they have treated the land in which they dwell, for we have now passed to the south of Hargh Gryghrgr, into the dismal nether-realms of their domain. A place we Cherines do not ever travel."

"Neither do the Pharsheeth," said Biddira. "There is nothing interesting here for us to see. Just dull, broken earth. We don't usually descend so far down the other side of the mountains, and I would never have chosen to, save for your request."

"And having fulfilled it, you are now free to return to your people," said Shaindor. "Your assistance has been gratefully received, for we could not have crossed the mountains without you. But the path that we follow grows more perilous by the day. We now make directly for Hargh Gryghrgr. You need accompany us no further."

Biddira considered Shaindor's statement before responding. "Your journey has become mine as well. As far as I am able to, I will stay with you."

So the three travellers turned to the north and began to make their way over the tortured ground. The journey was difficult. The constant trekking in and out of trenches and pits took its toll on Magnus's knees, while his feet were blistered by the hard, dry ground. Compounding the unpleasantness, they were soon set on by a host of ravenous, blood-tasting kwofferflies, horrid little insects who would suck up a mouthful of blood, swish it around in their mouths and then spit it out again, leaving itchy, blood-spattered sores all over their bodies.

As night fell, they found a particularly deep hole that offered good shelter. However, with no vegetable matter of any kind, a fire was out of the question. Instead, Shaindor and Magnus huddled together in order to keep warm.

"This place gives me the creeps," said Magnus. "All around me I can sense the presence of the Glurgs. Their smell and their feel. It is everywhere."

"I know what you mean," said Shaindor. "For having befouled this land, their miserable spirit cannot easily leave it. You see now how important our mission truly is. For should we at last be defeated, all of the land shall once more become like this."

"You say 'once more'," said Magnus. "Was there a time when all lands were like this?"

"Indeed," said Shaindor. "Long ago when the Glurgs ran unchallenged and ascendant over all lands. For you have heard about the great triumph of Ferelshine, but I have not yet told you what happened next."

So Shaindor told the story about the long wars that followed the battle of Ferelshine. As he did so, even Biddira came and sat beside them to listen intently to the tale.

"As I have said, we were triumphant at Ferelshine. But even we were not prepared for what followed, for we had no idea of their number, nor of the might of their forces. In those days they had many fortresses, of which Hargh Gryghrgr was not even the greatest. So they came upon us unawares, and the slaughter was great. Man, woman or child, they did not discriminate. All they wished to do was obliterate our race. We were forced to flee before them, finding whatever hiding spots we could. Still they pursued us, endlessly, remorselessly, destroying everything in their path and laying waste to all the lands. It seemed that there was no way for my people to escape their brutality.

"It was only by luck that the few survivors chanced upon the green hills of Gronadine. Then, within the sanctuary of those fair hills, a safe haven was founded, although you would not recognise that desperate settlement as the glorious Sweet Harmody of which you yourself have shared the wonders. Still, for years it withstood all attacks, standing firm as the tide of battle surged around and allowing my people to regain some semblance of their original strength. But the Glurgs were stronger still, and they massed their forces into the greatest army they had yet gathered. Out on the field of Phrill we faced that army, and thanks to the bravery of Gronfel the Brave, we won the battle against all odds.

"Since that glorious day, the fortunes of war turned in our favour. We were able to drive the Glurgs back and reclaim and heal the land. Under our stewardship, the earth was renewed and grew green and fertile again. And in time, other races, seeing that the land was rich and good, came and settled, establishing domains on the grounds that we had tended. Some even joined us in our continuing struggles against the Glurgs, although those that did not we do not judge any less.

"As for the fortresses of the Glurgs, these we destroyed utterly, save for one. Hargh Gryghrgr, the most remote of their cities, we could never reach. And so it remains like a sore, the last vestige of an evil disease that seems otherwise to be cured. Now the infection is once more spreading across the lands. But we will not let that happen. We will not stop until all traces of that sickness are removed at last."

After Shaindor had finished his story, all was silent for a while. Then he began to sing, very softly, the song Tharella had sung on Magnus's first night in Sweet Harmody, about the great victory on the field of Phrill. Midway through the first verse, Magnus began to sing along. Amazingly, Biddira did not complain, or even roll her eyes in annoyance. By the last verse, she too had joined in.

* * *

Early next morning, they resumed their march across the badlands. Barely an hour after setting off, the peril of their situation became apparent. Shaindor, with his sensitive eyes, was first to detect the danger.

"Glurg patrol to the east. Advancing quickly."

Fortunately, the tortured earth offered no shortage of hiding places, and the three were able to duck down into a deep trench before the patrol became visible. As they passed above, Magnus was forced to endure again the revolting sight of their twisted features and the putrefying stench that wafted around them. After the weeks of sanctuary in the mountains, it was a shock to be reminded of the vile nature of the enemy they were dealing with.

In the two days that followed, the patrols became more and more frequent. Progress began to be substantially delayed, as they were forced to spend more time in hiding than advancing towards the sinister fortress ahead. Still, slowly but surely, they continued on. With every step the sense of menace, the awareness that great evil lay before them, grew heavier on their hearts.

Then it happened. Late on the fourth day after they had left the mountains, as they descended into a particularly deep pit, the feeling of horror grew overwhelming. Gazing ahead over the lip of the hole, Shaindor was the first to see it. Immediately, he moaned and retreated back into the pit, covering his face with his hands. Biddira was next to look, and she too recoiled, her eyes bulging so wide they nearly popped out of her head. Finally, Magnus summoned up the courage to raise his eyes up over the rim, and then he too witnessed the sight which for so many days he had dreaded.

Hargh Gryghrgr lay before them, down the bottom of a long, but not particularly steep, incline. Its misshapen walls rose, sickeningly greeny-brown in colour, as if all the refuse of the world had been brought together, mixed and mashed into a fetid, reeking paste and then piled up at random. Magnus's senses reeled at the collected hideousness of the sight, and he collapsed back into the hole, gasping for air.

For a long while, nobody said a word. Each of them knew what this moment meant, but none wanted to be the first to say it. As the hours of the day ebbed away they remained motionless at the bottom of that hole, waiting for the others to speak.

At last, Shaindor patted Magnus on the back. "Night is falling," he said softly. "It will offer you the cover you need. Best not to delay this moment too long."

Magnus swallowed. For so long he had relied on Shaindor as a trusting and loyal guide. As day had followed day and week had followed week, he had been able to put aside his fear, barely considering the prospect that at some point they would be required to separate. Now the day had arrived, and in this moment of greatest peril he was about to lose the protection of the mighty Cherine and strike off on his own.

"Oh Shaindor," he said. "What am I going to do without you?"

"I know you're afraid," said Shaindor. "But look how far you've gotten. You've crossed the mighty Mountains of Mounji. You've faced perils that would cause even the mightiest of my noble race to pale in fear. You've already displayed all the strength and courage you could ever need."

"I do not feel like I have any courage in me at the moment."

"But it is there. All you need to do is search for it, and I know you will find a way."

The two embraced, and for a moment Magnus felt the strength of the Cherine flowing into him. Then he turned to Biddira.

"Goodbye, Magnus," she said. "On behalf of my race, I wish you success."

"Thank you, Biddira," he replied. "I couldn't have gotten this far without you." Then they too embraced, Magnus reluctant to let go of her twitching body, hoping to delay the moment of his leaving by every possible second.

At last, the moment could no longer be put off.

"Farewell to you both," he said. "You have both been worthy guides and companions. I hope beyond hope that I shall see you again."

"Of course you shall see us again," said Shaindor. "We are not planning to abandon you. When you have succeeded in your quest and discovered all you can about the Krpolg, we shall be waiting here to guide you back home again."

This news was a great relief to Magnus. He had given little thought to anything beyond the immediate completion of the mission. It was a comforting thought to know that as he journeyed into danger, his loyal friends would be remaining close by.

With a heavy heart, Magnus turned at last from his two companions and climbed out of the hole. For the first time since the nightmare of the Plergle Swamp, he was on his own again. Just one little Kertoobi against the might of the Glurgs, with every step taking him nearer and nearer to Hargh Gryghrgr.

Crouched at the top of the pit, Magnus felt himself hopelessly exposed, even beneath the gathering dark. Fearing to make a direct run at the frightful walls, he chose instead to dash to the nearest spot of shelter, even though it took him no closer to the gloomy city. There he remained, cowering in his hiding place for hour after hour. It had been one thing for Shaindor to tell him that the courage he needed was within him. It was quite another thing to be able to find it for himself.

Magnus placed his hand over his breast, wishing that he could somehow clutch onto some courage and pull it out. Underneath his vest, he could feel his heart beating. Inside each heartbeat was all of the grief, all of the pain, and all of the anger he had first felt, far back on the day when the Doosies had delivered their gruesome news. It might not have been courage, but it was just enough to overwhelm his fear at last. The moment of reckoning had arrived. It was time to show the Glurgs just who they had taken on when they had stolen his brother away.

Magnus rose to his feet and emerged from out of the trench. Then, keeping a wary ear out for any approaches, he crept towards the fortress, now a towering wall of darkness in front of him.

In less time than he had expected, he arrived at the foot of the city walls. He paused, considering what his next step should be. An initial visual inspection of the walls did not reveal any obvious break through which he might pass. He held out a reluctant hand to touch the looming barrier, then hastily withdrew it, shaking it in agitation to rid it of the cold, sticky slime that now clung to his fingers.

Slowly, carefully, Magnus began to creep along the wall, seeking for a way in. His ears were peeled for the slightest noise and his hands reached out before him, patting at the noxious stones in search of even the tiniest gap. Still nothing presented itself. The walls of Hargh Gryghrgr held fast against his admittedly somewhat limited assault. Magnus felt cold and desolate, revolted by the dank putrescence that covered his hands and the foul stink that permeated everything.

Suddenly, he heard gruff voices and footsteps. A patrol was headed his way. Panic gripped him and he turned to run. Too late, the footsteps were almost upon him. He lunged forward, trying for one last, desperate dash for freedom, but instead tripped and fell painfully on his shoulder. Now in utter terror, Magnus curled up on the ground. The voices were right above him. Surely the end had arrived.

Time seemed to stand still for Magnus. It was a very long moment before he realised that the voices were no longer directly above him, and the footsteps were actually receding into the distance. Magnus willed himself to open his eyes and barely stopped a sigh of relief escaping his mouth. By the most tremendous stroke of luck, he had managed to fall into a deep hole, right in the nick of time.

Too scared to even breathe, let alone move, he waited till the voices could no longer be discerned before he dared take a look around. He was lying at the bottom of what appeared to be a crevice at the foot of the wall. He clutched at the sides, attempting to heave himself out, but to no avail. The walls were too wet and slippery to get a decent grip, and, try as he might, he was not able to climb out. He sat down again, frustrated that his stroke of luck had turned itself into such an impediment.

Only then did he notice that his luck had not run out at all. The crevice was merely the opening to a narrow passage that seemed to lead directly under the walls. A passage that turned out to be just wide enough for a Kertoobi to squeeze into. Although the air was oppressive and the smell excruciating, Magnus managed to drag himself through, sometimes crawling and sometimes pushing along on his stomach. At last, the passage reached its end, and he emerged, gasping for air, through a tight opening. He was in Hargh Gryghrgr.

Magnus stood up. The first part of his mission was accomplished. He had actually gained entrance to the city of the Glurgs. For a moment, a feeling of elation swept over him. It didn't last long. The realities of his situation quickly wiped away any sense of relief. He still had the far more difficult task of finding out what the Krpolg might be. And he was now in the stronghold of his mortal enemies.

He began to walk, unsure of exactly where he might be going. Slinking beneath the cover of the deformed and distorted structures that rose up like silhouettes of mutated creatures all around, he trod warily down the muddy, pothole-filled streets. Occasionally, an armed patrol would march by, but Magnus had no trouble retreating into the shadows until they passed. No other residents roamed Hargh Gryghrgr at this late hour. The streets were shrouded in darkness. The only light to be seen seemed to be coming from somewhere deep within the heart of the city.

Without any thought or reason, Magnus found himself drawn to this light. As if in a trance he stumbled towards it, like a dragomoth attracted to a medium-sized active volcano. It was only when he neared the source of the light that his senses, jolted by the indescribable horror of the sight before him, came rushing back.

He was standing on the edge of what must pass for the public plaza of Hargh Gryghrgr. The entire space was illuminated by torches, revealing the full glory of the buildings that surrounded it, so grossly unformed that they seemed to be not so much built as hurled down from the sky and left where they had splattered onto the earth. Within this grotesque square was crammed what appeared to be the entire population of the city. From one side to the other, all that could be seen was a swollen sea of Glurgs, their repellent features twisting and warping under the dancing fires. But none of these faces was more repugnant than the one on the brute that stood on a platform in the centre of the square. A hulking figure almost twice the size of the other Glurgs, his eyes blazed with a beastly flame and his mouth snarled with rage as his words spewed out over the crowd.

"For too long, the Cherines have stolen what is rightfully ours. For too long, we have fled before them, letting them take from us what they will. For too long, we have cowered before them," he cried in a cruel, harsh voice as the crowd muttered in angry assent.

"But I tell you, my people, those days are no more," the monster continued. "It is time once more for them to fear us. Let us smite their armies."

At this, the crowd cried out their support with one voice.

"Let us tear down their towers."

Another great howl of approval.

"Let our mighty warriors put our enemies to the sword, driving all before them until there are none remaining to challenge the true supremacy of the great Glurg race."

With the last of these vicious words, the assembled Glurgs let out a roar so enormous that the whole city seemed to tremble. Then a chant began to rise through the crowd:

"Krpolg, Krpolg, Krpolg, Krpolg."

Louder and louder it grew, until it filled the whole square with its fury.

"Krpolg, Krpolg, Krpolg, Krpolg…"

Magnus felt sickened. Never before had he felt such utter, indiscriminate hatred. What this Krpolg that filled the savage hearts of the Glurgs with such delight might be, he could not conceive, could not even imagine without being immobilised by terror.

In a daze, he staggered away from the plaza. Even as he did so, a figure accosted him.

"Stop. Who are you?" cried a rough voice.

Magnus began to run. He had barely taken two steps before another figure appeared before him. There was nothing else for it. His hand reached out, groping blindly for his sword. Before he had the chance to raise it, other forms loomed out of the darkness. Their misshapen shadows rising up, cutting off the light from the torches, were the last things Magnus saw.

Klugrok

MAGNUS WOKE UP. Beyond the throbbing of his head and the aching in his back, he was able to discern little more than the fact that he was lying on a cold hard bench that was about as comfortable as the floor of the stone quarries of Qualambia.

The recollection of exactly where he was hit at around the same time he finally managed to summon enough energy to open his eyes, allowing him to greet his surroundings with a suitable degree of hopeless terror. The room was small, dark and filthy. The walls were composed of that slimy, brown matter that seemed to be the only building material utilised by the Glurgs, and there was no immediate source of either air or light within these dire surroundings. Overcome by shock, Magnus did the only reasonable thing in his power and proceeded to pass out again.

When he came to a second time, he decided to take a bit longer to open his eyes. Perhaps it was all just a dream. Perhaps this whole miserable journey had never actually happened, and he only had to pinch himself and he would be awakening back in his comfortable little kertottage.

He opened his eyes. Instantly, it became apparent that it wasn't a dream. Not only had his situation not improved, but it had actually managed to become even worse. Two pairs of beady eyes were peering at him through the gloom on the other side of the room. Without being able to help himself, he screamed loudly. Immediately, a rough voice from outside the room yelled out something, and the two pairs of eyes quickly disappeared.

This occurrence suggested to Magnus that passing out again was a pretty good option. But try as he might, unconsciousness evaded him. He was forced to deal with reality, and reality was not pleasant.

He had failed. There could be no doubt about that. He had totally and utterly failed. There was no bright side here. No silver lining to this cloud. Just ignominious, inexorable, undeniable failure. The quest that had begun with such high hopes had been brought to an end. He was now hopelessly, wretchedly, at the mercy of the enemy.

At the mercy of the Glurgs. The merest thought was enough to send a chill through his body, colder than the frigid draughts from the deepest depths of the underwater lake of Uldonte. Who could possibly imagine what horrors they had planned for him? Who could possibly entertain the tiniest skerrick of an idea of the sort of tortures that lay in store? Magnus did not dare try to hazard any guesses.

There was only one slim hope he struggled to cling to. Shaindor was waiting just outside the walls of the city. Surely he would be prepared to leap into action at the merest hint that his companion was in danger, but how was Magnus supposed to get a message to him? There did not seem to be any means of communication available. Shaindor was so close and yet still just out of reach. If Magnus was to entertain any hope of escaping, he would need to manage it all by himself.

But how? There was only one door in the room, and the guttural voices he could just make out coming from the other side made it clear that this was not a valid escape route. In desperation, he swept his eyes through the murk, hoping an alternative would present itself. Amazingly, just as he had all but abandoned hope, something actually did.

It was a tiny sliver of light creeping in from somewhere above his head, just strong enough to catch his attention. Magnus followed the light back to its source, which at first appeared to be little more than a small crack in the wall. Gradually, it resolved itself into the most desirous object he had ever seen – a small window, directly over the slab of stone he was lying on, so dirty that it barely stood out from the rest of the wall. It was high, but just in reach.

Magnus slowly got to his feet, taking care not to make any noise that might arouse the attention of his captors. Then he thrust his fingers into the crack where the light was creeping through, noticing immediately that it wasn't sealed. Was there a chance he could open it?

He pressed gently on the lower end of the pane but it did not budge. The window might not have been sealed, but it was wedged tightly. He tried again, pushing harder this time, but again it didn't move. Then, knowing that his very life depended on it, he took a deep breath and pushed with all his might.

With an almighty groan, the window shifted, perhaps by an inch or so. In an instant, the door opened. Magnus slumped back onto the bench as a large Glurg rushed into the room. It took one look at Magnus and grunted something unintelligible. Then it stepped onto the bench. Standing right above the cowering Kertoobi, it reached up to the window, which creaked and moaned under its rough fingers. Job complete, it stepped down, snarling a single word at Magnus.

"Klugrok."

Not getting a response, it repeated the word. "Klugrok."

When Magnus did nothing but continue to quake and tremble, the monster shrugged its shoulders and stomped out of the room, slamming the door behind itself.

It took over an hour for Magnus to stop shivering from the fear of this brief encounter. At last, despair was overwhelming him. Escape was well and truly cut off. Ruefully, he cast his eyes up to that firmly closed window, only to receive the surprise of his life.

The window wasn't closed. It was wide open. Magnus blinked, to make sure his eyes weren't deceiving him. How could that window be so open? Hadn't a Glurg just come in and closed it? Then Magnus remembered that he had been so busy trembling and shaking, he had not actually observed what the Glurg had been doing. Instead, he had made the obvious assumption that it must have closed the window, in order to cut off an escape option. What other reason could it possibly have had for coming into the room?

This inexplicable event threw Magnus's mind into confusion. Why should a Glurg come in and open a window? Did they actually want him to escape? Obviously, this was out of the question. Of course they didn't want him to escape. Perhaps this was all part of a trick they were playing. They hoped he would try to escape so they could capture him again and then accuse him of trying to escape. This seemed like a reasonable possibility so Magnus decided that in order to be safe, he should definitely avoid making any further attempts to try to get out through the window.

Still, the sight of that window, now gaping open, teased and taunted him. Freedom seemed to be just in his reach and yet agonisingly far away. Magnus's tormented brain seesawed between the two possibilities, until stuck somewhere in the middle, it came to the only logical conclusion. This must be exactly the effect the Glurgs were aiming for. They were messing with his mind, trying to soften him up before the real torture began. He would need to be on his guard, prepared for any other games they might try to play with him.

Magnus had little chance to pursue this line of thinking any further, because at that moment the door opened, and the Glurg came back in again. It held a bowl full of some vile-smelling gunk, which it placed on the floor beside the bench. As it turned to leave the room again, it made another rasping noise, from which Magnus was just able to decipher a single word.

"Food."

Magnus did not know how long it had been since he had last eaten. He'd lost all sense of time since waking up in this dingy prison, and he had no idea how long he'd been lying unconscious prior to that. Despite the gnawing hunger that was beginning to grip him, he felt no urge to even consider taking some of the putrid glop that filled the bowl. The very sight of it was enough to send his hunger off on a very long holiday, while the smell was so bad it made him seriously consider never eating again.

It was some hours before the Glurg returned. It took one look at the untouched bowl and then cast its malicious eyes back to Magnus.

"You have not eaten," it barked.

Magnus was still not capable of making any reply to his horrid captor.

"You must eat," said the Glurg, pointing a hooked claw towards the unpalatable contents of the bowl.

Magnus said nothing, but he did manage to cower just a little bit more.

The Glurg regarded Magnus for a moment. "You don't want to eat? Then don't eat," it grumbled. "If you wish to starve yourself, feel free to starve yourself."

The creature turned and walked back to the door. Before it exited the room, it snarled once more at Magnus. "But one thing I don't like is good food being wasted. I'll give you five more minutes, and then I'm taking it back."

Magnus sat up. He had now survived three encounters with a Glurg, but he wasn't sure he could handle another one. There was no doubt now in his mind that escape was the only option. Surely, five minutes would give him enough time to make his getaway.

He raised his arms, reaching up for the sides of the window. Then he tensed himself, preparing to leap up and out into the darkness.

"What do you think you're doing?"

Magnus fell back to the bench, too devastated to even register that it had been a ridiculously short five minutes. The Glurg was marching towards him again, an expression of perplexed fury etched across its foul features.

"I just opened that window," it croaked. "Now you want it closed again?" It reached up and began pulling on the window, all the while grumbling to itself. "There, are you happy now?" it snorted as, with one final slam, it shut both the window and any final plans Magnus might have had of escaping.

"And I see you still choose not to eat," it said as it stooped and collected the reeking bowl. It paused for a moment as if considering something. Then it rose up again, its ghastly face once more directed towards Magnus.

"I have an idea," growled the Glurg. "I think it's time you came out of this room and met the others. Maybe that will help you to find your tongue, and your appetite."

The Glurg reached out to grab Magnus's hand. Magnus tried to back away further, but by this stage he had retreated so far, there was nowhere left for him to go. Before he had a chance to resist, the brute had taken the trembling Kertoobi by the arm and was pulling him towards the door.

On the short journey from bench to door, Magnus was overwhelmed by the thoughts of what horrors awaited him outside this room. Inhospitable as it was, it suddenly didn't seem to be quite so unpleasant when compared to the unknowns on the other side of the door. Who were these others the Glurg referred to? What sort of diabolical threats was he about to face? How was he ever going to cope when he had found just a few seconds with a single Glurg to be so utterly terrifying?

Nothing could have prepared Magnus for the nightmare of the sight that greeted him. The room was considerably larger than Magnus's prison, but every bit as dirty and disgusting. In its centre, atop a decrepit, half-rotten table, a massive cauldron bubbled and boiled, sending out noxious fumes that filled the whole room. Around the table, preparing to tuck into this gruesome gruel, sat three other Glurgs.

"Allow me to introduce my family," said the Glurg. "This is my wife, Kruperke," and he pointed to the nearest of the three, a Glurg just as repellent as the first but distinguished by the long, scraggly hair that hung limply from her malformed head. "And these are our Glurglets, Rerglek and Lerchhle," he added, indicating in turn the two smaller Glurgs, who sat fidgeting at the far end of the table, their reduced size somehow adding to rather than detracting from the grotesqueness of their appearance.

"I must apologise for them disturbing you earlier," said the first Glurg. "They are but children and the sight of you fascinates them. Don't take offence, but we find your appearance somewhat unsightly. But that does not excuse rudeness to a guest."

"You speak of rudeness, but here you are, forcing him to stand while you yabber away," snapped Kruperke in a voice that was higher pitched but no less grating on the ears. "Come, Klugrok, let our guest sit."

"You are right, my dear," said the first Glurg, and he promptly forced Magnus into a chair which was so amazingly moulded as to be exquisitely uncomfortable in all places simultaneously. "Come, sit and enjoy some food with us. Kruperke is as fine a cook as you will find in all of Hargh Gryghrgr."

"And Klugrok is as fine a talker as you will find in all of Hargh Gryghrgr," said Kruperke as she ladled out a fresh helping of steaming muck into a bowl in front of Magnus. "Let's give our guest a rest from your voice for a moment. Can't you see he's starving?"

Klugrok! The word the Glurg had snarled at him earlier. That must be his name. Far from threatening him, the creature had actually been introducing himself. Still, this revelation did not do much to make Magnus feel more comfortable. He watched uneasily, not speaking or even moving, as the Glurgs tucked into their dinner.

Klugrok dipped a hand into his bowl and then stuffed it into his mouth. The gunk oozed out of the side of his lips and down his chin. Some of it dropped back into the bowl, but most of it fell on to the table top where it lay, largely indistinguishable from the rest of the mess that was already there.

"Not bad," he grunted. "Could do with a bit of seasoning." He leant over, produced a series of retching, coughing noises out of the back of his throat, and spat a massive ball of bright green phlegm into the bowl. Then he stirred it with a finger, picked up another handful, and shoved it into his ravenous jaws. "Mmmm, that's much better."

"You're right, it is a bit bland," said Kruperke. She too leant over her bowl and began to drool into it. Meanwhile one of the younger Glurgs was sticking his fingers as far up his nose as possible, dislodging a shower of thick dark mucous into his bowl, while the other was scratching at a large boil on the side of her face, sending a stream of gleaming yellow pus into hers.

Magnus watched in sickened fascination as this routine continued. There was not an orifice, from the smallest blister to the hugest bunion, that the Glurgs did not poke, pop or pick at in order to add further flavours to their food. As for table manners, they were definitely not a concept that had ever been introduced into Hargh Gryghrgr. Each of the family members took delight in talking with their mouths as full as possible, spitting, slobbering and dribbling with each bite they took, and continually hurling food from one side of the table to the other.

After several minutes of this performance, the family began to notice that something wasn't right. Someone at the table did not seem to be indulging themselves in the pleasures of this dinner.

"What, still not hungry?" enquired Kruperke of Magnus.

The others all turned to look at him. Trapped before the withering stares of those four repulsive faces, Magnus found himself incapable of any reasonable action. With a hand whose motion seemed to have become divorced from the workings of his mind, he reached into the bowl, scooped out a hot clammy handful, and thrust it into his mouth.

The Glurg food didn't taste as bad as it looked. It tasted a hundred times worse. It was like taking the mud from the Plergle Swamp, mixing it with the water from the cesspits of Swertania, and then allowing it to gently simmer inside the outfall of the sewers of Spondulik for fifty years. Only a hundred times worse. It was beyond horrible. It was beyond disgusting. Before Magnus could even control himself, he was spewing it back into the bowl.

The Glurgs all let out a great cry:
"He likes it!"

*   *   *

After the meal was over, Magnus found himself back in his, now slightly more airy, room. He sat on the edge of the hard stone bench, trying to make sense of the dinner he had just shared and his feelings towards this Glurg family.

There should not have been any difficulties in this regard. He was meant to hate the Glurgs. Hadn't they waged war on all of the civilised races for generations? Hadn't they cruelly murdered his brother? Wasn't the primary reason he had come here in the first place to seek revenge for this shocking crime?

Amazing as it seemed, he was actually finding it difficult to hate these particular Glurgs. True, their faces were hideous, their manners harsh and rough, and their personal habits extremely questionable. Yet, once these quite substantial deficiencies were taken into account, when it came down to it, they were actually rather…well…nice.

All through dinner, Klugrok and Kruperke had plied him with questions. Where was he from? How long did he plan to stay? What did he think of Hargh Gryghrgr so far? At first, Magnus had responded with sullen silence. But after a while, he could no longer resist their friendly openness, and he found himself joining in their conversations. He even managed to keep down a couple of handfuls of the dinner, and while it did not get to taste any better, it did imbue a certain amount of energy back into his system. However, while he eventually felt relaxed enough to reveal his name and the village of his birth, he told them nothing about the purpose of his visit to Hargh Gryghrgr.

Now back in his room, he tried to figure out what it could all mean. Perhaps it was all pretence after all, an attempt to trick him into revealing information about his mission. But they had seemed so genuine. If it was an act, it was an awfully good one. There was nothing to suggest that these were the vicious, savage beings he had spent his entire life believing all Glurgs to be. And for some reason, this idea was more than a little disquieting.

There was a knock on the door, and Klugrok came in.

"You're sure you want the window open?" he said.

Magnus nodded. "Definitely."

"Well, if that's how you like it," said the Glurg, sounding more than a little perplexed. "I myself prefer it dank and stuffy, but whatever my guest wants is fine by me. And I trust your bed is hard and uncomfortable enough for you?"

"Yes, it's fine," said Magnus without thinking.

"Good. See you in the morning then. Unpleasant dreams."

"No, wait," said Magnus suddenly.

"Is there a problem?" asked Klugrok.

"It's just that, where I come from, we prefer beds to be soft and comfortable."

"Really?" Klugrok seemed amazed at this concept. "Well, each to his own I say. Is there something I can get you to make it more...er... comfortable?"

Magnus explained the idea of sheets and mattresses to Klugrok, and while the Glurg wasn't sure that such things existed in Hargh Gryghrgr, he said he would see what he could find. He returned shortly afterwards with a couple of thick, dirty mats and some thin, hole-filled rags.

"Will these do?"

Magnus sighed. "I guess they'll have to."

As Magnus watched Klugrok make a bed of sorts for him, his mind wandered around in ever-increasing circles. How could he possibly reconcile this obliging host with the monsters that all other folk so feared and despised? How could this friendly family come from the same race as those beasts who had mindlessly unleashed violence upon the rest of the world for as long as anyone could remember?

"All finished," said Klugrok at last.

Magnus climbed onto the bed. It was still extremely uncomfortable but a lot better than just lying on a solid block of stone.

"Thank you, Klugrok," said Magnus.

"You're welcome, Magnus." Klugrok turned, preparing to leave the room. As he reached out to close the door behind him, Magnus found he could not resist asking the question topmost in his mind.

"Why do you hate the Cherines?"

Klugrok answered quickly without turning around. "Because they hate us."

"But you hated them first," said Magnus.

"What makes you say that?" asked the Glurg, now turning back to face Magnus.

"You attacked them for no reason on the field of Ferelshine."

"That is not true," said Klugrok, his eyes flashing. "We did not attack them."

"Yes you did."

"No, we did not. True, when these creatures first appeared in our lands we found their appearance so highly attractive as to be extremely repugnant. But how things appear is not of great importance to my people, so in keeping with our customs, we sent a small band of messengers to welcome these new arrivals. But how did these butchers respond to our peaceful greeting? By slaughtering every single one of our messengers, unprovoked and in cold blood."

"This is not how it was told to me. I was told that you attacked them, and that the Cherines only responded in self-defence."

"And by whom were you told this story?"

"By the Cherines."

Klugrok laughed a grim and throaty laugh. "Of course they would tell you that. My friend, you have been caught up in their deceits. Everything they have told you about that day is an out-and-out lie." Then, with a final, "Goodnight, and may all your dreams be nightmares," Klugrok left the room.

The Shkroulch

MAGNUS DID NOT HAVE any trouble fulfilling Klugrok's wishes. While it did take a substantial amount of time before he finally managed to get to sleep, his dreams were not pleasant.

He was back on the field of Ferelshine, but what he saw was far from the tale as described in the ballad upon the obelisk. It was now the Glurgs peacefully arranged on the field, preparing to begin their banquet when they were disturbed by a loud cry. High up on the hill stood a party of Cherines. With swords raised, they charged down into the field, stabbing and slashing at the defenceless Glurgs. In the midst of this carnage, the leader of the onslaught removed his helmet and let out a fearsome roar. At that moment, the face of this merciless brute became clearly visible.

It was Shaindor.

Magnus awoke, writhing and screaming on a hard bed. Firm hands were promptly laid on his shoulders, holding him down and comforting him.

"Oh, Shaindor," Magnus cried. "I've just had the most horrible dream."

"Who is Shaindor?" asked a gruff voice.

Magnus opened his eyes. Klugrok was standing over the bed, a puzzled expression on his gruesome face.

"Just a...a friend," stammered Magnus, unwilling to share any more information on that subject.

"I see," said Klugrok. "It is good that your dreams were bad. Perhaps you will join us now for breakfast?"

Seated around the table with the Glurgs, Magnus hardly touched his food. This was partly because the breakfast was no more appealing, either visually or gastronomically, than dinner had been. But it was mainly because Klugrok's final words the night before continued to twist around and around in his mind like a legless slitherskink.

Could it be true? Was it possible that it really was the Cherines, not the Glurgs, who were the aggressors on the field of Ferelshine? Klugrok had been absolutely adamant in that regard. Magnus did not doubt that he believed what he was saying.

But what of the Cherines? The prospect that they might have lied to him could not even be considered. The Cherines were so noble and wise, so utterly praiseworthy in every way. And what of Shaindor? The whole time they had been together, he had been nothing but the most trusted and loyal companion. It was not conceivable that his account of that ancient day could be deceitful.

So what was Magnus left with? Two races, both of whom had treated him with kindness and hospitality, producing two accounts of the same incident that were so divergent, they might as well be describing wholly separate occurrences. How could this be? How could a single event produce descriptions that conflicted so wildly? How could Magnus possibly resolve these differing versions into something that made even the slightest sense?

"Still not eating, Magnus?" tutted Kruperke. "Does it need a bit more snot?"

When Magnus didn't answer, she turned to her husband. "Klugrok, don't just sit there. Our guest looks miserable."

"You are right, my dear," cried Klugrok, leaping to his feet. "What is the matter, Magnus? Is there anything I can do?"

"No, really, I'm fine," said Magnus. What could he say? How was he meant to bring up these issues without offending his host?

"Perhaps he'd like a nice cup of flurball tea," suggested Kruperke.

She walked across to the stove where a small pot stood. Evil-looking liquid, mixed with globules of gunk and wads of dark hair, was bubbling out of the top, dribbling down the sides and onto the stove.

Observing this unappealing sight, Magnus began to think that maybe offending his host was not the worst thing that could happen to him. "Actually, Klugrok, there is something I'd like to talk to you about," he said quickly.

"Go ahead," replied Klugrok.

Magnus considered the best way to put this. "It's about what you told me last night. How the Cherines were the ones who attacked you on the field of Ferelshine."

"That is exactly how it happened," confirmed Klugrok. "Even the youngest of our Glurglets knows the truth of that dark day."

"But I just don't see why the Cherines should have lied to me about it."

"I would not put anything past the Cherines," muttered Klugrok. "They are vicious and cruel."

"No, they're not," protested Magnus. "At least not to me. They're friendly and loyal. Virtuous and wise."

Klugrok's eyes narrowed in suspicion. "These are the Cherines we're talking about?"

"Absolutely. I have spent many days in their city, noble Sweet Harmody. And many weeks travelling with a trusted companion of that race. I know the Cherines are not as you say."

"What's a nice boy like you doing spending time with those horrid Cherines?" said Kruperke as she returned from the stove with two mugs filled to the brim with flurball tea.

Klugrok picked up his mug and swilled a mouthful. "I think perhaps they have weaved some mischief with his mind. The Cherines have been our enemy since time immemorial. They have no redeeming qualities of any kind."

"Well, can I ask one more question?" said Magnus, trying to figure out what he could say to make Klugrok realise how mistaken he was.

"Anything you wish. I see it as my duty to reveal to you the truth about those vile butchers."

"Sh...the Cherine of whom I spoke told me also of what happened in the aftermath of the field of Ferelshine." Magnus continued by recounting Shaindor's tale of how the Glurgs had ruthlessly hunted down the Cherines. "Are you saying that this too is untrue?" he asked after he had finished.

Klugrok thought for a while before answering. "There is some truth in this story. As I have said, we are a peaceful people who do not choose to make war. But we also have our pride and could not be expected to ignore such a provocation. Plus the attack clearly showed to us that these Cherines were not a race with whom we could co-exist. If we did not take measures for our own defence, they would certainly wipe us out in time. And in this we were proven correct, for unfortunately, we failed in our mission. The butchers were not exterminated, and to this day, they continue to wage war on us, stealing our land and murdering our people."

As Magnus listened to Klugrok's words, he couldn't help noting an eerie feeling of familiarity. "But that is exactly what the Cherines say about you," he blurted out.

"That cannot be," said Klugrok. "Clearly they are the aggressors in this accursed war."

"It's the truth," said Magnus. "They also claim to be peace-loving and say they only act in self-defence."

Klugrok considered Magnus's words. "Could it really be as you say?" he said at last.

"I absolutely promise. Every word I say is true."

Klugrok looked away for a few moments. When he turned back to Magnus, it seemed that a new look filled his rheumy eyes. A look of decision.

"We are having a meeting tonight. Perhaps it would be worthwhile if you could come along. There are others in Hargh Gryghrgr who would be interested in hearing your words."

"What sort of meeting?"

"Glurgs who are not happy with our leadership. Not happy with the way the war against the Cherines is being waged."

"Will there be discussion about the Krpolg?" asked Magnus, suddenly reminded of his mission.

Klugrok gave Magnus a funny look. "Yes, there will most certainly be discussion about the Krpolg. We shall leave immediately after dinner. But now I must go to work. I will see you later."

Watching Klugrok leaving the house, Magnus felt strangely elated. Somehow, someway, in a manner that he could never have expected, his quest suddenly seemed to be back on course again.

* * *

Magnus spent the bulk of the day playing with Rerglek and Lerchhle. Their favourite was a grotty old board game called Glastriest which didn't seem to have any particular aim, but did require each participant to roll around in the filthiest corner of the room each time they passed Go. It turned out to be a surprisingly enjoyable way to pass the time, and before Magnus even noticed, night was falling and Klugrok had returned.

Despite Kruperke's fussing, Magnus still found himself struggling to eat any of the dinner. All he could think about was the upcoming meeting and the questions he was hoping to find answers for. What exactly was the Krpolg? What was the solution to the mystery of the differing accounts of the battle of Ferelshine? How could he convince the Glurgs that the Cherines were not the fearsome enemy they believed them to be?

After a while, Kruperke sighed and began removing dishes from the table. Interrupted from his mental preparations, Magnus noticed that Klugrok had also not touched his food. The Glurg was clearly agitated, his face a noticeably paler shade of sickly grey, as he stood up from the table and grunted.

"All right, Magnus. Are you ready to come with me?"

Magnus nodded nervously.

"Just remember," the Glurg continued, "there is danger in attending this meeting. All such gatherings are strictly forbidden. If we are caught, the penalty will be severe."

Magnus gulped. The reason for Klugrok's unease was now all too clear.

"It is probably better that you are not seen on the street. Suspicions are high during this time of war. There are many in this city who do not look kindly on unfamiliar faces, and although yours is not as disturbingly attractive as a Cherine's, it is insufficiently ugly to avert suspicion."

Klugrok went out the back door and then came back in wheeling a small cart.

"Climb on here," he ordered. "Lie down."

To Magnus's horror, he then proceeded to shower a sackful of stinking brown mud over the top of Magnus's body.

"What's the matter with you?" he growled as Magnus spat and spluttered and tried to wipe the muck from his face. "That's finest grade klongbuck dung."

"Klugrok is a manure deliverer," said Kruperke proudly. Such an occupation obviously carried a lot of prestige in Hargh Gryghrgr.

"Can we play in the dung too, please, daddy?" cried Rerglek and Lerchhle.

"Not now, Glurglets," barked Klugrok. "I'll bring some fresh dung tomorrow. This is for Magnus. Can you keep still? You must be totally covered. The streets are heavily patrolled at night and nobody must see you."

"Oh, do please be careful, Klugrok," said Kruperke, a look of great concern crossing her grotesque features.

"Don't worry, it will be all right," he replied, before picking up the handles of the cart and heading for the door.

Magnus tried to lie as still as possible as Klugrok wheeled him out of the house and into the cold night air. His eyes were closed tight, his fingers were clamped over his nose, and he did his best to ration his breathing to once every three or four minutes only. The cart bumped up and down over the rough, unpaved streets, and Magnus quickly lost count of the number of twists and turns Klugrok took as he wound through the back lanes of the city. The journey seemed never ending. Surely by now they must be near to their destination. Surely just one more turn and they would be able to step off these perilous streets and back into safety.

Then it happened. The moment Magnus had been dreading.

"Stop!" called a throaty voice.

Klugrok immediately stopped the cart. Magnus sank down as far as he could below the klongbuck dung, not daring to move even an eyelash as heavy footsteps approached.

"Out late tonight, Klugrok?" said the menacing voice.

"After-hours delivery," said Klugrok.

"Hmmm, let me check." Magnus could just discern a shadow hovering over him, and the sound of a long, drawn-out sniff.

"That's quality stuff you've got there."

"Nothing but the best," said Klugrok.

The shadow withdrew. "Very good," said the voice. "You may go."

The footsteps receded and Klugrok began pushing again. Even though the threat had dissipated, Magnus was still unwilling to refill his lungs as they turned through another three corners and then came to a stop.

Magnus heard Klugrok knock three times on a door. Instantly, three knocks could be heard coming from the other side of the door. Again,

Klugrok knocked three times, and again the knocks were answered from inside. Finally, Klugrok beat four times. The door immediately opened and the cart was wheeled inside.

"Well done, Magnus," whispered Klugrok. "We've made it."

Magnus raised his head up from out of the dung and took a deep breath, only to be confronted by a most frightening sight.

Four Glurgs were charging towards them, leaping up and down and flapping their arms around. Their eyes were wide and their faces distorted, beyond even the usual standard for Glurgs, and they were crying out at the tops of their voices.

Magnus turned to Klugrok, terrified that they had been found out, but Klugrok did not seem in the least bit worried. Instead of turning and fleeing, he began rushing towards the other Glurgs, all the while putting on a similar show. Only at the last minute, before they could crash into each other, did they reel off and stop.

"Greetings, Klugrok," said one of the other Glurgs.

"Greetings, Schnurqwel," replied Klugrok. "Tonight, I bring with me an honoured guest."

The Glurgs all turned to look at Magnus.

"What is that, a kverthog?" asked one of the Glurgs.

"A plodhound?" said another.

"The seldom seen but much discussed diperagoff?" wondered the Glurg Klugrok had identified as Schnurqwel.

"You're all wrong," laughed Klugrok. "This is Magnus, a visitor from the small homely village of Lower Kertoob. And he has some important news to share with us tonight."

"Welcome, Magnus, to our humble meeting," said Schnurqwel. "We look forward to hearing your news. Please come into the meeting room."

"Th-thank you," stammered Magnus, accepting Klugrok's hand as he stumbled off the cart.

"What's the matter with you?" asked Klugrok, sensing Magnus's anxiety.

"What was all that business before?" Magnus whispered to Klugrok.

"What business?" asked Klugrok.

"All that leaping about and shouting."

"Oh that. That was just the Shkroulch."

"The what?"

"The Shkroulch. It's a common greeting amongst us Glurgs."

"A greeting?"

"But of course. What did you think it was?"

"I don't know. It gave me a fright."

"No need to be frightened by the Shkroulch. It's a sign of great honour amongst my people. But come now, let us join the meeting."

Klugrok led Magnus down a dark corridor and through several doors until they arrived in a large room. The other four Glurgs were already there, sitting around a table.

"Magnus, let me introduce to you Schnurqwel, Kvishgrol, Lungsdek, and General Pchervlk." Klugrok pointed to each of the other Glurgs in turn, and each one let out a growl and waved their hands by way of introduction.

"Please repeat again, for our visitor's benefit, what you just said, Kvishgrol," said Schnurqwel, who seemed to be the leader of this group.

"I was just noting that the latest news from the front is good. We have now won through to the Eskivol River and the Flats of Ringobal have fallen without a fight."

"Your point being?" challenged Lungsdek.

"My point being that we are now barely a week's march from Sweet Harmody. Never in over a thousand years have we advanced so far. Do we really wish to withdraw when victory is so near?"

"Are you with us or not, Kvishgrol?" demanded Schnurqwel. "I trust we do not have a traitor in our midst."

"I have always been with you," said Kvishgrol. "But our successes in battle have made me reconsider my position. Why should we strive to prevent the greatest triumph in the history of our race?"

"You are young and foolish, Kvishgrol," said Lungsdek. "You have never been in battle, and you do not know the butchers. Other times we have been near to victory, only to be defeated at the last. I fear that they are luring us into a trap. Krpolg or not, I do not like this."

Magnus's ears pricked up at the mention of the Krpolg. Was he close at last to the information he sought?

"I might be young and foolish, but at least I am not old and cowardly," Kvishgrol retorted. "Is it not possible that the butchers are weakened and that Krpolg really can lead us to victory?"

"What do you say, General Pchervlk?" asked Klugrok. "You have been at the front recently. What impression do you get?"

"Yes, I have been at the front," said General Pchervlk. "And I do not like what I see. Our victories have come at little cost. Our enemies have offered barely any resistance. They are plotting something. What it is I cannot tell, but our intelligence tells us there are significant forces massed in Sweet Harmody. I cannot understand why they do not march, but I fear the worst."

"I know why they do not march," said Magnus.

All eyes turned towards him. Before he could say anything, there was a knock at the door. It flew open, and another Glurg ran into the room, puffing and panting. The others all got up and gave him a quick, impromptu Shkroulch.

"I have urgent tidings of great concern," cried the newcomer.

"Patience, Troghfel," said Schnurqwel. "It is the turn of our honoured visitor. Speak, Magnus. Tell us all that you know."

"You are right to say that there are forces massed in Sweet Harmody," said Magnus. "But the Cherines are holding them back. They have heard rumours of the Krpolg and its power. They choose not to unleash their armies until they learn what it is and how it can be defeated."

"This is interesting news," said Schnurqwel. "But why do you speak of Krpolg as an object?"

"I don't understand," said Magnus. "Is not the Krpolg some sort of deadly weapon wielded by the Glurg armies?"

A chuckle went around the table. "In some ways I guess you could say that this is right," said Klugrok. "But it is not *the* Krpolg. It is only Krpolg."

"You are jesting with me," said Magnus. "I cannot guess what that means."

"Krpolg is not an object but a person," said Schnurqwel. "The ruler of Hargh Gryghrgr and high commander of all the armies of the Glurgs."

"I saw a Glurg give a speech on the night I arrived in Hargh Gryghrgr," said Magnus. "Was that Krpolg?"

Klugrok nodded. "Krpolg addresses the people in a rally every week in the city plaza. Attendance by all is compulsory. It was outside such a rally that I found you."

"But his words were brutal, terrifying," said Magnus, shivering at the recollection.

"Krpolg's talent for speech drove his rise to power," said Schnurqwel. "The passion in his words filled our hearts with fire, and all who heard him could not help but be inspired. Our armies fought with a renewed courage, devastating all in their path, reclaiming lands we had not held for generations and restoring pride in our long downtrodden race. When he first became our ruler, there was not a soul in this city who did not believe with all their heart that he was good for the Glurgs. But now many of us are not so sure."

"Why not?" asked Magnus.

"For most of us," continued Schnurqwel, "the reclaiming of our land and our pride would have been enough. But for Krpolg it was not. He continues to call for ever more warfare and conquest. Nothing will satisfy him but the total destruction of our enemies."

"This in itself we would not protest," added Lungsdek. "But we know the strength of our foes. We fear that by taking the fight all the way to Sweet Harmody, Krpolg is leading our people into disaster."

"But Krpolg will not hear from any dissenters," said Klugrok. "All who disagree with him are locked away. There are many who think as we do, even from within the military." He paused, indicating General Pchervlk. "But few are prepared to speak up."

"I do not see why we should be gnashing our teeth about this," interjected Kvishgrol. "Did you not hear our visitor's words? The butchers are afraid. They fear we have a deadly weapon. Is this not the perfect time for us to unleash an offensive to destroy them utterly?"

"But you cannot destroy them utterly," said Magnus.

"Why not?" asked all of the Glurgs except Klugrok.

"You call them butchers, but you are wrong," said Magnus. "The Cherines are good and kind."

The Glurgs around the table all laughed. "This is preposterous," said Schnurqwel.

"No, it is not," protested Magnus. "I know them. They are worthy and noble. Steadfast and loyal till the end."

"You seem to know a lot about them," said General Pchervlk, fixing Magnus with a cold stare. "How is this so? Why have you come to Hargh Gryghrgr?"

"That is not important," said Magnus, reluctant at this time to reveal the reason for his mission. "The main thing I need to tell you is their desire for peace is as strong as yours."

"This makes no sense to us," said Kvishgrol. "Always in our history, the Cherines have been the aggressors, from the day they attacked us on the field of Ferelshine."

"But the Cherines claim the same thing. They say you were the ones who attacked them, and they only acted in self-defence."

The audacity of this suggestion seemed to upset the Glurgs.

"The facts of this tragic event are well established," said Schnurqwel. "There can be no doubt of the good intentions of our people on that day."

"The Cherines were welcomed with exactly the same greeting you witnessed on our arrival," confirmed Klugrok.

"You greeted them with the Shkroulch?" cried Magnus.

"But of course," said Schnurqwel. "It is the most honoured greeting our people can offer."

It was all starting to make sense to Magnus. The leaping and flapping of arms. The shrieking at the top of their voices. This was exactly how Shaindor had described the attack at Ferelshine.

"But the Cherines didn't know that," he said. "They thought they were being attacked."

"That is ridiculous," snorted Lungsdek. "Everybody knows the Shkroulch is a peaceful greeting."

"It did not look peaceful to the Cherines."

"The functions of the Shkroulch are plain for anyone to understand," said General Pchervlk. "We wave our arms to indicate that we carry no weapons. And we make as much noise as we possibly can in order to reveal ourselves and show we do not plan to make a surprise attack. Thus our peaceful intentions are made clear."

"But that's not how it appeared to the Cherines," said Magnus. "Remember that they'd never previously encountered your race. They did not know your ways. The sight of your messengers charging towards them frightened them terribly."

"Who could possibly be frightened of such a thing?" sniffed Kvishgrol in disdain.

"I was," said Magnus. "It scared the living daylights out of me."

"Magnus is right," said Klugrok. "I saw him afterwards. He was shaking."

"Don't you see," said Magnus. "It's all a big mix-up. The Cherines thought you were attacking them for no reason, so they attacked you back. This made you think they had attacked you for no reason, so you attacked them back. And it's all grown from there. You and the Cherines have been fighting a war for thousands of years over one silly misunderstanding."

Nobody said anything. The Glurgs all looked from one to the other. Eventually Schnurqwel spoke.

"Could these words be true?"

"Magnus has been a good and worthy guest," said Klugrok. "He has always spoken the truth to me. I would trust him."

"Then it would seem that a great tragedy has befallen both our peoples," said General Pchervlk.

"But what are we to do?" asked Schnurqwel. "How can we undo what has been done?"

"Let me speak to the Cherines," said Magnus.

"What good would that do?" said Kvishgrol.

"I will tell them what I have learnt. I know they will heed my words. Their leader, Tharella, is beautiful and wise."

"Beautiful *and* wise?" questioned Klugrok, as if such a combination could not possibly exist.

"Indeed. And she is advised by Phraedon, the kindly judge. When they hear my story they will be eager to make peace."

"Are you sure of this?" asked Schnurqwel.

"I would bet my life on it."

"Then this is the plan we will follow," said Schnurqwel. "Magnus shall return to Sweet Harmody immediately."

"But what of Krpolg?" asked Lungsdek. "I cannot see him approving any contact with the Cherines."

"No, he would not," said Schnurqwel. "And that is why we must do it. Yes, let us seek peace with our mortal enemies. It is the last thing Krpolg will expect and the best thing we can do if we wish to prevent him leading our race into catastrophe. General Pchervlk, can you arrange to have our troops pulled back? We must ensure that any planned attack on Sweet Harmody is delayed until Magnus has a chance to complete his mission."

"It will not be easy," said the General. "Krpolg is insistent that the attack occur without delay. But I still have the ear of most of the other generals. I should be able to hold it off in the short term, but for how long, I cannot say. Haste will be of the essence. Is there anything I or my troops can assist you with, Magnus?"

"Merely to pass unhindered through the city walls," replied Magnus. "My friend and guide, Shaindor, is waiting for me just outside," said Magnus. "Together, we shall return to Sweet Harmody so we can end this war forever."

The Glurg who had arrived late, Troghfel, cleared his throat. "I'm afraid there might be a problem with that."

"What sort of problem?" demanded Schnurqwel.

"This is the news I bring. Two spies were detected outside the city walls to the south. One was a Cherine, the other of a race we did not recognise."

"Shaindor and Biddira!" cried Magnus. "Are they all right?"

"I have no idea. They escaped and fled back into the mountains. But patrols now have been redoubled. They shall not again approach so near to the city."

"But what am I to do now?" wailed Magnus. "How am I to return? I cannot find my way back to Sweet Harmody unguided."

Again silence reigned over the table. For a moment, it seemed that the plan so recently devised was already threatening to collapse. Then Klugrok spoke five words that renewed the hope in Magnus's heart.

"I will go with you."

Urquarest

IT WAS DECIDED that Magnus would leave the following evening.

Kruperke helped Magnus prepare for the return stage of his mission. Although he maintained that he had more than enough in the way of supplies, still she spent the whole day stewing up a selection of dishes of varying degrees of noxiousness, and in the end, Magnus found himself unable to prevent her from forcing them into his pack.

After dinner, Schnurqwel paid a brief visit to offer his best wishes for the journey. He, Magnus, and Klugrok retired to the smaller room where they could speak in private.

"It is a great thing you are doing," said Schnurqwel to Magnus. "The hopes of all my people travel with you. You shall be known ever after as a friend of the Glurgs."

Magnus did not immediately reply. He had already decided that now was the time to come clean to the Glurgs about the real purpose of his visit to Hargh Gryghrgr. But finding the right words wasn't easy.

"When I first left home and set out on this journey, I never thought I would become a friend of the Glurgs," he began. "It pains me to say this, but the only feelings I ever had for your race were fear and loathing."

"Fear and loathing? Why ever would you feel like that?" asked Klugrok.

"Partly the way I was brought up, I guess. In my village we were always told that you were a brutal race that loved only fighting and killing."

"But these are nothing but lies," said Schnurqwel.

"I know that now. But before I came here I never considered looking at things from your perspective. I never even thought you might actually have a perspective." Magnus paused. This was the part that was really hard to say. "But there's more to it than that. There's another reason I held such a hatred for your race." He stopped again before blurting out the horrible truth. "A Glurg killed my brother."

"No," said Klugrok.

"That cannot be," croaked Schnurqwel.

"It is as I say," said Magnus, and he went on to describe the circumstances of Jangos's death.

"We can only offer our deepest condolences," said Klugrok after Magnus had finished.

"We had no fight with your family and meant no harm to your brother," said Schnurqwel. "Clearly, he was in the wrong place at the wrong time."

"But that's not how I saw it when I first found out," said Magnus. "All I could feel was anger and hate. I didn't want to tell you this before, but the main reason I came to your city was to seek vengeance for his death. But now that I know you, it is no longer what I crave. Once I thought all Glurgs were hideous and evil, but now I know that is wrong."

"Are you suggesting we're not hideous?" said Klugrok, affronted.

"No, you're certainly hideous, beyond all expectations. But you're not evil. You've been kind and welcoming to me. I'm sorry that I wasn't honest with you from the start."

Magnus stopped and waited, unsure of what sort of reaction his words might inspire.

"Well, that explains a lot," Klugrok grunted.

"What do you mean by that?" wondered Magnus.

"Your behaviour when we first met. I thought you were a little bit crazy. But now I understand."

"You mean you're not upset with me?"

Klugrok shrugged. "What's to be upset about?"

"Only good has come from your actions in the end," added Schnurqwel. "You have done no harm to our race."

Magnus thought about this with satisfaction. It was true. Despite his original intentions, he had not in the end caused any hurt to the Glurgs. Then a shocking realisation hit him. It was a lie. There was something that had happened, long before he had arrived at Hargh Gryghrgr. Something that had filled him with delight at the time, but which he now looked back on with horror. Something that he could not keep from his new friends, for the sake of his conscience.

"I wish there was truth in what you say," he mumbled, "but there is something else I need to tell you. I regret to say that I have killed a Glurg. I didn't mean to," he added quickly as the two Glurgs reacted with a start. Then he thought better of himself. "Actually, I did mean to." He paused, and then carefully recounted the details of the attack beside the field of Ferelshine.

It was immediately clear that this time neither Glurg was so willing to just shrug off Magnus's confession.

"This is evil news," growled Klugrok.

"Black was the day when you wandered onto that accursed field," rumbled Schnurqwel.

"I'm terribly sorry, I really am," said Magnus, suddenly fearful. Had he finally pushed these Glurgs too far?

The faces of the Glurgs softened, as far as two such ghastly faces could, at the sight of the terrified Kertoobi quailing before them.

"Do not worry, Magnus, we do not hold you to blame," said Schnurqwel.

"You acted in the heat of battle," said Klugrok. "From what you have told us, you had no other choice."

"But it would help us greatly if you could describe our fallen comrade," said Schnurqwel.

"Well," said Magnus, still breathing deeply to get over his shock. "He looked like a Glurg."

"Can't you give us a little more detail?"

Magnus wasn't sure that he could. He still did not find it easy to tell one Glurg apart from another. They all appeared equally unappealing. But Schnurqwel's tone was so urgent that he figured he ought to at least try.

"His eyes were sort of crooked this way. His mouth slanted down a bit like this. And his nose was kind of squashed, a bit like that." As he spoke, Magnus tried to use his hands for extra emphasis, but his description was so vague there was no way anybody could have made any sense from it.

Schnurqwel and Klugrok looked at each other. "Gropflug," they said in unison.

"We should pay a visit to his widow," said Schnurqwel. "It will be a great comfort to her."

After everything was prepared, it was time for goodbyes.

"Thank you so much for all your hospitality," Magnus said to Kruperke, and before he knew it, he was being squeezed tightly within her broad, clammy arms. The Glurglets too lined up for a farewell cuddle, but Magnus drew the line when Lerchhle requested he also hug her pets – three large and exceptionally slimy schkrungerfly maggots.

Finally, Klugrok and Kruperke shared one long embrace.

"Please take care," cried Kruperke.

"I will hurry back to your side," said Klugrok.

The couple then kissed, their lips making a loud, squelching glop.

Heaving his pack over his shoulder, Magnus followed Klugrok out of the house. Here they met the escort General Pchervlk had arranged to ensure they were able to depart the city unmolested, a detail that now seemed somewhat unnecessary given how utterly encrusted Magnus was in dirt, filth, and dung. Beneath the dim moonlight, he could easily pass for a rather short Glurg.

Before they left, they had one last errand to make; a visit to Gropflug's widow.

She met them at the door, a small, hunched-over Glurg carrying a screaming, dripping bundle of a baby in her arms.

"We have news of your husband," said Klugrok, "but I regret to say it is not good."

"I feared as such," she groaned.

Inside her house, Magnus hastily retold the story, his eyes permanently fixed to the floor.

"Please do not attach any blame to Magnus," added Klugrok, "for he acted only in self-defence."

"But that in no way diminishes my regret," said Magnus, thinking ruefully that there seemed to be an awful lot of self-defence in this conflict. "I am sorry."

She looked at him, but there was no hatred in her eyes. "I accept your apology," she said softly. "Thank you for telling me this."

"You spoke well," said Klugrok after they had left. "That cannot have been easy."

Magnus shook his head and wiped a tear from his eye. The recollection of that distant day, and the mindless exhilaration he had then felt, filled him with deep disgust. "There has been too much killing," he said. "It's time to put an end to it once and for all."

* * *

The initial stages of the return trip passed uneventfully. Magnus and Klugrok headed north from Hargh Gryghrgr, travelling by day and resting in trenches and holes at night. Over the next two weeks, they crossed the vast Plains of Plartoosis, the deserted stretch of nothingness that spread to the north of the city. All around, the signs of war were clear to see. A mass of Glurg encampments lay on either side, spread out as far as the horizon. But the soldiers within the camps were idle. It looked like General Pchervlk had achieved his objective. The advance of the Glurgs had ceased, at least for now.

As the plains ended, the travellers found themselves in a land of rolling hills. They were now approaching that place where Magnus and Shaindor had first viewed the approaching Glurg army, near to the field of Ferelshine, but the country was barely recognisable. Not a tree, nor a bush, nor even a blade of grass raised itself above the ashes. The land had been razed of vegetation, leaving nothing but a dry, burnt-out desert. Magnus could not help thinking of Shaindor's words as they had watched the advancing Glurgs on that day so long ago:

"Mindless destruction is the only thing they know."

"Why do you do this?" Magnus demanded of Klugrok. "Why do you wish to see this land destroyed?"

"It is not true that we wish to see this land destroyed," Klugrok growled.

"Then why did you do it? This land was lush and green. Now it is brown and desolate."

Klugrok looked around the broken land impassively. "Did I not tell you before that how things appear is not of importance to my people? What is important to us is the functions they may serve us."

"And what function can ruining this land possibly serve?"

"To strike fear and dread into the hearts of our enemies. Yes, it is true," the Glurg continued over Magnus's howl of protest. "While we are in a state of war, we do not think twice about destroying the land if it helps us drive away our foes."

"All the more reason for bringing this stupid, pointless war to an end," Magnus muttered.

"The land will grow again," said Klugrok offhandedly. "It is for lives lost that we should end this war."

Magnus did not reply. Though sorely troubled by Klugrok's words, he could find no reasonable argument with the statement the Glurg had made.

Three days from the end of the plains, they overtook the last of the Glurg armies. Now they travelled past the ruins of abandoned towns and villages. It all felt eerily similar to those other days, when Magnus had passed through this same country with Shaindor. Then, his eyes and ears had nervously sought out signs of Glurgs. Now, it was for Cherines that he and Klugrok kept alert, but they spied no other folk. Nobody was walking on the roads in these times of danger. For days upon days, they wandered in silence, until hearing a great commotion up ahead, they peered over a rise and beheld again other living beings.

It was the tail end of the great column fleeing the advance of the Glurgs. Peoples of many different races were scurrying along the road, making all the haste they could. Gleeprogs and Frungoles. Querks and Lothfarines. Doosies and Trongabores. All races known under the sun, as well as a few that seemed to have just been made up on the spot. Guiding this cavalcade, armed to the teeth and attempting to preserve some semblance of order, was a brigade of Cherine warriors.

Klugrok regarded this procession with some concern.

"This presents us with a problem," he said. "How are we to pass any further without attracting unwanted attention to ourselves?"

Magnus considered the possibilities. Klugrok's fears seemed warranted. It was far too risky to be discovered by the Cherines on the open road. Better that they completed the journey to Sweet Harmody before declaring themselves. How then could they pass any further? Magnus sat for a few moments thinking. Then something in the crowd caught his attention.

"Wait here for a moment," he said to Klugrok. "I think I have the answer."

He ran along the side of the road until he had caught up with the bustling crowds. At the very back of the procession, a covered wagon zigzagged back and forth across the road. Magnus hid by the side of the road as the wagon approached and then quietly called out to the tall figure who was towing it.

"Hey there, Shabandor. I have a deal for you."

The eyes of the tall figure shot around to the side of the road where Magnus stood. Cautiously, he scanned the road to make sure nobody was watching, before coming to a stop beside Magnus.

"What have you to offer me?" he asked, speaking in a low voice.

"You'll have to follow me to find out." Magnus turned and began walking back over the ridge.

The Shabandor's beady eyes followed Magnus for a moment, then turned back to the retreating column before him, considering his options. Finally, temptation got the better of him and he hurried to catch up with Magnus.

Shabandors, as Magnus well knew, were the sneakiest and greediest of all the races. Operating primarily as merchants, they travelled from town to town, towing their covered wagons full of odds and ends of indeterminate value. They would tell you that a diamond was a stone or a stone was a diamond, if they thought they could get some advantage out of the deception. Most races heartily despised them and the Cherines more than anybody. However, they were generally rudely tolerated, as amongst their mostly worthless trinkets, a gem of great worth, such as those much valued in Sweet Harmody, could occasionally be found.

Magnus indicated for Klugrok to duck down as the Shabandor approached. Like all of his race, his eyes were small and round, constantly sweeping from side to side beneath bushy brows. In fact, the eyes of a Shabandor were the only feature that defined the race. In all other ways, they were remarkably diverse in appearance. Shabandors could be short or tall, thin or stout, light- or dark-skinned. However, the eyes were always a giveaway, reflecting the devious nature of the soul inside; a devious nature that seemed to offer the best chance of their being smuggled through to Sweet Harmody.

The Shabandor crossed over the rise and for the first time noticed Magnus's companion.

"What is this? Treachery?" he cried in shock. Although scheming and crafty, Shabandors knew which side they were on, and it was definitely not the Glurgs'.

"No, wait, please," said Magnus. "I'm sure we can make this worth your while." He knew he was taking a risk here. The Shabandor could easily betray them by calling out to the Cherines. But Magnus knew that, like all Shabandors, this one would have his price. A Shabandor would sell his grandmother for the right price, and given the number of elderly female Shabandors that wandered aimlessly through a number of large cities, quite a few of them had.

"I have nothing to offer now, but if you transport us to Sweet Harmody, you will be richly rewarded."

The Shabandor laughed. "Oh, that's rich. Do you really think I'm falling for that one?"

"No, really," insisted Magnus. "I have news of great value to the Cherines. I promise you they will pay highly for it."

"You've got to be kidding. Do you think I was born yesterday?"

The Shabandor turned and began hurrying back up the road. Left with little choice, Magnus pulled out his sword and rushed after him. He held the blade up, glittering, before the Shabandor's wily eyes.

"Are you going to help us or do you wish to feel my cold steel?" he cried, hoping he sounded more forceful than he felt.

The Shabandor stopped. Even his eyes stopped. He looked down towards Magnus.

"Is that a blade of the Cherines?"

"It is. Do not make me use it."

"Such a blade would fetch a pretty price in the markets of Jiberpoth."

Magnus paused. This was not exactly the effect he had intended, but maybe it would serve him after all.

"And did you know it was once the blade of Gronfel himself?" he said.

"Gronfel the Brave?" said the Shabandor, his eyes now glowing with avarice.

"The one and only. Now, are we ready to make a deal or not?"

"Name your terms."

"I offer to you the sword of Gronfel but only as a surety. When we arrive in Sweet Harmody, you may set a price for its return. If the Cherines are not prepared to honour that price, the sword is yours."

The Shabandor considered for a minute, his eyes jerking frantically from side to side. Finally he spoke.

"My friend, I am at your service."

The Shabandor helped Magnus and Klugrok into the wagon. Once under its shelter, Magnus sat back. This would be perfect. The wagon was piled up with oddments, jewels, and stones of all varieties, most likely dropped or abandoned by the panicking villagers and carefully harvested in their wake by the Shabandor.

"Hide under this jewellery," Magnus said to Klugrok. "That way you can avoid detection by the Cherines."

Hiding under precious stones was clearly as distasteful to Klugrok as hiding under dung had been for Magnus, but he patiently acceded to Magnus's suggestion.

So they passed along the road, weaving through the throng like a glowershark through a school of werblefish. The Shabandor, being eager to receive his payment, made extremely good time, and the cover his trinket-filled wagon provided was so effective that they were not stopped or approached at any time. So it was that after a journey of a little over two weeks, Magnus peered out of the wagon and was delighted to recognise a high range of green hills.

"The green hills of Gronadine!" he cried with delight. "We are near at last to the noble city."

As they reached the top of the range, Magnus could not stop himself from leaping out of the wagon to behold once more that joyous sight. There lay Sweet Harmody, nestled safely amidst the circling hills, its towers gleaming more brightly than he could ever have remembered. But Klugrok looked out from the wagon with fear and distaste.

"I do not feel good about this, Magnus," he said.

"You have nothing to worry about," said Magnus.

"I'm sure you mean what you say, but the sight of this place fills me with unease. I do not yet wish to enter Sweet Harmody."

"Why must there be so much mistrust?" said Magnus. "This is exactly what we're trying to put an end to."

"I agree," said Klugrok. "But I feel that the time is not yet right. I will wait up here while you go on ahead to spread the news. Then, once the Cherines have learnt what we know, and I no longer have reason to fear them, you can send for me."

So Magnus returned at last into Sweet Harmody, but Klugrok was not beside him. Still, Magnus's heart soared as he directed the Shabandor through the winding streets. Spring had finally arrived, and the houses of the city shone under the renewed sun. When they arrived outside

Shaindor's small dwelling, he jumped from the wagon and knocked loudly at the door. After a few moments, shuffling footsteps could be heard inside and then the door opened.

Shaindor did not look well. His face, usually so bright and full of life, seemed weary and gaunt, while much weight had been shed from his previously robust frame. But when he saw Magnus, his eyes lit anew with their old fire.

"Magnus, is that really you?" he cried as if his eyes might be playing a trick on him.

Magnus nodded. "In the flesh," he said.

"What joy, what pure delight that you should return after all hope seemed lost. Let me touch you, that I may know it is not an illusion." Shaindor held out his arms to embrace his old friend. Almost as quickly, he withdrew again, wrinkling his nose in disgust.

"No doubt, you have a tale to tell," he said. "But let us get you cleaned up first. Come inside now that we may quickly wash away the stains of that foul place."

"Hmmm, hmmm." The Shabandor cleared his throat, forcing Shaindor to acknowledge him for the first time.

"Is there something I can do for you?"

"This Shabandor and I have a deal," explained Magnus. "He has provided me with great assistance, and in return I have told him he can name his price."

"Very well then, name it," said Shaindor curtly.

The Shabandor named his price. It was ridiculously, exorbitantly, excruciatingly high but Shaindor agreed to it without discussion. Magnus at once received his sword back, and the Shabandor left, grumbling as he went that the price he had set was clearly far too low.

Over four hours of concerted scrubbing were required to remove all the grime from Magnus's body, although even after that, some trace of the smell remained. Still, it felt indescribably good to finally put on some clean clothes and eat a proper meal. All the while, Shaindor attended to Magnus as if he was some great and powerful lord, remaining on bended knees as he offered up his heartfelt apologies.

"I cannot convey to you the deep pain I feel for having had to abandon you. But we were without a choice, for barely a day after you entered that dark fortress we were detected and forced to flee to the mountains. I surely would have returned, but the whole place was swarming with Glurgs. There was no chance to launch a rescue bid. With all hope seemingly gone, I saw no choice but to return, and in fact, have been back barely a day myself. Still, I curse the rotten luck and I curse myself even more for having let it happen."

"You don't have to curse yourself," said Magnus. "It's all worked out in the end."

"Indeed, it has. Though I cannot even imagine the horrors you must have faced to extricate yourself from that stronghold of evil."

"It's quite a story," said Magnus, "although less horrific than you might think. But more than that, I bring momentous news."

"The mission," cried Shaindor. "Was it successful? Did you find out the nature of the Krpolg?"

"That and much more."

"Do not tell me now. Let us go straight away to see the Prodiva and let Tharella share with us this extraordinary news."

In the Great Hall, Magnus was received with no less enraptured amazement.

"It is indeed a wondrous pleasure to be greeting you again, Magnus," said Tharella. "After the tidings Shaindor brought back we feared the worst."

"You are braver and more resourceful than we ever could have imagined," said Phraedon. "But now, what news of the mission?"

"I have discovered the nature of that which you know of as the Krpolg," begun Magnus, "and am glad to say that it is not at all as you feared." He then went on to tell them the whole story of the time he had spent in Hargh Gryghrgr, placing special emphasis on the hospitality of Klugrok and his family and the revelations concerning Ferelshine and the Shkroulch.

The end of his tale was greeted with stunned silence. Eventually it was Phraedon who spoke.

"Are you telling us that the Krpolg is not in fact a weapon that we should have reason to fear?"

"That is right," said Magnus. "It is not a weapon but the name of a Glurg – the ruler of their city and leader of their forces."

"You are certain of this?"

"Absolutely."

"Then we must send out our armies without delay."

"What did you say?" cried Magnus, not believing what his ears had just told him.

"My words are plain," said Phraedon. "We shall attack at once."

"Did you not hear a word I said?"

"I heard very well what you said. Thanks to you, we now know that the Glurgs possess no fearsome weapons. There is nothing to prevent us from launching our forces. Tharella, you must give the order now."

"But we should not be attacking them. We should be making peace with them."

"No, we shall never make peace with them," cried Phraedon. "We shall have no dealings with them except to slaughter them when we find them. And we shall never cease until they and everything of them is utterly destroyed and the horror of their filth no longer defiles this world."

"You cannot do that. They were good to me. They were kind and helpful."

"Do I hear the words of a traitor?" said Phraedon, his voice now soft again but no less frightening for that. "Do you thus consort with our enemies?"

"No, I..." Suddenly Magnus didn't know what to say. He had not expected a reaction like this. Not from the Cherines. All he could do was plead helplessly, "Shaindor, Tharella."

Before either could respond, Phraedon again cried out. "Tharella, you know our laws. When you accepted this office, you swore an oath to defend our people against all enemies. I demand that you now fulfill your duties by punishing this vile traitor."

"Magnus, I do not know what I can do..." said Tharella.

"Urqhuarest, Urqhuarest," screamed Phraedon, his face red with fury. "The penalty for treason is Urqhuarest."

"I'm sorry, Magnus, I must obey our laws." said Tharella, looking down to the floor as she spoke. "As a traitor to our race, I sentence you to Urqhuarest."

"Guards, take him away," ordered Phraedon. "Throw him in the deepest, darkest dungeon, never to be released."

Three towering Cherine soldiers rushed towards Magnus. In desperation, he turned towards his one remaining hope.

"Shaindor, please help me."

Shaindor only looked away, his head buried in his hands.

The guards were almost onto him. They reached out, preparing to grab him. But this was not the same fragile Kertoobi who had previously stood within this hall. Magnus was now lean and lithe, his body toughened by hard days on the road. So it was that he was able to twist free from those grasping hands, dodge clear of the hulking guards, and then flee down the length of the Great Hall and away.

Plombeth Jelly

MAGNUS HURTLED THROUGH the gates of the palace and out into the plaza, racing across the massive space as quickly as his short legs could carry him. No matter how fast he ran, the far side did not seem to be getting any closer, and the Cherine guards were now in close pursuit. There was no way he would be able to get even halfway across before they brought an end to this last dash for freedom.

Then something caught his eye. He changed direction, veering towards a squad of soldiers marching across the centre of the square. His pursuers quickly adjusted to his new course, reaching ever nearer and nearer. They had almost caught up with him. Magnus could feel their hot breath on his back.

Just in time, Magnus reached the parading troops. He ducked down underneath their legs, steering a path through the maze of striding feet. For his pursuers, this was not an option. Unable to stop themselves in time, they charged headlong into the platoon.

Chaos reigned in the great plaza. Cherines went falling left, right and centre, like a sparkly set of animated dominos. In all the pandemonium, Magnus was able to hurry away to the far side of the plaza and into the relative safety of the winding streets of the city.

He rushed from one twisting lane to the next, never going in the same direction for long and never stopping to look back. The guards had taken little time to recover their footing, and now the sound of their pursuing steps echoed through the alleyways behind. No matter how often Magnus veered this way and that, he didn't seem to be able to throw them. Finally, in desperation, he threw himself into a thin crack between two houses, just wide enough for a Kertoobi to squeeze into. It wasn't much of a hiding spot, but with those footsteps now so close, there didn't seem to be anything else Magnus could do.

No sooner had he concealed himself than the guards appeared. Peering intently from side to side, they advanced along the street. Closer and closer, they approached to Magnus's hiding place. Any second now and they would spot him.

But they didn't. Their gaze swept across the gap from one house to the next. Then they continued down the street and disappeared into an adjoining lane. For the time being at least, Magnus had escaped.

For the rest of that day, Magnus remained crouched down in his hiding spot, too scared to move even a fingernail. Several further search parties patrolled the street, but amazingly, he managed to avoid detection. As the long hours progressed, Magnus was left abandoned and alone, bereft of all except the companionship of his own thoughts. These were not pleasant company.

What hurt most was the betrayal. How could the Cherines have done this to him? He had always considered them to be the paragon of everything virtuous and wise, noble and good. How wrong he had been. Behind their fair faces, their hearts were black. Underneath their fine-sounding words lurked nothing but lies and deceptions. Even Shaindor, the one who had seemed his most faithful and trusted friend, had revealed his true nature, cruelly abandoning him in his hour of need.

Now, despite their professed love for peace, they were preparing to send their soldiers out to war. Clearly, the order had been given. Magnus could hear the signs even as he huddled, paralysed with misery and fear, in his narrow cubby-hole. The air was filled with the sounding of many trumpets, while the ground shook under innumerable marching feet. A massive army was now departing through the city gates and off to bloody battle.

Magnus couldn't help thinking of his new Glurgish friends– Klugrok, Kruperke, and their delightful children, who had treated him with such kindness; Schnurqwel, Lungsdek, Kvishgrol, and General Pchervlk, who had listened to his stories and been willing to help. Now, they had all been betrayed, and by whom? He was the one who had said the Cherines were trustworthy. He was the one who had claimed that they too would be eager to seek an end to this war. Even now, thanks to him, the Glurg armies were being held back, waiting for an overture of peace from the Cherines. When the Cherines arrived, there would be no offer of peace. The greeting the Glurgs received would be nothing but fierce hatred and cold hard steel.

* * *

As night fell, Magnus knew he could not remain hidden much longer. The Cherines had probably been distracted by the excitement of the departure of their armies, but no doubt the search would soon be resumed with renewed enthusiasm. Getting out of the city would not be easy, but unless he made an effort now, the only thing he had to look forward to was eventual recapture and then endless imprisonment.

Cautiously, he poked his head out into the street. It looked like the coast was clear. He forced his aching body up from its crouching position and set off. Two steps later, he realised he had been far too hasty. A lone figure was standing on the edge of the laneway, partly hidden in the darkness beneath the overhanging eaves. In a flash, Magnus leapt back into his hiding spot. It was too late. He had been spotted.

The figure walked quickly towards the gap between the houses. Now it stood directly in front of Magnus, blocking out the moonlight. It spoke, hissing softly.

"Come with me."

"Klugrok?" said Magnus hopefully, not imagining how his friend could have infiltrated the city of the Cherines.

"What did you say?" asked the figure. Shrouded in a heavy cloak and hood, it was not possible to observe a face. From the tone of the voice, it was clearly not a Glurg.

Before Magnus could make a move, the figure had reached down and hauled him out of his hiding spot. Utterly defeated, Magnus did not even resist as he found himself being led back towards the palace.

As they got near to that mighty tower, his captor took a detour. Instead of emerging into the plaza, Magnus was rushed down a series of back alleys, until eventually they arrived at the city wall. Here, the hooded figure took out a key and used it to unlock a small door. Once the door was open, he pushed Magnus roughly through the gap.

"Go now. Leave this city. Do not come back."

There was something about the voice that sounded familiar, but Magnus could not place it exactly.

"Who are you?" he asked.

"There is no time for talk," the figure insisted. "Leave now. Run and do not stop running until you are far, far away."

Magnus realised there was no point discussing it any further. He took the mysterious figure's advice and ran. Through the valley and up over the green hills of Gronadine he raced, not stopping for a last look at the now less than noble city. Onwards and on he ran, through the chill of the night. Though his head throbbed, his lungs ached, and his legs felt as weak as a flubbery sticklebear, still he did not dare to stop. Ever onwards he hurried, with no regard as to where he might be heading. The only urge that drove him on was the desire to get far, far away from the city of the Cherines.

As dim morning dawned, he at last allowed himself the luxury of a short rest, collapsing onto the moist ground. Everything he had once believed, all certainties and sureties, seemed no longer to hold. His friends were now his enemies, while his enemies had become his friends. What was he to do now in a world that had turned as topsy-turvy as the plumiferous grousehen that walked on its head and sang through its feet?

With feeling gradually returning to his exhausted limbs and air slowly seeping back into his lungs, his mind began to clear, and he became able at last to consider the course he should pursue. There was now no doubting where his allegiances lay. He had to get back to Klugrok. He had to pass on the message that the Cherines were not to be trusted, and warn him that their armies now marched to impending war. This was far easier said than done. How was he supposed to find his friend when he had no idea of where he was, or how far he had run, or which direction it was back to the city?

It was then that he took a quick look around to check out his surroundings, and for the first time, he realised where his nightlong dash had taken him.

He was sitting at the base of a high cliff, deep down at the bottom of a narrow ravine into which the light and warmth of the still-rising sun struggled to reach. Even in his state of semi-exhaustion, he did not have any trouble recognising this locale; a place of ill-repute from which he had barely escaped the last time he had entered. The dingy, dungy Drungledum Valley.

Terror immediately gripped him. He had to get out at once. But which way? How far in had he come? Was the deadly peril before him or had he already passed it by?

He got the answer to this question more quickly than he might have expected, but it was definitely not the answer he wanted. As he slowly raised his eyes, he saw first one stone and then another and then another, leading up like a giant staircase to a yawning black cave high up in the cliff–the den of the Blerchherchh.

Magnus leapt to his feet. If he was quick, he may yet escape. It was still early in the morning. Perhaps the hideous brute had not yet woken up yet.

Poised to flee, Magnus suddenly checked himself. What did it matter if the Blerchherchh was hideous? Why was it that goodness should correlate with attractiveness? If anything, in Magnus's experience, the opposite was true. The Cherines were exquisite in appearance, yet they had turned out to be his enemies. On the other hand, the Glurgs too were hideous, but they were now his friends. Why should it not be so with the Blerchherchh?

Before he was even aware of what he was doing, Magnus suddenly found himself calling out towards that dark cave in his loudest voice.

"Hey you, Blerchherchh!"

It took a few minutes for the beast to appear. Heaving itself out of its cave, it was obvious that it had just been roused from whatever might pass for a bed. Its movements were slow, its eyelids heavy, and all three of its mouths drooped and slavered. But once it spied the Kertoobi down below, it managed to quickly rouse itself, and three wide grins spread across its jaws.

"Mmmm," it roared. "I don't recall putting in an order for room service. But I'm not going to say no to breakfast knocking on my door first thing in the morning."

The monster licked its lips and took a step down the stone staircase.

"No wait, Blerchherchh," cried Magnus. "You don't really want to eat me."

"I don't?" The Blerchherchh sounded most surprised by this.

"No you don't," said Magnus. "I don't think you're evil. I don't think you're wicked at all, just because you're hideous and ugly."

"Who says I'm hideous and ugly?" protested the Blerchherchh.

"I do," said Magnus. "But that's no reason to fear and hate you. I'll bet that you've always been misjudged and mistreated, just because of the way you look. But I think that deep down underneath there's a different Blerchherchh. A kind and gentle Blerchherchh, just looking for a chance to reveal itself."

For a moment the Blerchherchh looked as if it couldn't believe what it was hearing. Then, suddenly, it burst into tears.

"Oh, you're so right," it blubbered. "I really am kind and gentle, but I've never had a chance to show it. All my life I've been reviled and detested. People flee whenever I so much as show my face. And for what? I can't help the way I look. It's not my fault that I'm big and horrible and ugly. Even my mother didn't love me. On the day I was born, she threw me out of the cave."

Magnus gazed in wonder at the weeping beast. Could it really be? Had he revealed the true nature of the Blerchherchh? Had he just made a new friend, even a powerful ally, who could aid him in his efforts to save the Glurgs from the Cherine forces?

"Could you…do you think you could…give me a hug?" asked the Blerchherchh.

It was certainly not high on the list of things Magnus most wanted to do, but the beast was gazing so plaintively at him that he found himself unable to say no. He threw his arms around the scaly skin and felt, in return, the powerful arms of the Blerchherchh wrapping around him.

"Mmmm, that feels so nice," murmured the Blerchherchh, still sobbing softly.

After a minute or so, Magnus tried to pull away, feeling that the Blerchherchh had had more than enough consolation.

"I think that's enough, Blerchherchh. You can let go."

But the Blerchherchh did not let go. If anything it seemed to be gripping him even more tightly.

"Ow, you're starting to hurt me. Please let go."

The Blerchherchh now had such a firm grip that Magnus could barely breathe. And as the sobbing grew louder, Magnus suddenly realised with a shock that it was not sobbing at all. It was laughter.

"Oh woe is me, nobody loves me," chortled the beast, now lifting Magnus up over its shoulder.

"Hey, what are you doing? Put me down," he cried.

The Blerchherchh laughed again. "You got me wrong, little one. There's nothing about me that's kind and gentle. I'm evil and rotten to the core. Being reviled and detested is what I love best of all. And people flee from me because I chase them away."

"But what about your mother?" cried Magnus. Surely if anything could bring out a softer side to this monster, it would be the memory of that cruel rejection.

"I ate her," crowed the brute. "Just like I'm now going to eat you."

Up the steps the Blerchherchh leapt, its prey trussed over its back like a sack of prompanapples. Over the hearth it stalked and into the black cave, then down a stinking corridor that led to an enormous cavern with a massive stove, a gigantic oven, and a wide bench, onto which it tossed the terrified Kertoobi. It found a length of wire, which it used to tie him tightly, and then it lifted him onto a metal spike that projected out from the wall, leaving him hanging high above the bench. All the while, it half growled and half sang to itself.

"Now, what do I feel like for breakfast today? Scrambled legs? Toast, lightly browned and smeared with gall-bladder paste? Knuckle porridge with warm milk and devilled eardrums? No wait, I have the perfect thing." The Blerchherchh paused for a moment, obviously well pleased with itself. "Kneecap pancakes with caramelised nostril syrup and plombeth jelly. Mmmm, mmmm. Let me just see what I need."

It began to potter around the cavern, sorting through pots and pans of various shapes and sizes, spatulas and whisks and numerous other implements of indeterminate but obviously unpleasant function, and the most extensive and alarming collection of knives that had likely ever been brought together. Poor Magnus could do little except clench his eyes tightly shut, to keep at bay the horrors of this gruesome kitchen.

Suddenly, the Blerchherchh let out an earth-shattering howl.

"Oh, great shock and misfortune!"

Magnus forced himself to open his eyes. The Blerchherchh was holding up an empty jar, a look of great dismay on its three wide mouths.

"Out of plombeths," it wailed. "And me with my stomach grumbling." It looked up towards Magnus, dangling ineffectually above. "I'm off for a spot of plombeth picking. But do not worry, I'll be back soon. Don't you go anywhere, little breakfast." It laughed a cruel laugh. "But I don't expect you will." Then it took the jar and stomped heavily out of the cavern, its footsteps receding as it departed its lair and descended the steps outside.

Magnus was alone. If there was any chance for escape, this was it. He writhed and squirmed as hard as he could, but it was no use. The bounds of the Blerchherchh were too tight for him to break. In desperation, he summoned all his strength, thrusting and pressing against the cold wire. He had to take advantage of this opportunity. Who knew how long before his foul captor would return.

Too late. He could hear footsteps climbing up the stairs, entering the cave, advancing down the corridor. Magnus slumped in despair as a shadow entered the room. Straightaway, he unslumped again. It was someone he had not expected, had not dreamed of ever seeing again. It was a figure of unsurpassed ugliness and yet, before Magnus's eyes, unbelievable beauty. It was Klugrok.

"Magnus, you're here," cried the Glurg.

"Klugrok, quick. You've got to get me down. The Blerchherchh will be back soon."

Klugrok rushed over and leapt onto the bench. He drew out a black dagger and reached up to cut Magnus's bindings.

Too late again. More footsteps could be heard on the steps outside. It looked like this time, Magnus's seemingly never ending cache of luck had finally expired. He and Klugrok turned to stare as another figure emerged into the cavern. But once again, Magnus's worst fears were not realised. It was not the Blerchherchh. It was...

"Shaindor?" cried Magnus in confused amazement.

"Praise be, Magnus, I've found you..." began Shaindor. Then he noticed Klugrok standing beside Magnus with his knife poised. His mouth dropped upon in shock and revulsion.

At that moment, Biddira also appeared. She looked across from Shaindor to Klugrok, each staring with hate-filled eyes at the other. A faint smile crossed her lips.

"This is going to be interesting," she said.

"Away from him, you filthy Glurg," cried Shaindor, drawing his sword.

"No, you stay away, vile Cherine," cried Klugrok, lowering his dagger and holding it at the ready.

"Shaindor, Klugrok, no," cried Magnus, but by this point, neither was interested in listening. Shaindor jumped onto the bench with his sword blazing, only to be met by the parrying dagger of Klugrok. Heedless to Magnus's protests, the two bitter rivals battled it out, the clashing of their blades ringing through the underground kitchen. Over the bench and onto the stove, through sieves and colanders and mortars and pestles, they fought. Magnus yelled and screamed at the top of his voice, but nothing he could say made any impact. It was only a much louder, deeper voice that finally brought the duel to a close.

"Well, well, well, this is my lucky day. What do we have here? Home delivery?"

The Blerchherchh stood in the doorway. It carried a jar full of purple fruit in its claws and a greedy, drooling smile on each of its mouths.

Shaindor was the first to leap into action. He lunged straight at the monster, sword uplifted. In response, the Blerchherchh swung its long arms, sending him hurtling off to the far corner of the cave.

Klugrok came next, charging towards the beast with dagger pointed. Again, the Blerchherchh swung its arms, sending the Glurg rolling into the opposite corner. Then it raised itself up to its full height and let out a great roar.

"All right, who's next?"

An ear-splitting 'clang' echoed through the cave. Biddira had come up from behind and smashed a large pan over the monster's head. For a moment, the Blerchherchh was dazed, but only for a moment. It turned and advanced on the hapless Pharsheeth, its brutal claws flashing.

In an instant, Shaindor was back up again, charging into the side of the Blerchherchh. For a third time, the Blerchherchh merely flicked its arm, sending the Cherine crashing into a mound of cutlery. Klugrok too had regained his feet, and he now leapt at the Blerchherchh, only to be easily swatted away, coming to rest inside a giant pot.

The Blerchherchh laughed and turned back to Biddira. In desperation, she attempted to fend it off, throwing beaters, blenders, graters, stirrers, and anything else she could find into its face. But nothing would deter her remorseless pursuer.

Again, into battle dove Shaindor, this time catching the Blerchherchh slightly off guard and carving a shallow wound in its side. The Blerchherchh winced, then viciously flung out its arm, sending the Cherine sliding across the floor and into a heavily laden shelf, whose contents of jars and bottles collapsed over his head.

In one step, the Blerchherchh stood over Shaindor. It raised a scimitar-sharp claw high in the air, ready to strike. Before there was time for the claw to descend, a black dagger was thrust into the flesh of its arm. The monster let out a yelp and then lashed out at Klugrok, who flew through the air, hitting his head against the front of the stove. Then the beast leapt over the helpless Glurg and again raised his claw. This time, it was the sword of Shaindor that smote at its arm, staying the deathly blow.

All this time, Magnus had been able to do little more than shout out encouragement and generally feel utterly useless as the other three bravely took the fight to the Blerchherchh. He could see that on their own, none of them had the strength to defeat it. Each of their assaults was random and uncoordinated, making it easy for the monster to fend them off in turn. Their only chance was to synchronise their attacks, to all strike the brute in the same moment, but there didn't seem to be any way for Magnus to communicate this to his allies.

Thump! Shaindor thudded into the bench below, sending a vibration up the wall. Magnus's whole body jerked up. For a second, it felt as if he had been set free. But no, he was still dangling up above the bench. Even though he wiggled and shook with all his might, that long thin spike held him firmly.

Thump! Klugrok too crashed into the bench. Again, the shock reverberated up the wall, jolting Magnus into the air. The spike still held him but only just. All he needed was to push his legs on the wall behind him and then...

Magnus dropped onto the bench. He rolled along the top and then fell onto the floor. The very next second, Biddira slammed into him. She had now armed herself with a long boning-knife, but it had done her little good.

"Cut the wire, quick," said Magnus.

Biddira deftly cut his bonds, leaving him free at last. Without wasting any time, he grabbed an enormous cleaver and leapt into the fray.

The Blerchherchh was wholly unaware that a new opponent had joined the fight, so intent was it on finishing off Shaindor and Klugrok, who both lay on the ground totally at its mercy. Magnus slashed as hard as he could at the monster's back, slicing a deep gash. The Blerchherchh let out a great howl and turned towards Magnus, its eyes alight with pain and rage. Before it could take even one step, it again felt the steel of its own cutlery as Biddira lashed out in turn.

By now, Shaindor and Klugrok had staggered back to their feet. Suddenly, the Blerchherchh found itself surrounded by four determined foes, each wielding a fearsome weapon.

"Everybody strike together," commanded Magnus.

Each of the four thrust at the Blerchherchh. Faced with blades coming from all directions at once, the Blerchherchh did not know which way to turn. It swung its claws wildly but ineffectually, powerless to prevent each of them striking a deadly blow.

"Once more," cried Magnus. Again, the four attacked, and again, the Blerchherchh was unable to stop the slashing, slicing blades that ripped and tore at its scaly skin and the tender flesh beneath.

A third time, the four blades struck. The Blerchherchh took two stumbling steps and collapsed onto the ground. At once, all four of its foes leapt atop that massive frame. Then they hacked and stabbed and carved and cleaved and sliced and diced with all their might until, at last, the Blerchherchh let out one final shuddering moan and moved no more.

Whounga Sunrise

THE FOUR FIGURES slowly extricated themselves from the massive carcass of the Blerchherchh. Klugrok and Shaindor immediately sought out far corners of the cavern and sat eyeing each other suspiciously. Only Magnus seemed to view the situation with any enthusiasm.

"We did it," he exclaimed. "I knew that if we all worked together we could defeat the Blerchherchh."

As nobody else was prepared to offer any further contribution to the discussion, Magnus had no choice but to continue.

"Well I guess I'd better make the introductions. Shaindor and Biddira, I'd like you to meet Klugrok."

Even though they had been introduced, it did not look like any of the others were ready to exchange pleasantries. Neither Shaindor nor Klugrok seemed prepared to even acknowledge the other while Biddira gazed towards each in turn, her round freckled face flushed the deepest red. Whether she found the situation to be interesting or not, she would not say.

"Isn't anyone going to say anything?" Magnus cried out in frustration.

At last Klugrok grunted. "You are the Cherine Magnus referred to. The one who journeyed with him from Sweet Harmody. You saved my life. I must thank you."

"And you must be the Glurg Magnus spoke of," replied Shaindor. "The one who provided shelter for him in Hargh Gryghrgr. I too must thank you for you also saved my life."

Klugrok nodded. "It would seem we are in each other's debt."

"Indeed." Shaindor then turned to Magnus. "So it was true. Everything you told us."

"I would not ever lie to you, Shaindor," said Magnus solemnly.

"And to think that I did not believe you," wailed the Cherine. "To think I would have let them take you down into the dungeons without even a word of protest. A poor friend and guide I have turned out to be. Twice now, I have abandoned you when you most needed my assistance."

"But more times have you been there, and many more times do I owe my life to you," said Magnus. "What matters is that you are here now, and you believe all that I have said."

"Could it really be that our whole history of warfare with the Glurgs is based on falsehoods and misconceptions?"

"It is true," confirmed Klugrok. "We did not seek to attack your people at Ferelshine. We had no idea that you might have found our greeting to be frightening."

Shaindor was silent for a while. Then, for the first time, he looked the Glurg directly in the eye as he spoke. "This is a hard thing for me to conceive, but I can see that you have been a good and loyal friend to Magnus. Though I cannot speak with the authority of all my people, if I could I would apologise for all the misdeeds of the past."

"And I would also," said Klugrok, returning the Cherine's gaze, "for though I doubted, I now see that you too have been a trusted companion to Magnus."

"You're both my friends," said Magnus. "But we cannot stay here. There is work to be done. Surely, the army of the Cherines has departed. Even from my hiding spot, I could hear the shock of their marching feet."

"So it is," confirmed Shaindor. "Long has that mighty force been ready. Tharella had but to give the order, at the insistence of Phraedon of course, and the army immediately set off."

"And the Pharsheeth with them," said Biddira. "Fifty-five battalions of our strongest, fiercest, and most excitingly energetic soldiers march amongst the Cherines."

"What of your people?" Magnus said to Klugrok. "How can we warn them of their peril?"

"Do not fear that my people will be taken unawares," replied Klugrok. "The armies of the Glurgs number no less than their opponents. They are combat-ready and ruthless. When both armies meet, the battle will be long and hard."

"Then we cannot let it happen," said Magnus.

"Why not?" asked Biddira. "Such a battle will surely be a most enthralling spectacle."

"Such a battle will be nothing but a bloodbath," said Shaindor.

"There will be no winners," said Klugrok. "Only the maimed and the dead."

'We cannot let it happen," repeated Magnus. "It's time we put an end to this bloodshed forever."

"But how are we to do that?" said Shaindor. Who could we possibly turn to for aid?"

"It is said that not far from this valley dwells the wisest of all beings," said Klugrok.

"The Great Oponium," exclaimed Shaindor. "Already we have sought his counsel on this quest. Perhaps it would be well if we were to seek again for his guidance."

"No" said Magnus firmly. After everything that had befallen him and all he had learnt, he now saw their visit to the Shrine of Oponite in a very different light. "The Great Oponium had nothing of worth to say to us when first we sought his advice. And he will not be able to help us now. It is up to the four of us to figure out what to do. But we can achieve nothing if all we do is sit here talking. Let us leave this house of death and follow after the army of the Cherines. Together we were able to conquer the Blerchherchh. Together we will find a way to prevent this battle and end the war."

So the four companions departed the cave of the Blerchherchh and made their way with all haste away from the dingy, dungy Drungledum Valley. They picked up the trail of the Cherine army without any trouble and then began their chase. What they would actually do when that mighty force was overtaken, none of them could say. But the army had the advantage of a day over them and was moving quickly, so for now, the only thing on their minds was to maintain their pursuit.

It was well after nightfall when they finally stopped. Then, over the crackling of the campfire, Magnus was able to ask the question that had been on his mind all day.

"So how did you come to find me?" he wondered, addressing the question to each of his saviours.

Klugrok was first to reply. "From my hiding spot in the hills, I witnessed the departure of the Cherine and Pharsheeth forces yesterday afternoon. I feared at once that you must be in peril, but I could not get near to the city in daylight. I waited until the sun set and then cautiously approached. As I circled the walls, seeking for some sort of entry, I saw a lone figure fleeing across the valley. My heart told me who it must be, so I followed as quickly as I could. And although I was not able to keep up with the pace you set, I found you soon enough."

"And I was most relieved that you did," said Magnus. "But what of you, Shaindor and Biddira?"

"Our story is as follows," said Shaindor. "At first, I grieved at your seeming betrayal of our people. But as I lay, inconsolable, I received a visitor: an old friend whom I deeply love and trust, the former Prodiva, Lipherel. He informed me, in the strictest confidence, that you had been found and removed from the city."

"Lipherel," cried Magnus, at last able to place the voice of the hooded figure he had encountered in the night. "He was the one who helped me escape from the city. But why?"

"He refused to believe there was merit in the charges against you and was not prepared to let you be taken into captivity. At this news, my sanity returned. I remembered again that we shared a common destiny and that my place should always be by your side. So I summoned Biddira, and we followed your tracks from the city walls until we found you."

"I am eternally grateful to all of you," said Magnus.

"But now I have a question," said Biddira. "I wish to know how it was that your flight should have led you into the kitchen of the Blerchherchh?"

"Not by intention, I can assure you," said Magnus. "The truth is, I was filled with such fright, I did not know where I was running to. Then, when I found myself trapped in the dingy, dungy Drungledum Valley, right outside the cave of the Blerchherchh, I tried to..." Magnus paused, embarrassed to reveal the next part of his tale. "I tried to make friends with it."

"You tried to make friends with the Blerchherchh?" said Klugrok, eyes wide in disbelief. "It's the single most vicious and evil monster in all of the lands."

"I can't tell you how foolish I feel just saying it," said Magnus. "I had this ridiculous idea that any creature that was horrible on the outside must be good deep down inside. Just like you, Klugrok. You're frightening to look at, but you're really good inside."

"Oh, Magnus," said Klugrok. "Just because someone is repulsively ugly doesn't mean they must be good. We Glurgs are as hideous as they come, but even we are not all good. You've already seen Krpolg for yourself. And there are many others in Hargh Gryghrgr who think like him. It was lucky for you that I was the one who found you that night outside the city plaza, for if it had been another, you may not have fared so well."

"You're right, Klugrok," said Magnus. "I was a fool to believe that anyone who was ugly had to be good, and anyone who was beautiful had to be evil. But it works the other way too. It's just as wrong to think that someone must be good because they're beautiful and evil because they're ugly. Isn't that right, Shaindor?"

"I...um...er..." Shaindor seemed to be utterly gobsmacked by this concept. "This is not something I have ever considered before," he managed to say at last. "Such a thing has always seemed to be the truth to me."

"Oh, Shaindor, is that truly how you would judge others?" said Magnus. The others too had turned to stare at the Cherine.

"Looking nice is important to me," said Shaindor, an almost apologetic tone in his voice. "Is there something so wrong about that?"

"No, I don't suppose there is," said Magnus. "But there's got to be more to us than just how we look."

"This is something we Glurgs have always understood," said Klugrok. "It is time you Cherines also realised that how things appear is not important."

"And then, perhaps, we could go out and destroy all things of beauty together," snapped Shaindor, stung by Klugrok's remark.

"We would never have had to destroy anything if you had not begun this killing spree," growled Klugrok.

"You say we began this killing spree," retorted Shaindor, "but our race could never match the zeal of yours as they hunted down and slaughtered our people."

Both Shaindor and Klugrok now stood on either side of the fire. The distaste for each other had returned to their eyes, and their hands were already reaching for their swords.

"Enough," cried Magnus. "The past is the past. Injustices have been committed by both sides. We cannot pretend otherwise. But there's nothing we can do about that now. We can't turn back the clock and change what's already happened. And we won't get anywhere if we spend all our time arguing about whose fault it was. We have to concentrate on the future if we want to make sure it never happens again."

Shaindor and Klugrok both stood motionless. Their hands relaxed and the madness that had blazed in their eyes was quenched.

"Magnus is right," said Klugrok. "I apologise for using the past against you."

"And I apologise to you," said Shaindor. "Truly, I can see that your desire is for peace. But I cannot say the same for all of my race. With my own ears, I have heard Phraedon, chief judge of our city, calling out for war. Now the wisdom in Magnus's words has been made clear to me at last. Never would I have thought a Cherine could be taught by a Kertoobi, but so it is. Let us fight no more."

"Must you always spoil things just as they are getting interesting, Magnus?" complained Biddira, but Magnus could hear the jest in her voice.

"We cannot let old grievances divide us," he said. "Only together can we achieve the peace we desire."

"Only together," agreed both Klugrok and Shaindor.

"Then let us shake hands and be done with it," said Magnus.

Neither of the adversaries seemed to be enthused by this course of action. Conversing together was one thing but actually touching was quite another. Each looked down at the other's arm, so repulsive in both sight and feel. So they might have stayed all night had Biddira not moved in, held one hand in each of hers, and then brought them together.

"I just had to see the looks on their faces," she confided in a whisper to Magnus.

Initially, the expression on both faces was one of utter horror. But as each realised that the other's touch could at least be tolerated, they relaxed, and a new look of understanding passed between them. Thus, for the first time ever, was physical contact of a non-violent nature between Cherine and Glurg achieved.

As Magnus lay down to bed he felt almost at peace. A huge step had been taken that day. Surely their ultimate goal lay in reach.

"You tried to make friends with the Blerchherchh," chuckled Biddira beside him. "Gillibub was wrong about you, Magnus. You're a lot more interesting than even I could have imagined."

*   *   *

Over the following days, there were no more flare-ups between Shaindor and Klugrok. While they both made sure to stay well away from the other while eating, at all other times they were able to conduct themselves with civility, if not open friendship.

For the next ten days, they chased the armies of the Cherines and Pharsheeth. Over highlands and lowlands and across rivers and streams they raced, gradually gaining ground with each day that passed. The footprints of the force that marched before them grew firmer and fresher and after a while their singing could be clearly heard ahead:

> *We go, we go, to meet our foe,*
> *To carve them up from scalp to toe,*
> *To hack their limbs and spill their blood,*
> *And leave their corpses in the mud.*
>
> *We go to fight, with all our might,*
> *Because we know that we are right,*
> *To slash and smite from foot to head,*
> *Till we have won and they are dead.*

Soon they could actually be seen, far across the plains. Their stride was sure and bold, their heads raised with pride and strength. The sun glistened on their shields and helmets, and their pennants and banners waved grandly in the wind. To most observers, it would have been a resplendent sight, but Magnus was not most observers. He was on a sworn mission to stop them from meeting their foes. And he was painfully aware that there were only the four of them against an army of thousands.

Every night, as they made camp, they would sit and discuss potential strategies, but none of them was able to come up with even the merest inkling of a plan. As day followed day, the debates grew more and more urgent, but still nothing came out of them.

"The armies of my people draw near," said Klugrok early on the twelfth day. "The battle we fear can be but days away."

"I do not see them," said Shaindor, keenly scanning the horizon.

"Your eyes may be strong, but my nose is stronger," replied the Glurg. "I can smell them close at hand. We do not have much time."

As evening fell and they made camp in a small hollow, even Magnus could detect the faint whiff of Glurgish odour in the air.

"They must be close if even I can smell them," he said despondently.

"The Glurgs are not the only thing that is close," said Shaindor.

"What does that mean?" asked Magnus.

Shaindor pointed to a series of ridges. "Yonder lies the course of the Flouphgraine River. Here, it is open, wide and fast-flowing. But not more than a few miles away, it cuts into the surrounding cliffs, forming a series of deep gorges. Truly marvellous are all of these gorges, it is said, but one in particular is especially famous throughout all lands. The Whounga Canyon."

"We are near to the Whounga Canyon?" gasped Magnus. Could it be true? Were they even now standing close to that marvel of scenic grandeur whose siren call had led his brother to his doom?

"Indeed," Shaindor said. "A short climb beyond the ridges over there will lead directly to the rim."

Magnus's mind spun. Thoughts of Jangos, so long buried by the urgency of his quest, now began to resurface. Magnus could see his brother clearly, that far-away look still in his eyes, as on the night when Jangos first described the yearning that had driven him to seek out this place. Suddenly, Magnus found himself overwhelmed by the same burning need. He had come so far, with all the worries of the world on his back. Must he now deny himself the chance to witness the one sight that surpassed all others in the known world? Did he not owe it to his brother's memory to take this one small detour from his chosen path?

"I wish to see it," he said at last.

"Are you sure?" said Shaindor.

Magnus nodded. "My brother did not get to witness the one site he most desired to view. In his stead, I would like to go and see it for myself, so that his soul may rest in peace."

"But do we have time?" said Klugrok.

"We have already overtaken the forces of Sweet Harmody and Pharnarest," said Shaindor, pointing over the ridge to where the soldiers made camp close by. "How far would you say the Glurg armies are?"

Klugrok sniffed the air. "I would say we have another two days at best."

"Then there is time," said Shaindor. "As we still have no better plans, I suggest we take early to sleep so we may rise before the dawn. Then we shall all see the fabled sunrise over Whounga Canyon. And perhaps that wondrous sight will provide us with the inspiration we need."

"We need more than inspiration," said Magnus grimly. "But I can only do what I can. After tomorrow, Jangos's journey will at last be over. But mine still has a long way to go. I am now more determined than ever to prevent this battle before us. Only then will I know that Jangos did not die in vain."

It was still night when Shaindor roused the others from sleep.

"Come, let us make haste," he urged as they yawned and protested. "We must give ourselves time to reach the canyon before the sun."

The four travellers stayed close together as they made their way to the rim of the Whounga Canyon. At first, the path was simple to follow, but it quickly became rocky and treacherous. As Shaindor was reluctant to allow a torch to be lit, in case they were spotted by soldiers from either army, every step forward became a nervous stumble in the dark.

"Be careful," he warned after over an hour of blind fumbling. "The rim of the canyon cannot be far now…"

Even as he spoke, he thrust the stick he was using as a guide into the ground ahead and found only thin air. He staggered and surely would have fallen into the abyss if the others had not immediately held him firmly.

"We are here," he coughed once his composure had returned. "Let us now sit and prepare for something the likes of which we will not ever see again."

So they sat down on the rim of the Whounga Canyon and waited for the sun. Daybreak was still some time away, so they passed the time by talking quietly amongst themselves.

"Do you think we actually have a chance of succeeding?" Magnus asked after a while.

"Should there be but a single mile left between the armies, then we still have a chance," replied Shaindor.

"I don't just mean that. Even if we are able to prevent this battle, do you think there can be true peace between your races? I have heard the songs of the Cherines as they march. And I have heard, on the other side, the speeches of Krpolg and the hatred he holds for all of Shaindor's race."

"You are right that Krpolg would not support the cause of peace," said Klugrok. "It is by harnessing our long grievances against the Cherines that he has built his power. But do not forget that my people have never known any better. If you were but to leave us alone and give us the space and the land that we need, then what grievances could he exploit? True, he would never stop trying to build up our fear and hatred, for only this way could he maintain his rule. But my people are not foolish. Many now see him for what he really is. Once they know they have a choice, they will choose the path of peace."

"It is not so with the Cherines," said Shaindor. "Long ago, we took steps to ensure no single ruler could wield such excessive power, for our leader, the Prodiva, can only serve for a single year."

"But what about he who selects the Prodiva?" asked Magnus. "What about Phraedon? How long is he allowed to serve?"

Shaindor looked like he had just been struck over the head. "There is no restriction on how long Phraedon may serve," he gasped. "And as I now recall, there has not been one occasion on which he has addressed us when he has not sought to feed our horror of the Glurgs." Suddenly, Shaindor began to chuckle. "The wool at last has been removed from my eyes. I see clearly how it has been. Our Phraedon is much like your Krpolg. He has exploited our fears and taken advantage of our customs, parading a series of puppets before us while he secretly holds power for himself. But no matter what he says, if you can show my people they have naught to fear, then they too will choose peace in the end."

"Enough talking," said Biddira. "I think something's about to happen." Something was indeed happening. A tiny sliver of sunlight had just leapt over the horizon, illuminating for the first time the view before their eyes. They sat on the edge of a deep cleft in the ground. Hundreds of feet below, the rushing water of the Flouphgraine could only just be seen, and before them, the far walls of the canyon rose, rocky and stark.

As they watched, a lone ray of light lit upon the wall in front of them. Where it struck, a small flare of brilliant golden orange blazed for an instant before fading. No sooner had it gone out than another beam hit, igniting another short-lasting flame upon the surface of the rock. By now, the sun had lifted itself higher, and its radiance began to pour down into the depths below. The sparks that it ignited upon the walls shone brighter and longer. Then, like seeds of light planted deep within the rock, they took root. A thousand flowers of flame blossomed and did not die but only grew. Veins of gold spread out across the cracks and seams of stone, joining each of those glowing flowers until it was as if the whole of the canyon wall was afire.

For nearly an hour, the walls gleamed thus. Spellbound, the travellers stared at the sight before them. Never still but constantly changing, each subtle shift of the sun revealed new details and intricacies in the play of light across the rocks. Only as the sun passed higher up did the fire start to dim, slowly dying out until what they saw before them once again was nothing but a wide brown defile in the earth.

No one spoke for quite a long time. Magnus sat, his feet dangling over the side of the canyon, too overcome to even move. Shaindor stared out into the space before him, a glazed look in his eyes. Biddira's face was almost as red as the canyon walls, her hair stood on end, and she breathed deeply. Only Klugrok seemed less than enthused.

"Not bad if that's the sort of thing that appeals to you," he grunted. "Personally, I prefer it when it's dull and rocky."

The others looked at him in disbelief but nobody said anything. There didn't seem to be any point.

Eventually Shaindor stood up. "Time we were going. The armies will have departed by now. We have some chasing to do."

Biddira and Klugrok also got to their feet but Magnus remained sitting.

"Coming, Magnus?" called Klugrok.

"I'd like a little time here alone. I'll catch up," said Magnus.

Left to himself, Magnus looked out over the vast canyon.

"I understand, Jangos," he said softly. "I can see what it was that drew you to this place. Now it's over for you at last, but for me it seems like there's no end in sight. What am I to do? How am I to stop this war?"

A moving speck caught Magnus's eye far below. It was a bird, a glor-eagle, gliding in the updrafts of the canyon. Such a massive bird of prey had a wingspan of over twenty feet, but deep within the canyon it appeared tiny. Then, flying lower, it disappeared completely amidst the rocks.

"I need a canyon that can make two whole armies disappear," muttered Magnus. "Disappear so completely that they'll never be able to find each other."

But this canyon was wide and vast. No great army could remain hidden here for long. Magnus looked down to the churning water of the Flouphgraine. He tried to follow its path out of the far end of the canyon. Beyond these great rock walls, the river flowed for many miles through dusty plains before entering…

Magnus jumped to his feet. He remembered exactly where the Flouphgraine passed beyond the dusty plains. Suddenly, the smallest fraction of the merest beginning of the tiniest inkling of a plan began to cross his mind.

Trupitompsit

MAGNUS HURRIED AFTER the others, finally catching them about halfway back to the campsite.

"How far are we from the gorges of Trupitompsit?" he puffed.

"The Labyrinths of Trupitompsit?" replied Shaindor. "They are a good four days march from here. But why do you ask?"

"I have an idea. We need to send both armies into the labyrinths. It's the only chance we have to prevent them from running into each other."

"And what do we do then?" asked Biddira.

"I do not know. But at least it will buy us a bit more time. Klugrok, do you think there's a way we can divert the Glurg armies towards Trupitompsit?"

"The Glurg armies are drawing near," said Klugrok. "If I leave now, I should be able to reach them in time. I can try to make up a story that the enemy is moving into the labyrinths, but I cannot guarantee it will work. My people will most likely have scouts spying on the position of Cherines. If what they see contradicts what I say, it will not be believed."

"Do not worry about the Cherines," said Magnus. "I know a sure-fire way to get them to change direction."

"Then I shall go now," said Klugrok. "I guess this is farewell."

"I guess it is," said Magnus.

"Goodbye, Magnus," said Klugrok. "I shall never forget what you have done for my people. Your name will always be held in honour in Hargh Gryghrgr." He held out his arms and pulled Magnus into a tight embrace.

"Goodbye, Klugrok," said Magnus, no longer paying any heed to the Glurg's unappealing appearance or odour as he returned the embrace. "You have been a worthy companion and a true friend. I will miss you."

The others were not prepared to farewell Klugrok with quite the same vigour, but they did offer parting greetings that came from the heart.

"Good luck to you all," said the Glurg at last. "Perhaps we shall meet again in the Labyrinths of Trupitompsit."

Then he turned and hurried away, quickly disappearing amongst the stony ridges.

"Once again, we are three," said Shaindor.

"Come on now," urged Magnus. "We must catch up to that army without delay."

"By what means are you so convinced we shall be able to get the Cherines to change their direction?" said Shaindor as they set off again. "Surely such a great army will not be easy to sway."

Magnus quickly explained his plan to the others as they ran. When he had finished, even Shaindor had to admit it was a stroke of genius.

They caught up with the Cherine and Pharsheeth armies just as the sun was reaching its highest point. The great force had stopped briefly for lunch as the three companions approached. Cautiously, they skirted the mighty host, keeping carefully hidden in the surrounding scrub.

Finally, Magnus spied what he had been seeking. Two figures, neither Cherine nor Pharsheeth, sat slightly apart from the rest of the troops. Such stout figures could always be found in the near vicinity of any advancing army, even though they were not dressed for war. They sought not glory on the battlefield but merely to be present when great events occurred. Thus, they might pass on their stories to others of like kind, embellishing, misinterpreting, and generally reinventing, until all people in all lands were suitably misinformed about exactly what had not actually come to pass.

The hypersensitive ears of one of the Doosies quivered slightly at the sound of creeping in the undergrowth. Out of sight of the soldiers but just within earshot of the Doosies, Magnus prepared to put his plan into action. He pitched his voice as low as he could, ensuring that his words could be heard only by the two nearby figures.

"I hear that the Glurgs have taken fright at the merest rumour of the awesome host that pursues them," he whispered.

It had the desired effect. All three ears on each of the Doosies instantly shot up and their noses began sniffing around towards them.

"Indeed," replied Shaindor just as softly. "They flee before the might of the great Cherine army."

"Do you mark where they run to?" asked Biddira, her voice cracking under the strain of trying to speak so quietly.

"They seek, in their cowardice, to hide deep within the Labyrinths of Trupitompsit," whispered Magnus.

The Doosies leapt to their feet and hurried away as quickly as their stubby legs would carry them, searching for someone, anyone, they could share their information with. There was nothing for the three companions to do now except wait. Before too long, the news would be all about the camp, from the lowliest foot-soldier to the Cherine High Command. By then, even though it had been based on nothing but an overheard whisper, it would have gained such authority that it could not be regarded as anything but the absolute, verifiable truth. For, as the popular Kertoobi rhyme stated:

If you wish to spread a rumour fast,
Tell a Doosie first, not last.

Not a particularly good rhyme, but it did capture the essence of Magnus's plan. He watched from his hiding place as the news fermented its way through the resting army. The troops remained for several hours, engaged only in agitated discussion, while the generals of both races debated the most appropriate response to this new intelligence. Around late afternoon, a decision seemed to have been made at last. The soldiers jumped up and resumed their advance, but no longer in the direction they had been heading. They were now marching directly for the course of the Flouphgraine River.

Carefully concealed away from sight, the three travellers grinned at each other. Magnus's plan had worked.

By the end of that day, the army had reached the banks of the Flouphgraine, meeting the river as it leapt in swirling rapids from the mouth of the Whounga Canyon. For the next four days, they followed the course of that mighty waterway as it meandered through the drylands and plains beyond. Magnus, Shaindor, and Biddira trailed behind, carefully keeping their distance. With Klugrok gone, their concealment was not such a vital issue, but still they felt it better to avoid discovery for now.

On the fifth day, the land began to rise and grow sparser and rockier. Once again, the river plunged between stony cliffs, but these were less high than the majestic canyon of Whounga, and much narrower and darker.

So they arrived at the Labyrinths of Trupitompsit, a series of winding gorges carved out by the snaking, coiling waters of the Flouphgraine. Measuring barely ten miles in a direct line from start to end, travellers following the course of the river would cover over two hundred miles before emerging from the other side, but only so long as they did not get hopelessly lost on the way. Within these gorges, there were many offshoots and tributaries from the main course that forked off in all directions. Sometimes, they wound back to meet the river again, but more often, they just petered out into blank cliff walls. Merely keeping to the true course was the greatest challenge of all.

Such was the place that Magnus had led the two opposing forces. A place in which two armies could march for months, even years, and never see a sign of the other.

The army of Cherines and Pharsheeth paused for a while at the dark entrance to the labyrinths as the generals once again debated their best course of action. These gorges were not the ideal location for battle. Their twisting cliffs and tight, constricted passages offered many opportunities for ambushes and surprise assaults. Eventually, the allure of taking on an enemy that cowered somewhere within became too much for them to resist. With a furious cry, the soldiers of Sweet Harmody and Pharnarest took up their arms and advanced with a rush into the narrow opening.

After the last of the armies had disappeared, Magnus, Biddira, and Shaindor followed through the gap. Inside the labyrinths, the air was cool and moist. The river, now a narrow stream, raced alongside, its spray splashing their faces. But the path was rough and wet, and the cliffs that rose above them seemed to lean inward, cutting off all but the thinnest slivers of light. Cold and dull were the passages within the Labyrinths of Trupitompsit.

"So we have arrived at last," said Shaindor, looking around the gloomy gorge with distaste.

"Okay, Magnus, what's the next step?" asked Biddira.

"I do not know," said Magnus. "My plan did not extend beyond getting here. But for now, we should have some extra time to work something out. I'm trusting it will be a while before the two armies are able to find each other in here."

"Let us not leave that to fate," said Shaindor. "We should now march ahead rather than behind. If there is any chance that the Glurgs are nearby, we must make sure we are the first to know it."

So that night, while the soldiers slept, the three companions crept through their ranks. From then on, they marched at the head of the army, but no comment was raised about their presence. Both Shaindor and Biddira were well known in their respective cities and it was assumed that they were doing no more than taking their place amongst the hosts of their people.

*   *   *

For days unnumbered, the great army wandered the twisting-turning paths of the labyrinths. At first, spirits were high. The Cherines sang their marching songs as they strode ahead, confident their foes were no further away than the next bend. But as each day passed with no sign of the enemy before them, the mood began to sink. The songs became more leaden and dirge-like and eventually disappeared altogether, while the pacing of the march grew slower and slower. The paths they trod seemed to get ever less firm and more slippery underfoot while the feral carrion birds that dwelt within the gorges, the thrungs, blugthrushes, and khrows, tormented them from above, swooping at their heads, pecking at their faces, and most grievously, mussing up the perfectly coiffed hair of the Cherines.

As time went on, morale continued to sink. The battle, so long looked forward to, now became a source of dread. The soldiers no longer strode forward, eager for the chance to take on their cowering enemy, but hung back before every slight turn in the passage, fearful that a surprise attack lurked just around the corner.

Little did they know that it was only by the artifice of Magnus, Shaindor, and Biddira that such an attack never occurred. The three friends kept a constant vigil, making regular forays ahead to ensure the coast was clear. On a number of occasions, they had actually spied the Glurg armies wandering just as aimlessly some way ahead, and had hastily engineered a change of course. Several times, the two forces had ended up marching down adjacent passageways, separated only by thin rock walls. But the footfalls of both armies so swirled and echoed within the claustrophobic corridors that each remained blissfully unaware their enemies passed barely yards away.

The only consolation those heart-stopping near misses brought was that they did provide opportunities to make brief contact with Klugrok. However, the news he bore did not make them feel any better. As with the Cherines and Pharsheeth, the Glurg armies were rapidly losing patience with this futile hunt. Tempers were frayed, quarrels frequent, and morale had dropped lower than the water levels of the dry sea of Wudgheriee.

"This does not go well," said Shaindor as the three of them convened in the evening to discuss how best to proceed. "I do not believe our armies can remain in this dismal maze for many more days."

"But we don't have a choice," protested Magnus. "They must remain here, at least until we've been able to work out another plan."

"Can't we just let them meet and get it over with?" muttered Biddira. Of the three, she was finding the tedium hardest to bear. Her face had lost its ruddy glow and her normally frizzy hair now drooped down the sides of her face.

"No, we cannot," said Magnus, annoyed. "We must do everything we can to prevent that happening. And keeping them here is still the best way to do that."

"If something doesn't happen soon, we'll have a different battle on our hands," said Shaindor. "The Cherines and Pharsheeth will rip each other to shreds."

Magnus knew Shaindor was right. Relations between the two races were fast approaching breaking point. The Pharsheeth had resorted to dealing with the unending boredom of this seemingly fruitless quest by playing a series of practical jokes on their allies. They disguised themselves as Glurgs, hid behind corners, and leapt out in front of unsuspecting Cherines. They placed dead blugthrushes inside Cherine backpacks. Worst of all, they took to hiding the Cherine's vast assortment of cosmetics, beauty products, and hand mirrors. Unsurprisingly, the Cherines did not react well to these provocations, and the sound of numerous petty arguments reverberated through the labyrinths. It was clear that the two races could not remain confined together within these narrow canyons for more than another day or two.

Magnus sat on the stony floor, his head in his hands. His plan was falling apart. From what Klugrok had said, the Glurgs too would most likely choose to depart the labyrinths soon. Then where would they be? Right back where they had started. Two forces, armed and ready to fight, and nothing Magnus and his friends could do to keep them apart. In the end, it seemed they had as much chance of preventing this battle as a tzepperfly had of catching, skinning, and cooking a giant giflogadon.

"Can we just give it a few more days?" he said at last.

"I do not think we have a choice," said Shaindor. "It is no longer in our control. If things remain as they are for another day, I cannot believe the Cherine High Command will allow this situation to continue."

Fortunately, something did happen the very next day.

Early in the morning, not long after the day's march began, something was discovered on the path ahead.

"Footprints," cried the soldiers in the front columns. "At last our foes are found."

But even this discovery was treated with some scepticism.

"So many times have we traversed this endless maze, most likely it is our own footsteps we have come back upon," complained others.

Shaindor rushed up to look at the markings on the track. After close examination, he turned to the disbelievers.

"These are not the footprints of any Cherine or Pharsheeth," he said. "Notice how the toes splay out, like talons. See how the ends are marked by sharp claws. None of either of our races has feet shaped so beastly. These are clearly the footprints of our foul enemy. But see how they flee before us. Let us make speed and catch them, for they cannot now be far away."

At this news, all about were greatly heartened. Suddenly, heads were raised and marching feet lifted high again. Now with rekindled zeal and haste, the great force followed in the direction the tracks led.

Only Magnus was somewhat distressed by this turn of events.

"Why did you do this?" he hissed to Shaindor. "Why would you encourage them to try to catch up to the Glurgs?"

Shaindor merely smiled. "So desperate are they to end this, they do not pay close regard to these tracks. They are not fresh. Many days have passed since the Glurgs made these prints. Even if we tripled our pace, I do not think we will catch them soon."

So it turned out to be. After two days of following the Glurg footprints, any renewed zest had completely evaporated. The tracks only seemed to lead them on another merry chase around the labyrinths. By the end of the second day, all the gripes had returned, even more loudly than before.

"Our enemies toy with us," said some. "They lead us on a foolish dance while our leaders do nothing but sing along."

At this, Shaindor leapt before them. "We must persist," he cried. "Surely now, our enemy is near at hand."

Magnus was watching the others as Shaindor spoke. He couldn't help noticing the weariness and despair in their eyes; the way shoulders sagged and heads drooped, and uniforms, once kept so meticulously spotless, were now ragged and dirty. Very different this miserable bunch now seemed from the proud force that had departed Sweet Harmody. Anyone looking at them now would think they were a defeated force, utterly spent. With this sudden awareness, an idea flashed into his mind. He called the others over.

"I have a new plan," he said. "But before I can set it into action, I need to send a message to Klugrok. Can you think of a way we can contact him?"

"There is a stock of messenger flythrops," said Shaindor, "but they are reserved for Cherine High Command."

"Then how are we to get one?"

"Not a problem," laughed Biddira. "Leave that to me. I know exactly what we need to do."

With Biddira providing a distraction, by performing a complicated series of handstands, cartwheels, and somersaults, while singing a Pharsheeth love ballad at the top of her voice, Magnus was able to quickly steal a flythrop from the small cage in which they were housed. He hurriedly scrawled out a series of instructions on some parchment, describing in detail exactly what he needed Klugrok to say and do. Then, on the other side, he attempted to draw a picture of the Glurg. The resulting image resembled nothing so much as a badly deformed stick figure, but Magnus had no doubt the flythrop would be able to deliver the message to its desired recipient.

"Now what is your plan?" asked Shaindor once the bird had been released.

"We have to get the army out of the labyrinths," said Magnus.

"But won't that just leave us where we were at the start?"

"Trust me, the time to keep them in the labyrinths is past. We have to get them out the same way they came in. But we can't have them think they're just giving up. We have to make them believe it's really the Glurgs who are desperate to get out of this place. Can you think of a way to do this?"

"I do not believe they'll take too much convincing," replied Shaindor.

Once again, he stood before the soldiers. "My friends, I have misread the signs," he declared. "Our enemies have doubled back. They seek to evade us by fleeing from these labyrinths, leaving us caught in their tangled pathways. Let us now make haste to pursue them back to the entrance of this doleful chasm."

So eager were the troops to extricate themselves at last from the dark labyrinths that they barely even waited for High Command to approve the order before letting out a roar of approval, turning on their heels, and hurrying back the way they had come.

"So what of your plan?" asked Shaindor as they set off. "What message did you send to Klugrok?"

"To do exactly as we are doing," said Magnus. "To lead the Glurgs out of the labyrinths."

"But what will happen if we overtake them on the way?" said Biddira."

"I don't think that will happen," said Magnus. "They are not going the same way as us. I told Klugrok to take them downstream, to the opposite exit."

*   *   *

Finding the way out proved substantially less difficult than finding another lost and wandering army within the labyrinth. It took less than three days of following the various winding streams back to their sources before they rounded one final corner and were met by sunlight, the first they had seen for weeks, streaming through the gap in the cliffs. Overcome by relief, the soldiers rushed out of the darkness, staggering heedlessly into the light.

The moment of truth had arrived. The success or failure of Magnus's plan was about to be revealed. So many unknowns were at play. Had Klugrok received the message? Would he be able to get the Glurgs out of the labyrinths in time? Would the two races respond the way Magnus had anticipated? This was the last chance. If things did not work out as he hoped, there was no chance of battle being prevented.

Shaindor had by now been apprised of his role in the plan, and he played the part to perfection. He urged the leaders of the Cherines and Pharsheeth to climb up to the top of the cliffs beside the entrance to the gorges. From this high lookout, a view of the whole of the Labyrinths of Trupitompsit spread out before them; a wide plateau deeply scored and scarred with twisting, weaving, winding, grooves. In the distance, the Flouphgraine River could just be seen as it tumbled out of the other end of the gorges, continuing on its way to the faraway sea.

But the Flouphgraine was not the only thing departing from the far end of labyrinths. Beside the gleaming water, a great army could be made out issuing from that exit.

"Do you see," cried Shaindor. "The Glurgs are fleeing. Even the rumour of our approach is enough to send them scampering back to their rat holes. They are vanquished, utterly defeated."

To the others, there seemed to be truth in Shaindor's words. Under the sharp gaze of the Cherines, the enemy appeared not the deadly force so feared but a dishevilled, ragtag lot, scurrying with undue haste onto the flats beyond the gorges. None who saw them thought anything but that the Glurgs were retreating in shame and ignominy.

Then some among them called out that they should make chase, seeking to take advantage of this opportunity and wipe out the Glurg armies once and for all. Shaindor replied that such a course was not necessary.

'We have done what we sought to do. We have seen off the threat of the Glurgs. Let us now return home."

At this, the greater part of the host cried out in support. The long days of futile trooping through the labyrinths had well and truly snuffed out the lust for battle that had once burnt so strongly in each of their hearts. Thoughts for most now turned back to home and hearth, to loved ones cherished and missed. It did not take long for High Command to make their decision.

"Our task is achieved," they declared. "The enemy has been dispatched. We return now to Sweet Harmody in triumph."

Little did they know that many miles away, the leaders of the Glurgs observed the Cherine armies hurrying out from the labyrinths, a bedraggled force in apparent disarray. None of the great commanders of the Cherines had the faintest inkling that a similar debate had ensued amongst their opposing officers. But under the urgings of Klugrok and General Pchervlk, the Glurgs too concluded that their enemies fled in despair, and they resolved to march, victorious, back to Hargh Gryghrgr.

Thus ended the battle of the Labyrinths of Trupitompsit, unique amongst all of the battles in the long war between the Cherines and the Glurgs in that at the end of the day, both sides claimed victory for themselves. But what really set this battle apart was that apart from a few stubbed toes, twisted ankles, and grazed knees, there was not a single casualty.

Barglefest

THE GREAT GATES of Sweet Harmody swung open in greeting as the mighty army of the Cherines and Pharsheeth marched in triumph towards those shimmering walls. The sound of music rang through the air, and many of the troops were already breaking ranks and charging into the city to embrace a wife or hurl a child into the air. As Magnus approached the gates, his heart swelled with pride. After the humiliation of his previous exit, it felt fine to be returning to the noble city such a grand manner. He couldn't wait to join in the celebrations.

But Magnus never made it into Sweet Harmody.

Before he had a chance to pass under that broad archway, strong hands were laid upon his shoulders. He struggled with all his might, but there was no way he could fight off the burly Cherine guard who now held him firmly.

"These three," said a rough voice. "These are the ones who led us away from battle when victory was within our grasp."

Magnus ceased his wriggling and looked up. The speaker was a Cherine general, one of those, Magnus recalled, who had called most loudly for the continued pursuit and annihilation of the Glurgs. As he spoke, he pointed, not just towards Magnus, but also to Shaindor and Biddira who had been similarly detained. And the one he directed those words to was Tharella.

She stood just outside the gates, clad as always in the ceremonial garb of her position. Her beauty was no less than the first time Magnus had seen her, but in her eyes was a look as hard as the iron cliffs of Howlishium.

"You have done well to bring them to me," she said. "I will deal with them now as the power vested in my position requires."

The general bowed and disappeared into the city. Tharella looked at each of the prisoners in turn, but when she spoke, her words were addressed to the guards who held them.

"This Pharsheeth will be returned to her own people. Let the elders of Pharnarest choose a suitable fate for her."

The guard holding Biddira nodded and began dragging her into the city, although being Biddira, she put up a fine show of resistance.

"As for Shaindor, he will be imprisoned while the evidence against him is considered. When I have a better idea of the crimes he has committed, I will pronounce sentence accordingly."

"Very good, oh great Prodiva," said the guard, and he too disappeared through the gates, leading Shaindor behind him.

"Shall I bring this one in too, great Prodiva?" asked Magnus's captor.

Tharella shook her head. "This Kertoobi shall not be permitted to enter our city. He must be barred, exiled forever. Leave him here now, for he shall not ever pass through these gates again." Without even a second glance at Magnus, she turned and walked back into the city.

Then Magnus was thrown down to the ground, and the gates of Sweet Harmody were slammed firmly shut behind him.

Magnus remained on the road for some time, paralysed by sorrow and impotent rage. His plan to prevent the battle had succeeded beyond his wildest dreams, but for what? The Cherines neither knew nor cared about what he had done for them. How they celebrated now, not even knowing the true nature of the events that had transpired. This should have been his victory. He was the one who had engineered it, along with Shaindor and Biddira. Yet, rather than being honoured as heroes, his friends were now captives of their own people, while he had been crudely ejected like a piece of garbage tossed out on the giant refuse piles of Ponghonia.

At last, he picked himself up and dusted himself down. Then, he began to walk away from the city of the Cherines. Not once did he look back. After many long days of wandering, nothing in the outside world held any appeal any longer. There were no more marvellous sights he wished to see. Whatever remained of the Grompets had been well and truly beaten out of him. Now all he wanted to do was go home.

So began the final stage of the journey of Magnus Mandalora. And if he encountered no dangers on this last road, he did not enjoy the comforts of any company either. At last, on the evening of a bright summer's day, the road passed beside the steaming reek of the Plergle Swamp and below the high hill of Upper Kertoob. And there, spread out before him like a child's plaything, was the small homely village of Lower Kertoob.

Magnus did not broadcast his return to the village. He made straight for his kertottage and did not leave his bed for the next three days. Eventually, it was necessity, or to be more precise hunger, that drove him out of his home and into the village square.

Not surprisingly, his fellow villagers did not exactly welcome him with open arms. Sneaking out of the village under the cover of night and then not coming back for months on end was certainly not appropriate behaviour for a Kertoobi. In addition, there had been the matter of the extraordinary ingratitude he had displayed in rejecting their generously offered prompanapples, most of which still lay, mouldy and rotten, just outside his front doors. Such actions certainly could not be encouraged, or worse still rewarded, by any kind of warm reception.

As time went on, he was gradually accepted back into the community. And if he tended not to make a lot of effort to participate in village activities, no objections were raised. Though he blocked up one of his doors, in order to reduce by half the number of visitors he received, and he persistently declined all offers of sleepovers, still nobody was prepared to speak ill of him. He was regarded as a bit odd, rather grumpy, (particularly by the children who thought it a funny thing to occasionally knock on his boarded-up door) and extremely private, but as the Kertoobis were by and large a tolerant lot, this was all fine by them.

*   *   *

An uneventful year passed. Few travellers passed through the village, although those that did reported that tensions remained high in the world outside. It seemed the armies of the Cherines were still at battle stations, armed and ready to march at the slightest provocation.

So it came to pass that a touring party of Cherines visited the village. As was always the case with such esteemed guests, a massive banquet, Barglefest, was put on by the Kertoobis. Magnus, however, had no inclination to join in the celebrations, being less than eager to socialise with anyone from Sweet Harmody. Instead, he decided to remain inside, cooking and eating his own pflugberry pies while enjoying the company of himself and no other.

Late in the evening there was a knock at the door. Magnus chose to ignore it, concentrating instead on the more pressing matter of the next slice of pie. Several moments later, the knock repeated itself, slightly more forcefully. Magnus responded by taking a slightly more forceful bite of his pie. After the third knock, he began to get annoyed. He slammed down the pie, stomped to the door, and threw it open.

"If you do that one more time, I'm going to tell your mother to…" he began, but it was not a child, nor even an adult Kertoobi at the door. It was Shaindor.

"Hello, Magnus," said the Cherine.

"Shaindor, you're free," cried Magnus, overjoyed to see his friend.

"Indeed I am," said Shaindor. "But what is it you wish to tell my mother?"

"Why nothing. I just thought that…oh it doesn't matter. Come in, come in. It's so good to see you."

Magnus grabbed Shaindor's strong hand and tugged him into the kertottage. As he did so, he noticed that another Cherine also stood outside his door. In a flash, the smile fell from his face.

"Greetings, Magnus," said Tharella. "I understand why you are less pleased to see me. But would you please also allow me the honour of entering your house?"

Magnus looked to Shaindor, who nodded. He turned back to Tharella, motioning for her to come in and bowing stiffly as she passed.

"It is all right," she chuckled. "You do not need to bow. I am no longer Prodiva."

"Remember that position is held for one year only," said Shaindor.

"Is Phraedon still judge?" asked Magnus.

"He is," replied Shaindor, frowning.

"And that title will not be easily prised from him," said Tharella. "But let us not speak of that now. We have other business. May we sit?"

Since she had entered the room, Magnus had stood by the door, seemingly unable to move. Now at last rediscovering the power of his muscles, he hurried over to find some chairs for his guests.

"First," said Tharella as she sat down, "there is the simple matter of an apology."

"I will not apologise," said Magnus, still standing. "I do not believe I've done anything wrong."

"It is not you who needs to apologise to me," said Tharella solemnly. "It is I who must now apologise to you. You have been wronged, greatly wronged. You should be acclaimed, not punished. Your name should be shouted out from the highest towers of Sweet Harmody, but instead, you are rudely expelled from our city. I do not expect you to forgive me. All I ask is that you listen to my words and understand why I had to take the seemingly cruel actions that I did. But please sit. You look so uncomfortable."

Magnus at last allowed himself to take a seat as Tharella continued.

"When first you returned from Hargh Gryghrgr, the tale you told was so outlandish, so unbelievable that I did not know how to respond. When Phraedon straight away invoked the penalty of Urqhuarest, I had no time to think clearly. Our laws are very clear in this regard, and I did not see that I had any option but to do as he commanded. But I was deeply troubled, and I relayed my fears to Lipherel, who fortunately took matters into his own hands. His engineering of your escape lifted a great burden from my mind. I believed at that point that the issue was finished, and though I grieved at your passing from our city in such a fashion, I was pleased that you had retained your freedom. Little did I expect that you should return so soon and in such circumstances.

"Fortunately, when you returned at last with our triumphant armies, I was better prepared. Shaindor had sent me a message by flythrop, alerting me to all that had transpired. He confirmed that everything you had said to us, fantastic and outrageous as it seemed, was in fact the truth. He told me much about the steadfast integrity of your friend, Klugrok. But, most importantly, he told me all about your courage and presence of mind in the face of impending battle, and your brilliance in finding a way to lead us to victory without the loss of a single drop of blood."

Magnus turned to Shaindor. "You said all this?"

"Indeed," replied Shaindor. "I was concerned about how we would be received when we returned to Sweet Harmody. I believed that Tharella needed to be informed of the true situation before we arrived."

"A wise decision," said Tharella, "for it gave me time to come up with a plan of my own. Well did I know that if Phraedon became aware of your actions, your penalties would be severe, for nothing would ever satisfy him but the complete destruction of the Glurg race. Therefore I resolved to act quickly, to ensure you could not fall into his hands. Thus it was that you found me waiting outside the gates, prepared to cut you off before you entered the city.

"I did not have any concerns in handing Biddira over to her people. For the Pharsheeth, the only crime is not being interesting, and that is not something you could ever say about her. Likewise for Shaindor, I did not hold any fears. He would likely be incarcerated for a brief time, but as there was no evidence of his having conspired directly with the enemy, I knew that any charge against him could not be sustained. You, on the other hand, were my greatest worry.

"The evidence against you was plain for we had already heard from your own lips of your intimate involvement with the Glurgs. The penalty of Urqhuarest, once handed down, cannot ever be withdrawn, so if you had passed through the gates, I would have had no choice but to again have you thrown into our deepest, darkest dungeon. The only thing I could possibly do to prevent that happening was to stop you entering the city. And if you felt perhaps that it was done in a manner more heartless than necessary, my only defence is that I wanted to make sure you should never again attempt to come to our city, for I wanted to ensure your continued freedom.

"So that, Magnus, is my story. That is the only explanation I can offer as to why you were thrown from our city like a common criminal when you should have been hailed as a hero. As I said, I do not seek your forgiveness, just your understanding. I have done the best I could. I am sorry I could not do better."

"Then you are not the only one who needs to apologise," said Magnus at last. "I admit that since that day I have thought ill of you, but until today, I did not recognise the difficult position you were in. I should instead thank you, for without your intervention I would still be languishing in your deepest, darkest cell."

"Well spoken, Magnus," said Shaindor. "Tharella took a great risk on our behalves. We both have much to thank her for."

"But I think I have much more to thank the two of you for," said Tharella.

"I don't know," said Magnus shaking his head. "I don't feel like we achieved much in the end. I thought that if we prevented that battle we'd have a real chance to bring peace between your people and the Glurgs. But in the end, nothing much seems to have changed."

"But you're wrong," said Tharella. "You've achieved so much. Thanks to you, there are hundreds, maybe even thousands of Cherines and Glurgs who live and breathe when otherwise they would not. Thanks to you, there are those who walk on two legs who would otherwise be limping on one, and those who have still the use of their two hands when maybe they would not have either. Wives have their husbands and children have their fathers. Each of these is a mighty thing, but that is not all you have achieved.

"Most grievous of those wounds your actions have prevented are the injuries to the heart, the nursing of hatreds and grievances, and the raging desire for revenge. For such injuries do not always heal, as wounds of the flesh will, but rather linger, growing stronger by the year and passing even to the children and to the children of these. Thus it is that these conflicts can go on and on, for generation after generation, until the reasons for the original injuries have long since passed out of memory. But by stopping this one battle, it is possible that we have taken the first step towards breaking this pointless cycle and at last ending the brutal, wasteful war between our people."

Magnus considered her words carefully. "At the Whounga Canyon, both Klugrok and Shaindor said that given a choice, their people would choose peace. I have wondered many times since if that would really be the case. You and the Glurgs still hate each other. And Phraedon still wields great power in Sweet Harmody, ready to send your armies off at a moment's notice. Do you really think there can be true peace between your people and the Glurgs?"

"That is not a question I can easily answer," said Tharella. "Merely preventing a single battle is not going to bring peace. True peace does not just happen. It must be encouraged, nurtured. Fear and hate are its natural enemies. And within our people, there is still much of both for the Glurgs. Others, like you, have suffered at their hands, and not all are as willing to forgive as you were. The idea that the Glurgs are not mindless beasts committed to our destruction, but fellow beings who, like us, crave peace, is so violently opposite to the common view that most of our people will not easily accept it.

"But difficult though the fire of peace may be to kindle, once it begins to burn, it cannot easily be put out. There will always be those, such as Phraedon and Krpolg, who will try, seeking to feed the fear and hate till it blankets our cities in a shroud of darkness. But they will not win. The flame will never be extinguished. For thanks to you, Magnus, that spark is lit."

"Do you recall," said Shaindor, "how I found you in the Plergle Swamp? At the time, I stated that such events happen for a reason. Now I can clearly see why we were meant to meet, for it was your fate to show our people the path to peace."

"Indeed," nodded Tharella. "That is the gift that long ago I predicted you would bring to our city. Without you, our people could never have imagined that peace with the Glurgs was possible. Now, thanks to you, we are slowly taking the first steps down the road you have brought us to."

"It is true," cried Shaindor in excitement. "Already we have had a meeting with the Glurgs."

"How did you get Phraedon to agree to that?" asked Magnus in delighted amazement.

"He did not, of course," said Tharella. "Phraedon would never agree to such a meeting taking place. It was arranged in strict secrecy."

"But it's still fantastic," said Magnus. "Who did you meet with? How did it go?"

"In response to your first question," said Shaindor, "we met with a small delegation which included Schnurqwel, General Pchervlk, and of course, Klugrok. In answer to your second question, I'd be lying if I were to say it went particularly well. There are many differences of opinion, many difficult issues we still need to resolve."

"We are not like the Glurgs," said Tharella. "There are many things about them that are not appealing to us. Their appearance is vile, their manner uncouth, and their way of life deeply disturbing. Therefore, I do not think our races can ever be close. But we can surely learn to accept these differences and to look beyond them to find instead the things that we have in common. For only then will it be possible for us to live peaceably together."

"How is Klugrok?" asked Magnus, eager to hear news of his old friend.

"Perhaps we should let him answer directly," said Shaindor. "Here is a letter he gave me to pass on to you."

Shaindor passed a shabby-looking piece of parchment to him. He quickly unfolded it and squinted at the raggedy writing that could barely be discerned over the general grottiness of the page.

Dear Magnus,

Much has passed since we last met. Krpolg still reigns in Hargh Gryghrgr but his power over the city is slowly slipping. Schnurqwel and the rest of us are doing what we can to inform our people of the truth, spreading the word to all who will listen. Although it is still too early for us to reveal ourselves, we are gaining more supporters every day. It will not be long before we are able to openly challenge Krpolg and bring his tyranny to an end. And then, at last, we can seek the peace we desire so much, and your name will receive the glory it truly deserves. We are even talking about building a statue in your honour in the middle of the main plaza after we are victorious.

Kruperke and the Glurglets say hello. I hope you enjoy the food. Kruperke insisted I take it along. She still worries that you don't eat enough.

May your dreams always be dark and yucky,
Klugrok

Magnus could not wipe the smile from his face as he read the letter. This all sounded so promising. To think that one day there might even be a statue of himself in the middle of Hargh Gryghrgr. Although, come to think of it, given the Glurgs' tastes, maybe that was not such a great idea.

"But what happened to the food?" he asked.

"What food?" said Shaindor.

"In the letter, Klugrok said he had brought some food to give me."

"We saw no food," said Tharella. "There was some noxious substance that he attempted to hand to us, but we got rid of it as quickly as we could. Did we do wrong?"

"No, you did not," chuckled Magnus. "The Glurgs have many qualities to recommend them, but their cooking is not one of them."

"It is good to see you cheering up at last," said Shaindor.

"I feel a lot better now," said Magnus. "But how could I not, seeing such worthy friends again."

"And you are a worthy friend of the Cherines, though most do not know it yet," said Tharella. "There is much work to be done, but we will get there in the end. Though we begin with nothing but two small groups meeting together in secret, still we will continue to speak the language of peace, letting it flow amongst our peoples until it has grown into a raging flood which none can resist. And when that day comes, you and all your deeds will be properly recognised in Sweet Harmody. But until then, on behalf of my people, I wish to say thank you."

"You're welcome," replied Magnus. What else was he meant to say? Suddenly a loud horn sounded outside.

"That is the sign that our party is departing," said Shaindor, jumping to his feet. "I fear it is time to leave. Good-bye, Magnus, until we meet again."

"Farewell, Magnus," said Tharella, also standing. "May your pflugberry bushes always blossom and your pies be forever unmatched in Lower Kertoob."

Magnus embraced each of the Cherines in turn. Then, as they departed through the one remaining door, he hurried after them.

"Wait for me. I'm coming too."

"But you cannot return to Sweet Harmody," said Tharella. "I have told you your sentence still stands."

"I don't want to return to Sweet Harmody," laughed Magnus. "I'm only going as far as the village square. It's Barglefest tonight. There's going to be one enormous pflugberry pie fight. And I don't want to miss out."

Acknowledgments

Lliam Amor – for design awesomeness

Elizabeth Braithwaite – for fantastic feedback and story suggestions

Tracy Jennings and also Catherine – for editorial wisdom

Fiona Gould and Toddie Brown – for helping polish up the text

The wonderful people at Booktrope, especially Katherine Sears, Jesse James Freeman, Emily Price, Melody Paris, Andy Roberts, Adam Bodendieck, and Kelsey Wong – for holding out their hands and bringing me on-board

Book Club Questions

The chances of *Magnus Opum* ever being featured in a book club are about as likely as the chances of a Cherine and a Glurg doing a slow dance together. But just in case, here are some possible questions that may serve as food for discussion:

1. Is there a causal relationship between excessive consumption of pflugberries and reported cases of the Grompets?
2. What is the significance of the minor key chord progressions favoured by Cherine song writers?
3. What impact do Doosie nasal inflections have on regular news transmission?
4. Is there anything the Great Oponium doesn't know, and are you a complete idiot for even considering the question?
5. Discuss the aesthetic of the Pharsheeth, in a loud sing-song voice, while standing on your head and balancing a ball on your knee.
6. If you were ever captured by the Blerchherchh, would you rather be marinated in a red wine sauce or seared, steamed, and served in dumplings?
7. Would you classify the bodily fluids of a Glurg as offensive weapons?
8. Whose borse does have the least lean?
9. A Gleeprog, a Shabandor, and a Klunkarian walk into a bar. What happens next?
10. The seldom seen but much discussed diperagoff: discuss.

MORE GREAT READS FROM BOOKTROPE

Dead of Knight **by Nicole J. Persun** (Fantasy) King Orson and King Odell are power-stricken, grieving, and mad. As they wage war against a rebel army led by Elise des Eresther, it appears as though they're merely in it for the glory. But their struggles are deeper and darker.

Doublesight **by Terry Persun** (Fantasy) In a world where shape shifters are feared, and murder appears to be the way to eliminate them, finding and destroying the source of the fear is all the doublesight can do.

Forecast **by Elise Stephens** (Young Adult, Fantasy) When teenager Calvin finds a portal that will grant him the power of prophecy, he must battle the legacies of the past and the shadows of the future to protect what is most important: his family.

The Mad Lord Lucian (A Portals of Destiny Novella) **by Shay West** (Fantasy) A young magician is at risk of being corrupted by dark magic, a magic more powerful and dangerous than any he has ever known. Will an old story of a lord, a dark magician, and the man who dared to stand up to the Mad Lord Lucian be enough to change his path?

Of Stardust **by February Grace** (Fantasy) At the age of twenty-six single, geeky bookseller Till Nesbitt inherits the shock of a lifetime: a huge Victorian farmhouse filled with unique tenants, and the knowledge that there is a reason she's always been different. She's destined to become a fairy godmother, because the skills are written into her DNA.

Discover more books and learn about our new approach to publishing at www.booktrope.com

Made in the USA
Lexington, KY
19 February 2015